Emily didn't know what to say to that. More than anything, she hoped he would see her for the woman she was. But all he saw was a potential Unionist.

"Thank you for your assistance," she said.

She filled a cup, intent on carrying it to the first soldier she found awake. Dr. Mackay thought the water was for him. His long fingers brushed hers as he took it. Emily felt a shiver travel straight up her arm.

"Thank you," he said. "You have always been very kind."

Something significant passed between them in that moment. So much so that Emily once again had difficulty breathing. She felt as though the real Evan Mackay was standing before her, the honorable, gifted physician who had served God and humanity before distrust and disgust had darkened his heart.

She did not break his gaze. "I am praying for you, Evan."

He gave her hand a quick yet gentle squeeze; then he moved for the door. Emily felt the warmth of his touch long after he had exited the ward.

Books by Shannon Farrington

Love Inspired Historical

Her Rebel Heart
An Unlikely Union

SHANNON FARRINGTON

is a former teacher with family ties to both sides of the Civil War. She and her husband of over eighteen years are active members in their local church and enjoy pointing out God's hand in American history to the next generation. (Especially their own children!)

When Shannon isn't researching or writing, you can find her knitting, gardening or participating in living history reenactments. She and her family live in Maryland.

An Unlikely Union

SHANNON FARRINGTON

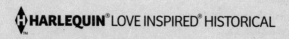

™ LOVE INSPIRED BOOKS

Recycling programs
for this product may
not exist in your area.

ISBN-13: 978-0-373-82986-6

AN UNLIKELY UNION

Copyright © 2013 by Shannon Farrington

www.LoveInspiredBooks.com

Printed in U.S.A.

And be ye kind one to another,
tenderhearted, forgiving one another,
even as God for Christ's sake hath forgiven you.
—*Ephesians* 4:32

For Eric
The man of courage, faith and compassion
that I always knew I would marry

Chapter One

Baltimore, Maryland
1863

Emily Elizabeth Davis stood in the dark, narrow corridor between the hospital wards and prayed for strength. Weary as she was, she wanted to remain strong for the sake of her friend and fellow nurse, Sally Hastings. The poor woman had given way to tears. Emily couldn't blame her. She was near tears herself.

For days now the wounded soldiers had been arriving, thousands of them, train after train, crammed in like cattle. They were dying of thirst, of infection and despair. When word reached Baltimore that General Lee's forces had met the Army of the Potomac in the farm fields of Pennsylvania, the entire city held its breath. Would Maryland soon behold her sons in liberating glory or by the horrors of the casualty lists? For a state divided between Federal and Confederate sympathies, it turned out to be both.

Emily and the other nurses had anticipated the soldiers' arrival, but it didn't make caring for them any less painful.

"I thought I could do this," Sally cried, "but I don't think I can."

This was not the first time the pair had nursed wounded men. Following the battle of Antietam, one year earlier, they had gone down to the office of the U.S. Christian Commission and volunteered. They were subsequently placed in the West's Buildings, a cotton warehouse on Pratt Street that had been converted to a U.S. Army General Hospital. Emily and Sally had cared for scores of bleeding men, Confederate and Federal alike, but this time the task was more difficult. The men they presently nursed were their own schoolmates and neighbors.

The members of the Maryland Guard, once so dashing in their butternut uniforms, now occupied these bleak, crowded rooms. Although Baltimore was their home, the Confederate men were held by armed guards, deemed prisoners of war.

Sally wept upon her shoulder. "First Stephen…now this…"

Sally's brother, Captain Stephen Hastings, had been listed as missing in the great battle at Gettysburg, and, only moments ago, the man she hoped to one day marry had lost his left arm.

"Oh, Em, I am absolutely wicked."

"No, you are not," Emily said gently. "Why ever would you say such a thing?"

"When the stewards returned Edward to his bed, all I could think of was, 'He will never waltz with me again.'"

Emily blinked back tears of her own, sympathizing with her friend's pain. Edward Stanton had danced the farewell waltz with Sally at the last ball before the Pratt Street Riot, the day Federal soldiers had come to

Baltimore and opened fire on innocent civilians. It was the first bloodshed of the war. Outraged at the soldiers' attack, Edward, and many others, had headed south to enlist right away.

The days of silk dresses and white-gloved escorts had given way to months of broken bodies and blood-stained petticoats. Mirth and merriment surrendered to weariness and worry.

"Try not to fret," Emily said. "Edward will dance with you again."

At least she prayed that would be the case. It was only one of the numerous petitions she had whispered during her time at the hospital. As a believer and a volunteer nurse, Emily desperately longed to bring comfort to those she came in contact with. She wanted to be a light in this dark, battle-weary world.

"Remember, God is the great physician. He can—"

The door to the opposite ward pushed open, hitting the wall with a forceful thud. Evan Mackay, a newly arrived Federal doctor from Pennsylvania, glared at them.

"Rebels!" he said, angrily spitting the word. "Shouldn't you women be tending to them?"

The man was as tall as Abraham Lincoln himself, with shoulders as broad as a ditchdigger's. Although he spoke with a Scottish accent, which Emily thought was a dialect straight out of poetry, she was severely disappointed. Evidently not all Scotsmen were as noble or heroic as the men Robert Burns had written about. She couldn't imagine Dr. Mackay had ever even stopped to look at a red, red rose much less compare his love for his sweetheart to one.

I seriously doubt the man even knows the meaning of the word love.

Of all the physicians in this hospital, he displayed

the most hostile attitude; he had an open disdain for the Confederate men. Emily felt it her duty as a Southerner to protect the wounded from Dr. Mackay's wrath.

She felt it her duty to protect Sally now.

"We were just returning," she said politely. "Were we not, Nurse Hastings?"

Sally quickly wiped her eyes, her back now ramrod-straight as though she herself were a member of the Federal army. "Yes, indeed."

Dr. Mackay crossed his arms over his chest and scowled. "Aye," he said slowly. "Then do so directly."

"Yes, Doctor," the women said in unison.

The army physician moved by them and into the next room. Emily caught Sally's eye as the tornado blew past. Both were tempted to make a remark concerning the rude bluecoat, but they did not indulge in the luxury.

The Confederate prisoners needed care.

Flickering oil lamps hung from the rafters as Evan stepped into the remaining ward. There were six buildings in this former cotton warehouse, 425 beds. Most of them were crammed with rebels. His mouth soured just thinking of it. Evan knew firsthand that the field hospitals in Gettysburg were bursting at the seams with brave boys in blue that deserved beds. *Boys like Andrew.*

He sighed. *Yet even if there was room, I wouldn't bring our men here, not to this city. It is one full of barbarians trying to pass themselves off as loyal members of the Union.*

His collar grew tight and his head warm. The reaction wasn't caused by the stifling July heat. It was the memory of his younger brother and the brief time he had endured in Baltimore. Evan had heard the story from Andrew's comrades, the men of the Twenty-Sixth and

Twenty-Seventh Pennsylvania Volunteer Infantry, "The Washington Brigade."

"They simply surrounded us!"

"They cut us off from the rest of the regiment!"

"They were ready to tear us to shreds!"

Rioters and murderers, every last one of them, Evan thought. *And now I must put them back together. The army could have kept me in Pennsylvania. They could have let me tend to our men. They need every surgeon available.*

But Providence had not allowed him to remain in Gettysburg, and Evan had his suspicions why.

I am doing penance for my actions, in the worst possible way.

He cast a glance in the direction of one particular rebel, a major. He was a Maryland man. Evan had seen what remained of his butternut uniform when he'd first arrived. The Johnny's left arm had just been amputated because a vile infection had set in. Evan had performed the surgery. He had done his best to save the reb's life. His duty to God and his Hippocratic oath to do no harm compelled such. But he took no pride in the task. After discharge from the hospital, rebels like this one would be sent to prison, but upon parole many would return to their regiments only to fire upon U.S. soldiers again.

At least this one won't be picking up a musket, he told himself.

The major was still with fever and under the effects of the ether so he continued through the ward. Those prisoners who asked for water or voiced other requests he left to the nurses. That was their job. Most of them were rebel women anyway. Why his superiors permitted their presence in a U.S. Army hospital was beyond his comprehension. They had each signed oaths of loyalty, but it was rumored that several had altered the document. Finding certain lines disagreeable, they had supposedly crossed them out.

If loyalty to the government of the United States of America, to its Constitution, is so abhorrent, they have no business nursing prisoners of war. If Evan had his way, he would have all secessionist nurses tossed out to the street and the rebel wounded held in prison until the end of the war.

They deserved it after what they had done to his brother.

Emily drew in a deep breath, forcing herself to ignore the odors of blood, ether and rotting fish from the nearby docks. This massive warehouse had little means of ventilation, and the air grew more pungent by the day.

Sally had returned to her own section of the hospital. Emily now prepared to step into hers. She smoothed out her pinner apron. Though it pained her, she smiled. It would do the men no good to see a downcast face. They needed hope. They needed cheer.

Lord, help me to be a light. Help me to show Your love.

She had no intention of fostering romantic feelings among the soldiers, but a pretty smile and a little lilac water did wonders in the wards. Some men had been removed from sisters, mothers and sweethearts for so long that they had forgotten the fairer points of civilized society. Emily wanted to remind them there was more to life than this war. Whenever she wasn't assisting doctors or changing soiled bandages, she tried to do so.

She had written countless letters on behalf of men too sick to do so for themselves. She recited Bible verses and poetry. She also spent a great deal of time fanning the suffering, an effort to break the sweltering mid-summer heat.

Emily's friend Julia Ward was doing so now. She was seated at her brother's bedside. Edward still slept heavily from his surgery. Looking at him, Emily sighed. He was once the most confident, dashing man of her neighborhood and had captured ladies' hearts with ease. Injury, illness and two years of war, however, had ravaged his chiseled face and muscular frame. Emily wondered just what Edward would think when he woke to find his left arm was no more.

Each man reacted differently to the devastating reality of amputation. Some cried out for their missing limbs; others simply turned in silence toward the wall. Whichever Edward's reaction, she hoped he would realize that his family and friends still cared for him. Emily moved closer to his bed. Julia looked up. Fatigue lined her eyes.

"Has there been any change?" Emily asked.

"No."

She could hear the discouragement in her friend's voice. Emily tried to reassure her. "Sometimes it takes quite a while for the ether to wear off."

"He isn't any cooler. At least not yet."

Emily felt Edward's forehead for herself. "It is still early."

"Would you bring me a basin and some cool water?" Julia asked. "I'll sponge his face and neck."

"That would be very helpful, but be careful not to overdo."

"I won't."

Edward's sister had faithfully attended him since his arrival yet she was not a nurse. Emily knew exactly why Julia had not volunteered. Although her sacque bodice and gored skirts concealed any evidence from the average passerby, Emily and her closest friends knew the truth. Julia was expecting a child.

"Em?" she asked.

"Yes?"

"When Edward begins to stir…will he be sick to his stomach…or have strange visions? I have heard that some men do."

"Not necessarily, but we should keep watch. The best thing you can do for now is stay beside him. Alert me the moment he begins to wake."

Commotion at the far end of the ward caught Emily's attention. Dr. Mackay was barking orders to two of the Federal stewards.

"I told you to deliver him to surgery! Do so immediately!"

She swallowed back the lump in her throat and watched as the young men in blue scrambled to obey. The man in question had severe shrapnel wounds to his leg.

"Tell the surgeon to cut the leg now or he'll have another dead man on his hands!"

Emily gasped. The poor man about to undergo the procedure was so delirious with wound fever that he knew not what was about to happen, but everyone else in the room did. Their faces went pale. Even the stewards cringed at the doctor's harsh tone.

Forcing herself to continue, she found Julia a sponge and basin, then moved on. A soldier several beds down from Edward asked for a drink. Emily brought him a cupful of the freshest water she could find. His face immediately brightened.

"Bless you, Miss Emily."

"God bless you, Jimmy."

He drank his fill, then leaned back upon his pillow. Dark curls flopped about his forehead. "Is the surgeon really gonna take Freddy's leg?" he asked.

Freddy was Jimmy's comrade and unfortunately the subject of Dr. Mackay's recent tirade. Emily hoped her tone sounded encouraging despite the news.

"I am afraid so, Jimmy, but it is what is best for him, in order to save his life."

His chin quivered ever so slightly. Emily didn't know how old he was exactly, but he looked barely beyond boyhood.

"Me and Freddy come up together," he said. "All the way from Saint Mary's City."

Emily recognized the name of the southern Maryland town; she had once visited the place when her father, a lawyer, had business there.

"Is that where your family is from?" she asked as she straightened his bed coverings.

"Yes'um. Freddy's, too." His thoughts then shifted. "Reckon they will send us both to that new prison camp they've made? The one at Point Lookout?"

She would not allow herself to dwell on what would happen after these men were discharged from the hospital. More than likely, they would be sent to one of two Federal prison camps, either Fort Delaware or the one Jimmy had mentioned at the mouth of the Potomac River.

"I don't know where they will send you," she said honestly. "But I hope that your stay there will be short."

"Well, if I gotta go to prison, I hope it's Point Lookout. At least then I'll be closer to home."

She smoothed back his dark curls as a mother would do, tucking a small child in for the night. The gesture had a dual purpose, comfort for him and evaluation of potential fever. Thankfully, Jimmy's forehead was cool.

"It would do you well right now to try and dream of home," she said.

"Yes'um. I reckon it would. But before you go… would you mind prayin' for Freddy? I know you bein' a lady and a volunteer from the Christian Commission… Well, would you please?"

She was touched by his request and the concern for his friend which was so evident in his eyes. "I would be honored to do so."

He reached for her hand. Had they been conversing at dinner or a society ball, the gesture would be entirely too forward. Yet here in the hospital, Emily often cast society's rules aside for the sake of grace and compassion. She clasped his hand and prayed for Freddy. She prayed for Jimmy as well. When she had finished, she whispered, "Try not to fret. God already has looked after your friend, for Dr. Turner is now the surgeon on duty. He's a kind and capable man."

His face brightened somewhat. "Thank you, Miss Emily. That's right good to hear. Some docs are better than others 'round here."

She knew which doctor he was referring to, and although she probably should have defended Dr. Mackay's skills, she let the opportunity pass. She stood, pleased that the worry in Jimmy's eyes had faded.

"Rest well," she said to him.

He smiled and turned to his side. Emily straightened his coverings once more, then turned, as well, only to crash directly into the chest of the angry Scotsman.

Words were quick to shape in his mind, but Evan held his tongue as his blue wool collided with her Southern-grown, Baltimore-milled cotton. The woman came no higher than his breastbone. After staring seemingly transfixed at his brass buttons, she dared to raise her eyes. Her cheeks were pink with embarrassment.

He stared down at her.

What is she waiting for? An apology? Did the little Southern miss expect him to play the part of a gentleman and beg her forgiveness for the improper contact? She'd get no such courtesy from him. Why should she? She'd had no trouble holding hands with a rebel just moments ago.

Perhaps it is her close proximity to a Yankee that fills her with such shame.

Evan wasn't a gambling man, but if he were, he'd lay money down that she was one of the nurses who'd altered her oath of loyalty.

"Haven't you duties to attend to?" he asked.

"Yes, Dr. Mackay."

"Then see to them." He pointed to the water buckets on the table in the corner. "Fill them with fresh water, then scrub the floor. It is a nesting ground for disease!" Lucky for her, she did not need to be told twice. She scurried away, skirt and petticoats swishing.

Incompetent little socialite, he thought. *Little Miss Baltimore. She's probably never worn anything less than silk before now.*

"You shouldn't treat her that way."

Evan turned in the direction of the weak yet determined voice. Boyish curls framed a scowling pair of eyes.

Aye. Her love-struck suitor. "Were you speaking to me?"

The rebel pushed up on his elbows, trying to marshal what was left of his Southern pride. "I am, sir, and

I will kindly ask you not to speak that way to her. She is the finest nurse here. And, I might add, she's been here longer than you."

Evan turned his back, stepping away. He cared not how many months of service the woman had.

"You could learn a lesson from her," the boy called. "A little compassion would do you no harm!"

Evan's ire rose. His fists clenched at his side, but he didn't give the boy the satisfaction of knowing the words had affected him. *You didn't show any compassion when your mob surrounded my brother,* he thought. *When they bashed him with paving stones!*

He told himself the Maryland rebel wasn't worth his time, and he moved on. There were wounds to probe and minié balls still to extract. As he made his way through the rows of iron cots, he cast a glance in Little Miss Baltimore's direction. The water had been replenished. She was currently on her hands and knees, scrubbing the vile floor.

Another experience I doubt she's had the pleasure of until now, he thought. *We shall see how well she handles it.*

As Emily raked the scrub brush across the filthy floor she dealt with Dr. Mackay's temper the only way she knew how. She prayed for him. Actually, she prayed more for herself than for the man.

Oh Lord, please give me grace. I can't work alongside him without it.

Dealing with the Federal army's disdainful attitude toward Confederate men was nothing new, but most of the guards, doctors and hospital commanding officers were professional enough to keep their words to themselves or at least voice their condemnation outside the wards.

Some even took pity on the wounded souls and showed them kindness. Jeremiah Wainwright, a young steward who Emily knew to be a Christian, was such a man. Dr. Jacob Turner was another. He was a good-natured New Englander who treated the Confederates not as prisoners or scientific studies, but as men.

Just yesterday Emily had been called to his section, to assist as he probed a North Carolina man's back for shrapnel. The poor soldier had leaned upon her, trying not to flinch while Dr. Turner carefully extracted the metal.

"Do I hurt you?" the old man had asked considerately.

"Not too terribly," the soldier had said.

Emily had known by the tightness of his muscles that the Carolina man wasn't exactly telling the truth, but because of Dr. Turner's gentle demeanor and a story of snapping New England lobsters, he'd been able to endure the painful procedure without crying out or fainting.

If only Dr. Mackay could be more like that, she thought. *A little kindness would go a long way to promote healing and to foster interest in eternal matters.*

Though a few ragtag Bibles lay at the bedsides of the men, Emily knew many in this hospital were starved for spiritual comfort. In the past year, she had held the hands of the dying, both Confederate and Federal alike. She had sat with those who'd lost their dearest friends on the battlefield, who then asked, "Where is God in all this terrible suffering?"

She gave them the only answer she could. "Right here grieving with you."

The will of God made no sense at times to Emily. Why He had allowed war to come instead of an end to slavery, then a peaceful compromise of ideals, was unknown to her.

She dared to glance at Dr. Mackay. *How long the hostilities continue will, I suppose, depend on men like him.* The intimidating physician was now standing at Edward's bed, perusing his wounds with a look of cold indifference. Julia sat her post, pale and frightened. Emily hurried to finish her scrubbing so she might join her friend. In her delicate condition the last thing Julia needed was to hear that man's sharp, condemning tongue.

The dinner bell rang, calling all officers to the dining hall. Emily breathed a sigh of relief when Dr. Mackay exited the room. She put away her brush and bucket and went to her friend.

"What a horrible man," Julia whispered. "There is no compassion in him. He looked at Edward as if he were nothing more than a stray dog."

"I know. I'm sorry." Emily touched Edward's forehead gently. The fever was going down. "He is much cooler."

"Oh, thank the Lord."

Within a matter of moments the rest of their friends appeared: Sally and the Martin sisters, Trudy and Elizabeth, and Rebekah Van der Geld, the only one of them who staunchly supported the Federal army's occupation of Baltimore. Each had come to inquire of Edward. As they clustered around his bed, Emily couldn't help but remember with fondness the times the six of them had met for knitting and needlework in each other's homes.

Such happy times.

But the joyful emotions of the past were tempered

by today's reality. The girls had not gathered to decide which dress pattern from *Godey's Lady's Book* would attract a handsome beau's attention, nor were they there to knit socks for their glorious, invincible army.

We are here to tend to one of its wounded, she thought sadly.

Try as she might, Emily's eyes kept drifting to the place where Edward's left arm should be. Apparently Sally was having the same difficulty. Her eyes were watering.

"He stirred slightly," Julia told them. "When that doctor was standing over him."

"That is good," Emily said. "Soon he will wake."

Sally drew in a quick breath and lifted her chin. "We should pray for him and then go about our business. It won't fare him well to have us all hovering over him when he wakes."

Emily agreed. They should give Edward his privacy. She couldn't help but also think, *And if Dr. Mackay returns from his meal to find us clustered about instead of busy with some task, he will surely spew his venom upon us all. That won't be good for Julia or her child.*

Trudy, Elizabeth and Rebekah all nodded in agreement. Rebekah offered to begin the prayer. The women clasped hands. One by one they prayed for Edward's recovery and for the rest of the wounded men of this hospital. When no Federal soldier was close enough to overhear, Elizabeth and Trudy each whispered a plea for their brother, George, also a member of the Maryland Guard. As far as everyone knew, he had survived the Pennsylvania battle and returned safely to Virginia. Sally then prayed for Stephen; his whereabouts were still unknown.

"Try to keep faith," Trudy said, hugging her after they had finished. "God knows exactly where Stephen is."

"I know. I take comfort in that."

Before they could go their separate ways, Jeremiah Wainwright approached. "Ladies," he said, "forgive me for intruding, but I've just come from the dining hall. They are presently serving the nurses. If you don't go quickly, there won't be anything left for you to eat."

They all knew he was speaking truth. They had each learned the hard way to eat when called or go hungry.

"Thank you, Jeremiah," Emily said. "We appreciate the warning."

He smiled and tipped his blue kepi. "You are quite welcome. And don't worry, I'll keep track of your charges, especially the major here."

She believed he would, and so Emily turned to Julia.

"Come with us. Have a bite to eat."

She shook her head, unwilling to leave her brother's side. "I'll stay. Samuel will arrive shortly and I want to be here when Edward wakes."

Her husband, Samuel, joined her each day after his work as a teacher at the Rolland Park men's seminary was complete. Her parents came in the early evening, as well. Julia's father, Dr. Thomas Stanton, worked in the private hospital across town. He was busy caring for his own load of wounded, most of them Federal soldiers from wealthy families or those with high political connections.

"I understand. Shall I fetch you something?"

"No. Thank you. I am not hungry."

Emily gave her hand a squeeze. Then she followed her fellow nurses to the dining hall.

* * *

His food wasn't sitting well. Evan wondered if it was the stewed blackberries, which had obviously been picked too early, or the sight of the carts and laborers moving along Pratt Street. He stared out the window.

The army supply wagons and the countless crates stamped *U.S. Christian Commission* bore witness to the activities of today, but all Evan could think about was a day two years ago last April. His brother, Andrew, was newly trained and eager for action. He was unaware that such would come by way of a bloodthirsty mob while he and his regiment were en route to Washington.

Andrew had been one of the first to answer President Lincoln's call for volunteers. He'd wanted to preserve the Union. When he and his fellow soldiers had tried to pass through Baltimore, the local citizens made it quite apparent which side they had chosen. As Andrew and the others had marched toward the Washington trains, a crowd had surrounded them. They were soon pelted with rocks, bottles and paving stones.

The Northern men had exercised restraint, but when the citizens had grabbed for their guns, the soldiers did what anyone would have done. They'd defended themselves. When the smoke had cleared, several boys in blue were dead, along with eleven rebels. The Baltimoreans had then had the audacity to claim the shots fired were unprovoked.

Just thinking of what had taken place made Evan's fists clench. He knew he should leave the window, spend his remaining moments of the dining break in some other place, but try as he might, he could not pull his eyes from the street. Where exactly had Andrew fallen?

His eyes scanned the street before him. Traffic pulsed. City life moved at a steady pace. Men in scrap shirts with slouch hats set low on their foreheads lugged sacks of grain to and from the nearby wharf.

Were any of them present that day? Were any of them part of that murderous mob?

He bit down hard, teeth against teeth. The only emotion stronger than the anger he felt toward rebels was the emptiness in his heart.

If only I had been there. I could have saved him. I would have recognized the signs that the pressure was building in his brain. I could have drained the blood. He didn't have to die.

And then his thoughts turned to another. *Mary...*

The memory of her face, her pleading words, burned through his mind. Just as he'd never forgive those thugs for Andrew's death, he would never forgive himself for leaving his wife behind.

By the time Emily returned to the ward, Edward had opened his eyes. Her initial joy was tempered by the quiet pain she heard in Julia's voice.

"I promise you, Edward. It will be all right."

He turned from her sharply, setting his face toward the wall. The bandaged knob at the end of his shoulder stood out like a regimental flag.

A lump wedged in the back of Emily's throat, but she moved toward him. She bent to his level, her skirts folding to the floor.

"Edward," she said softly. "It is me, Emily."

His blue eyes, once so gallant and full of life, were now vacant, almost spiritless. He blinked but did not acknowledge her presence.

"Are you in any pain?"

He blinked again. Emily's heart was breaking. She knew Julia's was, as well. She dared not look to her grief-stricken face. Emily knew if she did, she herself would break down. *I have to remain strong. I am here to give comfort, not to be in need of it myself.*

Carefully, methodically, she felt his forehead. He was much cooler. *Thank You, Lord.*

"Here," Emily said to him. "Let me fetch you something to drink. I am certain you are thirsty."

She reached for a nearby pitcher and filled a tin cup with water. She offered it to him, but Edward simply stared past her, no reply. By now Emily was beginning to wonder if he was even aware of her presence.

Perhaps it is the effects of the ether. She set the cup on the table, peered closely into his face. Edward's eyes registered a startled reaction. They held hers for a quick second, then pulled away. In that brief time Emily saw a storm of emotions there.

He is aware of his reality, she thought. *All too well.*

There were times when it was wise to draw a man out of his solitude, but Emily sensed this was not one of them. She could only guess what Edward had witnessed on the battlefield, what actions had led to this place. She wanted to ask about Stephen but knew there would be time for questions later.

She brushed her fingers gently through his hair. "Perhaps you will feel up to taking water later on. For now, just rest."

Still he only blinked. Emily drew the sheet to his chest, mindful of his bandages, then moved to the side of the bed where Julia stood. She stared pitifully at her brother's back. Emily gave her a gentle squeeze.

"Try not to be discouraged," she whispered. "He is alert and the fever has broken."

Julia nodded slowly but her face was as pale as January snow. "Will you send for our father?"

"Of course. Straightaway." Emily agreed with her friend's assessment. Edward needed his family now.

She moved toward the door. Sally was peeking through it.

"Is he awake?" she asked the moment Emily stepped into the corridor.

"Yes."

Sally breathed a shallow sigh. "Is he speaking? Did he mention Stephen?"

Emily did not wish to upset her, but she knew the truth was best. If she were in Sally's place, she would want to know.

"I am afraid he has not spoken at all. That is why I did not think it wise to ask about Stephen just yet. The battle seems to have damaged not only Edward's body but his mind, as well."

Her chin began to quiver.

"I'm sorry," Emily said gently.

Sally quickly wiped her eyes and garnered her composure. "Is there anything we can do?"

"Julia requested that we send for her father."

"I will see to that."

"Can you manage? We could ask one of the other volunteers."

Sally shook her head. "Dr. Turner will not mind. He has a soft spot for me. He knows Edward is our friend, and he told me if I had need of anything only to ask."

Thank the Lord for small kindnesses, Emily thought.

"Tell Julia I will be as quick as I can." She turned and descended the staircase. Emily quickly went back to the ward. Dr. Mackay had also returned.

"Nurse!" he called, waving her over.

I do have a name, she thought.

Nevertheless, she went to him. He was in the process of resetting a Virginia man's broken leg. Having placed the limb in the fracture box, Dr. Mackay handed her a small sack. It looked as if it had come from the hospital kitchen.

"Fill the box with oat bran. It will support the leg and collect any further drainage from the wound."

"Yes, Dr. Mackay."

Emily promptly went to work, trying her best to smile at the wounded Virginian while ignoring the scowling Federal doctor beside her. When she finished the task, she looked to him. She expected another order, but he simply grunted and moved on to the next man.

She went back to Edward.

Her friend still lay with his back to his sister. Julia held her place in the chair beside him, a palmetto fan in one hand, a Bible in the other. She waved the fan faithfully over his head while she sought her own comfort in Scripture.

Emily watched them for a moment, but when Julia made no gesture or request she quietly backed away. Concern weighed heavily upon her. Edward's mind-set *was* disturbing. She had seen some soldiers following the battle of Antietam who had recovered physically from their wounds but were never able to reenter life. When the memories of mortar shells and musket fire became too vivid, they often retreated into dark, private worlds, where no loved one or enemy could ever find them again.

"The water pitchers need to be filled," she heard Dr. Mackay say as he brushed past her.

For a moment Emily considered reporting her observations but she realized any competent physician would have already recognized Edward's condition. If she spoke up it would seem that she doubted his skills.

She dare not call his judgment into question—at least not yet. For now, Emily thought it best just to keep her eye on her friend and stay out of the ill-tempered doctor's way.

Chapter Two

All meals were now finished. Emily helped Jeremiah and the orderlies remove the last of the men's food trays. Afterward she changed three dressings, then wrote a letter for another Maryland man.

As soon as she had completed that task, Freddy was brought in from surgery. He was already awake, sick to his stomach and shivering with fever. Emily was thankful he was still alive, but it grieved her to see him suffering so. She sat beside him with a basin and repeatedly wiped his face as he emptied what precious little was in his stomach. When the violence finally subsided, she settled him in his bed, then went to comfort Jimmy, who had been watching the entire time.

"He gonna be all right, Miss Emily? Will the sickness pass soon?"

"It will," she promised. "In fact, his eyes are already clearing."

"That's good." He fell back to his pillow. "Thank you for prayin' for him. It's hard seein' him without his leg, but I'm real grateful the Good Lord's left him here with me."

"Indeed, Jimmy. So am I."

She tucked him in and moved on. The day had been long and difficult. Fatigue slowed her steps and worry darkened her mind.

Where is Sally's brother? she wondered. *Is he misplaced in one of the field hospitals? Has he been captured or is he wandering around somewhere cut off from the Confederate army?*

"Lord, please bring Stephen home. Please comfort Edward—"

"Miss Emily?"

She turned to see Private Robert Stone, another Maryland man, looking at her. Emily immediately went to him. A minié ball had shattered his right knee.

"Are you in pain?" she asked.

"No, miss. I'm alright. I just heard you praying for Major Stanton and Captain Hastings."

Emily blushed. She had not meant to speak the prayer aloud. *I must be more careful.* She was, after all, a volunteer in a Federal army hospital. There were many here who would disapprove of her prayers for Confederate soldiers.

"I know the major's not doing so well," Rob said. "I think perhaps, well…I think he feels responsible."

Her skin prickled. *Responsible?* She sat down on the edge of his bed. "What exactly do you mean?"

"I think he feels responsible for the captain and the others."

Emily's pulse quickened. This was the first time anyone had mentioned Sally's brother. Did Rob know what had become of him? She glanced about for Dr. Mackay. If Stephen was hiding out somewhere, she didn't want that man or anyone else in blue to know.

The Scotsman was at the far end of the room, checking on a sergeant with a terrible cough. His ears were plugged by his stethoscope. Jeremiah had gone to the kitchen, and the sentinel at the door was well out of earshot.

Emily looked back at Rob. "Captain Hastings was reported on the lists as missing. Do you know what has become of him?"

He swallowed. "I'm afraid I do, miss."

Her heart immediately sank. *Oh, no.* Rob was undoubtedly struggling to tell her what she could already guess.

"Is he dead?"

For a moment he looked almost relieved. The gentleman in him did not wish to break such news to a lady. "I'm afraid so…but he died bravely. A hero."

Tears filled her eyes. Emily shut them for a moment. When she regained her composure she asked the man to tell what he knew. There was no longer any fear of Federal eavesdropping. Plotting to help a Confederate soldier would be considered treason, but Stephen was beyond any aid or shelter she could offer him now. Any details Rob could provide about his demise may bring a small measure of comfort to Sally, and perhaps hold the key to Edward's solitude.

"Were you with them on the battlefield?"

He nodded. "Me and what was left of the old Maryland Guard. First Maryland Infantry Battalion we are now." He shifted his position, wincing slightly. "Captain Hastings, well…it was a bad scrap. We don't blame Major Stanton. He was just following General Stewart's orders. Things just happen like that sometimes."

Her heart beat faster. "What things?" she asked. "What orders?"

"To take the hill, miss. Culp's Hill." He gestured battle movements with his hands. "You see, we were all lined up. The bluecoats were above us and we were fightin' our way through the trees, over the rocks. That's when it happened."

"What did?"

"Captain Hastings was with Major Stanton in the front. Right in front of me, in fact. They charged valiantly, yelling for us to follow. Gave the rest of us real courage, it did."

Emily had expected no less. Stephen and Edward were the bravest of the brave. At least Sally and the rest of them could take solace in that.

Private Nash continued. "Captain Hastings took a bullet to the chest. I know 'cause it spun him around. Major Stanton took one in the arm just about the same time. They fell together. The next one had my name on it."

She was grateful he spared her the gruesome details, although she had little difficulty imagining the sight. Emily had seen what hot lead could do to a man. "I am certain your comrades appreciated your sacrifice," she said, her voice quivering slightly. "Were you successful in taking the hill?"

"No, miss. We had to fall back."

Tears spilled over once again, and frustration filled her soul. *Such loss, such sacrifice for nothing gained! Stephen died for ground unclaimed, ground that even the Federal army probably no longer occupies!*

"Our men tried to gather us," Rob insisted, "but they couldn't get us all. The Yankees were just too quick."

"Is that when you were captured?"

"Yes. Major Stanton shielded the captain just in case any of the bluecoats used their bayonets, but I believe he was already dead by then. When the major realized, he was shook up real bad. You could see it in his eyes.

He held it together for the rest of us, though, tried to encourage us as we were being rounded up. But then we learned we'd been fightin' the First Eastern Shore."

He looked at her as if she should know what that meant. Emily had no idea.

"I'm sorry. I don't understand."

"The First Eastern Shore is Maryland Infantry, miss. We, the First Maryland, were fightin' against men from *our own* state.

Emily sucked in air. Rob continued.

"When Major Stanton learned that, the fire just went out of him. All he could say was 'it was my fault.' To my knowledge he hasn't spoken a word since."

Waves of nausea rolled through her.

"I can sure understand it," he said. "We're all torn up inside. Sergeant Moore told me he'd seen his own cousin bearing the colors for the First Eastern Shore."

Emily was afraid she was going to be literally sick. It was bad enough these men were fighting against their own countrymen, but Marylanders spilling Maryland blood? No wonder Edward could not speak.

"Miss Emily? Will you do something for me?"

She tried to rein in her feelings. She could do nothing about what had happened on that hill, but perhaps she might be able to do something for Rob, for Edward.

"Of course."

"Will you tell Major Stanton that he's one of the bravest men I ever served under? And that I'd be proud to do so again."

She was struck by his loyalty, his compassion for his officer. "I will do so. Is there anything else that I may do for you?"

"No, miss. Don't fret over me. There's plenty of other fellas here worse off."

"Thank you for telling me," Emily said.

"You're welcome."

He offered her a hint of a smile and she gave him one in return, but they both knew the other's heart was heavy.

Gathering her skirts, Emily rose slowly, feeling as though she had twenty petticoats and two sacks of flour tied about her legs. She had promised Rob that she would convey his message, but would the words comfort Edward or be another painful reminder of what had taken place on the battlefield?

Just as she stepped away from the bed, Dr. Mackay made his way across the ward. He must have seen the look on her face and recognized something was wrong.

"Are you ill?" he asked.

Ill didn't even begin to describe how she felt. *Men from my state are shooting at their neighbors, their own relatives! And Sally...her brother has been killed! Now I must tell her the terrible news!*

But Emily swallowed back her emotions. It would do no good to tell Dr. Mackay such things. He would offer her no sympathy. He'd probably say her friends deserved what had become of them.

"A nurse in danger of swooning is of no use to me in this ward."

Her backbone stiffened. "You need not worry," she assured him. "I am not given to such tendencies."

His left eyebrow arched as if he doubted that, but before he could speak, a soldier's cry commanded his attention.

"Doc! Doc! Come quick!"

Emily turned, as well. A young Kentucky man was bent over the bed, holding his brother—a soldier who had been wounded in the neck and jaw.

"He's turnin' blue!" the man cried.

Dr. Mackay raced to the Confederate man's side. Taking one look at him, he ordered Emily to fetch water and lint packing. She hurried to obey while he ran for the locked cabinet at the end of the ward. She gathered her items, he a surgical tray.

"Hold on there, Billy," the brother encouraged. "Doc's comin'."

"Step back!" the Scotsman commanded. To Emily, he said, "Remove those bandages so his wound is exposed."

She deposited the basin and packing on the table beside them and quickly carried out his instructions. Her heart was pounding, for Billy was staring wide-eyed at her, silently begging for help.

Then he closed his eyes.

Oh! Oh! "Dr. Mackay!"

The instant Emily had seen to the last bandage, the doctor moved in with his scalpel. She watched as he made an incision in Billy's neck just below his maze of black battle scars and inserted a small tube. Dr. Mackay then blew his own breath into the man's throat.

Emily had never seen such a thing before. The blue in Billy's face faded to gray, then finally a more natural shade.

After several more breaths, Dr. Mackay straightened up. Still holding the tube in place, he asked for the packing.

"Do you wish for it to be cut into smaller strips?" she asked.

"Aye."

She did so, handing them over one at a time. While he secured the tube, Emily couldn't help but wonder, on what was this soldier choking? He was one of the men who had been prescribed a low diet, only beef tea and a little milk. She had followed Dr. Mackay's orders precisely concerning that. One of the man's comrades must have given him something else to eat.

"Were you able to dislodge what he swallowed?" she asked.

"He isn't choking on food."

"He isn't?"

"'Twas the swelling from the wound which constricted his airway." Dr. Mackay spoke with confidence, as if he performed this sort of thing daily and in doing so had saved countless lives. Emily prayed that was indeed the case. Much to her relief, after a few moments Billy's eyes fluttered open. She dared breathed a sigh, knowing the immediate crisis had passed.

Emily touched his shoulder. "Just lay still," she encouraged. "You'll be all right."

She hoped Dr. Mackay would confirm her words, but he did not. Plugging his ears with his stethoscope, he listened to Billy's chest. Thankfully, he looked pleased with what he heard.

Emily's heart slowed somewhat. The Northern physician would not spend his breath comforting a Southern man but he *had* preserved his life. For that, she was thankful.

Evan watched her exhale. The sight of such procedures had sent many of his past assistants to the floor, but *she'd* managed to keep on her feet and follow his instructions. For that, he commended her. With so many prisoners to tend to however, he could not be concerned with her health. She had clearly been troubled before this case, and even now she was still a ghostly shade of pale.

Removing his stethoscope, he told her, "Take a moment to yourself and get some air."

Still too overcome to respond, she could only blink.

"Go on, now," he said.

Slowly, she turned. The Johnny in the bed beside them thanked her for her help. She patted his arm silently, then walked away.

The reb then turned to him.

"Thank you, Doc. I'm real grateful to you for savin' my brother's life."

With those words Evan wasn't certain what he should feel—gratification or anger. If it wasn't for brothers such as these, ones willing to make war on their own nation, *his brother* would not have died. Not knowing how to respond, he ignored the comment altogether.

He signaled for the steward. "Fetch me some ice," he told him.

"Yes, sir."

He'd see if that would bring the swelling under control. If not the reb's brother would have to return to the operating room.

Emily stepped into the corridor. Her heart was still pounding. Try as she might, the breath she repeatedly drew just didn't seem to be enough to fill her lungs. Heading straight for the small window, she pushed it open. The air drifting in from the harbor was not fresh by any means but at least it was a little cooler.

Contrary to what Dr. Mackay may think, the sight of blood had not caused her distress. It was thinking of how the poor wounded man had come upon his injury. She did not know where Billy and his brother had been during the recent Pennsylvania battle, but she knew by looking at them that their experience had been just as horrific as Edward's and Stephen's.

Oh, Lord, I beg you. End this war...please...

"Em, are you all right?"

She turned to find Julia standing in the hall.

"What troubles you? Is it that poor soldier? He looks much improved now."

Emily sighed. Julia was the last person she wished to burden with such distressing news, but she realized she needed to know. "I have received some information concerning Stephen."

Her friend's shoulders dropped with a long sigh of her own. "He's gone, isn't he?"

"Yes."

"I suspected such. Especially when Edward wouldn't speak. Poor Sally...but why would Stephen have been reported as 'missing'?"

"A misidentification, I suppose."

"Then it's likely he is buried somewhere on the battlefield?"

"I would imagine."

Sorrow fell over them both like a shroud. The sound of wounded soldiers groaning echoed through the halls. An armed sentinel passed by on his way to duty, and they could hear an officer shouting orders on the floor below.

"Private Stone saw him fall," Emily said. "He told me the entire story."

"What did he say?"

She explained what she had learned. When Emily got to the part about Maryland men fighting their own neighbors, in some cases their own flesh and blood, all color drained from Julia's face.

"Gracious," she breathed. "Edward chose to fight

in *defense* of his state and now battle lines have forced him to fire upon our own citizens? Does he know this?"

"Apparently so. Private Stone says Edward feels responsible. He overheard him remark it was all his fault."

Julia wiped her eyes with a lace-trimmed handkerchief. Emily dabbed at her own eyes with her apron. The sights and sounds of war continued to swirl around them.

"We need to tell Sally," Julia finally said.

"Yes." Though Emily dreaded having to be the one to do so, she volunteered anyway.

"No," Julia said. "It should come from me. I will tell her when she returns. Do you think Private Stone would mind if I spoke with him? I would like to hear the story for myself."

"I don't believe he would." Emily paused. "There was one other thing." She told Julia how Private Stone had asked her to deliver a message to Edward. "But I am not certain now that I should."

"What kind of message?"

As Emily explained, tears spilled over Julia's long, dark lashes. "Tell my brother what the soldier said."

"Are you certain?"

"Yes. I believe it will help."

They both turned back for the ward. Emily introduced Julia to Rob, then stopped to check on Billy. Crushed ice had been placed around his neck. Dr. Mackay was nowhere in sight, but Jeremiah Wainwright was sitting at the soldier's bedside. Emily asked if he had need of any assistance. When the steward politely declined, she moved on to Edward.

Her friend was staring at the dust-covered rafters above him. She surveyed his tight bandages but only with her eyes. Then she poured him a fresh cup of water and drew close. All he did was blink.

Setting the cup aside, Emily quietly moved in closer. "Edward," she said softly. "I understand that you do not wish to speak to me or to Julia right now, but know that we are here should you change your mind."

She waited, hoping for a response of any kind. There was none.

"And know this…God waits patiently, as well."

His lips tightened into a thin line. His jaw twitched. It was the first real indication he had given that he was listening to anything she said.

Emily leaned a little closer. She could see the pain in his eyes. Her heart ached for him. He had been her schoolmate, her childhood friend. He had teased her and tugged at her curls. She had once bandaged his wrist when he'd cut a gash in it after jumping from the tree in her backyard.

I mended his wound then, but how do I do so now? How does one even begin to ease the guilt a soldier feels over the death of his friend?

There was no change in his eyes, but she felt compelled to continue. "Private Stone asked me to deliver a message to you.…"

Slowly, his eyes shifted from the rafters to her. Emily drew hope from the movement.

"He said to tell you that you are the best man he has ever served under, and he would be proud to do so again."

What she'd hoped would bring encouragement had just the opposite effect. Edward's jaw clenched and Emily watched helplessly as his eyes welled up with tears.

He shook his head no.

Her heart squeezed as she whispered, "I know what happened on Culp's Hill. I know what happened to Stephen...to the other Maryland men."

"It was...my fault...Emmy."

His voice was distant, defeated, but he had referred to her by her childhood name, a memory of a happier time. She used his, as well.

"No, Eddie. You mustn't blame yourself. We are at war. Terrible things happen. There was nothing you could do—"

"How dare you!"

Emily felt the blood drain from her face. She need not wonder who had spoken the fierce words. She already knew. How long Dr. Mackay had been standing behind her and how much of the conversation he had heard, she was not certain, but it had been long enough to rouse his fury. Swallowing hard, she turned. He stood towering above her, fists clenched at his sides.

"What do you think you are doing?"

When she didn't answer immediately, he pointed to the door.

"Get outside!"

Emily chanced a glance at Edward. Just as she had feared, the blank stare had returned. *I have made things worse.*

Torn between comforting her friend and following the doctor's orders, she hesitated. She shouldn't have.

"Now, Nurse!"

Emily's legs were as wobbly as a freshly cooked batch of mint jelly and walking the distance to the doorway seemed to take an eternity. All around her, the wounded stared, surely wondering what was about to happen. Even the Federal guard at the entryway showed sympathy on his face. Emily wasn't afraid of

Dr. Mackay physically, but she feared that he in his position of authority would hinder her from ministering to the Confederate men.

She stepped outside. He was immediately on her heels, catching the hem of her skirt with his long stride. Emily turned to free herself before his clumsiness ripped the fabric. Losing her footing, she was captured by his massive hands.

"You little rebel!"

"Unhand me, sir!" she commanded.

He did but only to stick a long, sharp finger in her face. "I will not have that kind of talk in my ward! Do you understand? How dare you tell that dirty Johnny it isn't his fault! They *started* this war! The blood of thousands is on their heads!"

Emily sucked in her breath, fire building inside her. Her parents had raised her to be respectful, to be gentle. She had never been one to argue before, but this man, this *Yankee,* brought out a fierceness she didn't know existed.

"*They* started this war? I beg to differ with you, sir. It was *your* soldiers who opened fire upon *our* civilians, and that is why a good many of these men took up arms in the first place! They wished to defend our state from tyrants like *you!*"

He looked shocked. Surely no woman had ever talked this way to him before. His eyes then narrowed. "I assume you are referring to the riot on Pratt Street."

"I am."

"Then you had better get your facts straight."

Emily held her ground. "Oh, I am completely aware of the facts, Doctor. Major Stanton and his sister, her husband as well, were caught in that riot."

"Aye. That explains quite a bit. All of you are as guilty as sin."

Her blood was boiling. How dare he speak that way about her friends! "They are guilty of nothing more than meeting the Philadelphia train. Julia was nearly trampled to death when your Massachusetts soldiers emptied their muskets in an act of barbarous cruelty!"

The veins in his neck were bulging. His side whiskers rose like the barbs of a porcupine. His chest swelled so that Emily expected his brass buttons would fire off at any moment.

"Did your rebel friends tell you that the shooting took place only *after* the Pennsylvania volunteers were cut off from the rest of the Federal forces? *After* they had been pelted by missiles and cut by shattering glass?"

Emily held her tongue, though she was silently questioning his words. She had never heard of these supposed Pennsylvania men. She doubted Julia had, either. Was it true?

Dr. Mackay stepped closer, his anger seething. "Did they tell you that my brother, an *unarmed* man, had his head bashed by a paving stone? That he died twelve hours later?"

The disgust she felt instantly evaporated. Whether his facts concerning the riot were entirely accurate or not was not the issue. He had suffered the loss of a loved one. He was suffering still.

His anger must be his attempt to manage the pain. Her heart squeezed. "Dr. Mackay, I—"

"Do not lecture me, miss, about your good citizens of Baltimore! I know perfectly well what you all are capable of."

He stared at her, his gray eyes as sharp as any bayonet. She held his gaze.

"I apologize for my hasty words, Dr. Mackay. I am truly sorry for your loss. How many years had your brother?"

The old proverb about a soft answer turning away wrath proved true. He looked surprised that she would even ask. His stance softened just a little.

"He was nineteen."

She grieved any loss of life, Confederate or Federal. The cost of war was much too high. "Too young," she whispered.

"Aye. 'Twas much too young indeed."

The color was slowly fading from his face. Dr. Mackay raked back his dark brown hair, looking as if he didn't know what to say next.

Emily waited, wondering. *Will he regain his temper, or will he dismiss me without further word?*

He did not have time for either. A steward from Sally and Elizabeth's section appeared at the door. "Doctor, come quick! Your assistance is needed."

The call of duty snapped him back to his determined, unyielding state. His shoulders straightened and the commanding physician immediately turned. Emily stared after his broad back until the door closed behind him. Breathing a sigh of relief, she then returned to her own ward.

Chapter Three

By the time Emily stepped back into the ward, Edward's parents had arrived. Mrs. Stanton was seated in a chair next to her son's bed, talking to him in soothing tones. Dr. Stanton was standing beside her. Emily did not see Julia anywhere in the room. She wondered if she had gone to break the horrible news to Sally concerning Stephen's death.

Emily moved to where Edward lay. Ignoring everyone, he had once again turned his eyes to the wall. His parents, however, greeted her warmly.

"Look," Mrs. Stanton said to her son. "Emily has returned."

Yes, she thought as heat crept into her cheeks. *I have returned.* She felt terrible about what had just happened in the corridor. She wondered when exactly the Stantons had arrived, how much of her altercation with Dr. Mackay they had overheard. She knew her voice had carried. She could tell by the grins on the Confederate men's faces. They all seemed pleased she had put the Federal doctor in his place.

Emily was not pleased. She knew she had set a terrible example, and her timing with Edward had caused him more pain. She knelt beside him.

"Eddie, I am so very sorry for the disturbance earlier. So very sorry about it all."

He continued to stare at the cracked plaster wall. She dared not say any more. She looked to his parents. Mrs. Stanton had tears in her eyes. Her husband's face also showed concern.

"Can I fetch you anything?" Emily asked them.

"Some fresh water," Dr. Stanton said. He picked up the nearby pitcher. "This one is empty."

She reached for it.

"No," he said with a kind smile. "That's all right. Just show me where."

She led him to the water buckets at the opposite end of the room. Dr. Stanton ladled the liquid into the pitcher.

"Julia told us about the battle," he said. "Would you tell me what happened with Edward just before we arrived?"

Emily did so, right up to the part where Dr. Mackay breathed out his fire.

"And Edward held your gaze?"

"Yes. He spoke to me, although it was a negative response."

"It was still a response and for that I am grateful." He smiled at her. "You did well, Emily. Don't blame yourself for what happened after the doctor's intrusion."

She appreciated his encouragement yet felt burdened at the same time. Surely Dr. Stanton was just as concerned as she. She knew he wished to be caring for Edward himself in the private hospital, but the Federal army would not allow it. The Stanton family did not have the political connections to change the army's mind.

"I am glad you are here to look after him," he said.

"Thank you, sir. If I may ask, where is Julia?"

"She has gone to see Sally. Sam has, as well." He turned from the table. "They are taking her home."

Good, she thought. *He will look after them both.* Emily thought how blessed Julia was to have a husband like Sam. He was a man of strong conviction, and compassion, as well. Emily hoped she would one day find someone of equal character.

Her parents did, too, and the sooner the better.

Though at twenty-four she was hardly an old maid, they repeatedly encouraged her not to spend all her time volunteering in the hospital.

"Life is not all service and duty," her mother insisted. "The occasional ball or outing will do you no harm. You are young and pretty, and you should give consideration to your future."

Emily sighed. She missed the days of music and laughter and she liked silk and satin as well as any other girl, but the young men in her social circle, the sons of lawyers and city politicians, held little interest for her. She had always imagined her heart belonging to some preacher or backwoods missionary rather than a polished gentleman of Southern society.

I want to serve God and His human creation with my whole heart, she thought. A smile tugged at the corners of her mouth. *My husband will be a man of faith, of courage and compassion.*

She didn't know where or when she might find such a man, but Emily knew one thing for certain. She would recognize him when she did.

But such dreams must be postponed until the end of the war. For now, I must do my duty.

The evening bell chimed and the night matron came on duty. Mrs. Danforth was a round little woman of about fifty or so who never lacked a smile.

"Good evening, dearie," she said. "And how are the boys today?"

Emily quickly gave her an overview of each man's condition. Although the woman was dedicated to the Union and wore a blue rosette on her apron proclaiming such, Emily had no hesitancy in leaving the Confederate men in her charge. She was a kind, Christian woman.

She was anxious, however, concerning Dr. Mackay. He still had not returned from the emergency in the next room. Though she had no desire to run the risk of being lectured by him again, she was reluctant to leave Mrs. Danforth shorthanded, especially given what had just happened with Billy.

"Should I stay until he returns?"

The older woman waved her off. "Bless ya, no. He may be hours still. He's been called to surgery. Some poor Texas boy is in a difficult way."

Emily's heart sank. She knew by what she'd witnessed that afternoon that Dr. Mackay was a capable physician, but the poor man now under his knife would need more than skillful surgery. He would need encouragement, compassion—and those were things the Federal doctor would *not* give.

"Fetch your basket, dearie," Mrs. Danforth urged. "Your family will be expecting you."

That was certain. Her parents would worry if she was late and she did not want Joshua, their driver, to be kept waiting at the dock. Gathering her personal items, she bid everyone good-night and left the ward.

Reverend Zachariah Henry and his wife, Eliza, both delegates of the Christian Commission, were departing, as well. Emily met them at the main entrance. Reverend Henry tipped his topper. He smiled.

"Well, Miss Davis, how was your day?"

"Well enough," she said as they descended the long wooden ramp leading to the street.

Eliza patted her arm. She must have sensed Emily's thoughts were still with the wounded men. "You must learn to leave your charges in God's hands," she said gently. "He will watch over them."

She was right of course, but it was a task easier said than done. "Are the two of you going home for the evening?" she asked.

"Shortly," Reverend Henry said. "First we will stop at Apollo Hall."

The Baltimore chapter of the commission had rented several floors of the building for the sorting and distribution of Bibles and supplies. The items were given to Federal soldiers and sailors in town and in the nearby army camps. The commission also cared for the prisoners of war in the hospitals and forts. The reverend and his wife had the opportunity to personally minister to wounded men on the battlefield following Antietam. Emily respected the couple greatly.

"We want to see how many cases are ready for distribution," he said.

Emily knew what he was referring to. She had helped to pack a few of those cases herself. The long numbered boxes looked as though they carried muskets, but in reality they were full of foodstuffs and medical supplies.

"Do you need any assistance?" she asked.

"Oh no," Eliza answered. "We'll see to it. You go

home and rest. One never knows what opportunities tomorrow will bring."

Opportunities was the word Eliza always used in the place of *challenges* or *difficulties*. The latter, she insisted, were invitations to see God's hand at work, to draw on His strength. Emily smiled slightly. She wondered how many *opportunities* Dr. Mackay would present her with tomorrow.

"Oh, there's Joshua," Eliza said. "We will see you in the morning."

Emily bid the Henrys a good-night, then walked toward her father's carriage. Her muscles ached. Her eyes were heavy. She hoped she would be able to stay awake long enough to reach home.

Despite his best efforts, the surgery was not successful. A pair of orderlies carried the dead man out. Nurses now prepared his bed for another. Exhausted, Evan took a moment to catch his breath before beginning evening rounds. He stared out the window. Sunset was upon the city, painting the warehouses in a softer glow.

Back in Pennsylvania, before the war, this was his favorite time of the day. He'd put his office in order, saddle his stallion and gallop for home. He would race back to Mary and her smile, to Andrew and whatever outrageous tale he would spin that day.

But that was before Baltimore.

Evan's eyes fell upon a woman below. He recognized her as his nurse, the one who'd dared go toe-to-toe with him in the corridor. He watched as she climbed into a carriage manned by what looked to be a slave and was promptly whisked away. He grunted.

I was right about her. She may have shown compassion in regards to Andrew, but she is no different than any other Maryland rebel, still holding on to her slaves even though President Lincoln has issued his Emancipation Proclamation.

And rebel slaveholders serving as nurses, whispering anti-Unionist words, was poison in this place. The woman may have somehow won the respect of the commission and the officers here in charge, but not him.

The Federal commander at Fort McHenry should have made good on his threat at the beginning of the war to fire his guns on Baltimore. If he had quelled the Southern ladies and gentlemen's taste for rebellion, the war would be over now. Countless lives could have been saved.

It would have been too late for Andrew but perhaps not for Mary. Instead he had lost both of them.

"Dr. Mackay?"

A female voice invaded his thoughts. He turned to find the night matron, a good patriotic woman, standing before him.

"Beg your pardon, Doctor, but it's time for the evening medication."

"Aye," he said. "Of course."

They went back to the ward. She had already secured a tray. Evan walked to the locked cabinet at the far end of the room. He took out a key from his inner vest pocket, unlocked the door, then started laying out the various pills and powders.

He made his rounds, distributing the necessary medication to each prisoner. When he came to the bed of the rebel major, the one Little Miss Baltimore was so bent on comforting, he told the family, "Visiting hours are now over."

The father, gray-headed and wearing spectacles,

politely protested. "Doctor, I am a physician myself. I would like to stay. Perhaps I can be of service to you."

You should have been of service two years ago, when the streets ran red with patriotic blood. "I am afraid that is impossible, sir," Evan said, deliberately disregarding the man's title. Professional courtesy did not extend to rebel doctors. "You may return on the morrow."

The man looked as though he would argue the point. Evan stretched to his full height. He stood a good six inches above the man. He leveled his most scrutinizing glare.

"Very well, then," the rebel doctor said, and he encouraged his wife to say goodbye.

She did so, though the boy in the bed simply stared past her. The pair was slow in exiting, but Evan stood his ground until the door shut solidly behind them. He then took what was left from the dispensary tray and sent the nurse away. He inspected the Johnny's wound. The site was healing satisfactorily, so Evan replaced the bandages, then moved on.

When his rounds were complete, he tramped off to his quarters, a postage-stamp room with a cot, a wash basin and a view of the city he so detested. After pulling off his soiled shirt, he lay down and tried to find a comfortable position. The bed was much too short for his body.

Despite being exhausted, he struggled for hours to find peace. When sleep finally did claim him, he dreamed of Andrew and then Mary.

Emily was awakened by Abigail's gentle nudge.

"Rise and shine. You don't wanna be late, now. I've drawn you a cool bath and laid out a fresh dress for you to wear."

Though the precious hours of sleep had not been nearly long enough, Emily gave her friend a smile. After tending all day to wounded men it was nice to have someone look after her.

"Bless you, Abigail. You are a treasure."

The woman's dark, round face lit up with a wide smile. Abigail had come into service in Emily's home only a year ago. She and her husband, Joshua, recently married, had been slaves in the household of one of Emily's father's clients. When the man had died, he had left a considerable amount of debt. As a lawyer it was her father's job to oversee distribution of the estate, to make peace with the man's creditors.

Rather than see Abigail and Joshua sold once again on the slave auction block, he ransomed the pair himself. Because he found slavery so abhorrent, he then promptly drew up papers granting Joshua and Abigail their freedom.

"We knowed right away your father was a good man," Abigail once told Emily. "So we asked to come to work for him."

Emily was so glad they had. As an only child, with parents heavily involved in professional and civic responsibilities, the house at times could be quite lonely. Abigail became the older sister Emily had never had. They laughed. They shared secrets. They encouraged one another in their faith.

"Hurry now," Abigail urged. "Your mama will have breakfast on the table shortly."

Emily readied herself, then stepped into a gray cotton day dress with tight-fitting coat sleeves. The simple style would serve her well in the hospital.

"That shorter hemline will work better for you, I believe," Abigail said. "Your dress from the other day is still soakin'. That dark ring 'round the bottom hasn't yet come clean."

"No matter how many times they scrub, that hospital floor is still filthy," Emily said. The West's Buildings needed an army of scrub maids alone just to keep up with the task. She wondered if Dr. Mackay would permanently transfer her to that brigade after what she had said to him yesterday.

Emily fastened the hooks and eyes of her bodice, then adjusted her collar. Abigail smiled. "I declare, you are just as pretty in gray cotton as in pink silk. You'll be cheerin' those poor men right nicely."

The thought of Dr. Mackay's grief-stricken face suddenly passed through Emily's mind. He had looked so lost when she inquired of his brother.

"You be thinkin' of a particular soldier?" her friend asked.

"No. Well, I suppose so. A Yankee doctor."

"Um-hmm," Abigail said as she took the brush from Emily's hand and began to arrange her hair. "He handsome?"

"Handsome?" He wasn't particularly *ugly,* yet then again, how could Emily really say? She had only seen him once, for sixty seconds at the most, without a scowl on his face. "He's a big tall tree of a man. A Scotsman."

"Um-hmm. Like them ones in your poetry book?"

Emily let out a laugh, knowing where Abigail's thoughts were headed. "Oh, far from it! All this man does is bark orders and frown. He makes more work for us than any other doctor. Do you know he insists on washing his hands after tending to each man?"

"Does he?"

"Yes, and not in the wash basin, mind you. Fresh water each time. Our ward goes through more buckets than the entire hospital combined. He is dreadful to work with and he treats us all as enemies."

She stopped, realizing how foolish she sounded. Whatever she'd had to endure at the hand of Dr. Mackay was nothing compared to what Abigail and Joshua had faced.

"I'm sorry. That was thoughtless of me to complain so."

Abigail's face, however, showed not the slightest offence. "He just sounds like a soldier in need of cheerin' to me."

Her kindness often amazed Emily. Of anyone, Abigail had the most reason to be bitter. Lincoln's Emancipation Proclamation had taken effect earlier that year, but the document only proclaimed freedom to slaves in states of rebellion. Maryland had been kept in the Union by force. Since the state had not seceded, slavery was still legal, and the occupying army didn't appear to be in any hurry to change that.

Furthermore, while many on the Confederate side did not support slavery, a great many did. Emily once asked Abigail what she thought of her tending to such men.

"Please be honest with me. Does it trouble you?"

"At times," she admitted. "But then I think 'bout that verse in the Bible. 'Love your enemies. Bless them that curse you.' I don't reckon this world will change much if we don't start takin' the Lord's message to heart."

Abigail finished setting the pins in Emily's hair. "Your kindness to that Yankee doctor and to them other soldiers could go a long way," she insisted. "You remember that."

Emily nodded. She would try.

After breakfast the family went their separate ways.

Emily's mother was off to a bandage drive for the local hospitals, and her father had business at Fort McHenry.

Joshua drove her to the harbor, where a ghastly sight met her eyes. The Westminster trains had brought new wounded. Scores of bleeding, sick men lay once more along the docks. She could hear them begging for water and other simple necessities. Army personnel and many volunteers scurried about.

"Shall I stay with ya, Miss Emily?" Joshua offered. "Looks like ya could use the help."

She wanted to say yes but feared in this chaotic environment Joshua would soon be commandeered as a slave, at least temporarily.

"Thank you, Joshua, but no. Perhaps you should return home."

He nodded and tipped his slouch hat. "I'll be by at sunset to collect you."

"Thank you."

It was only after he had rolled away that Emily realized that in her shock over the sight before her, she'd left her basket and bonnet in the carriage. She would need covering from the sun as the day wore on.

But a few freckles will do me no harm, she thought. *I'll make do.* She turned for the docks.

Her heart broke. The cries of suffering rose around her and it was almost impossible to walk without stepping on a wounded man. Swallowing back her emotions, she found a water bucket and went to work. Emily doled out the precious liquid and gently wiped dust-caked faces. While doing so, she glanced down the dock. Trudy, Elizabeth and Rebekah had each arrived. They were doing the same.

Surgeons raced back and forth. Confederates and Federal soldiers alike were begging for their attention.

The injured men were in desperate need of pain medication. Although they had been tended to in the field hospitals, many also needed suturing. In some cases the train to Baltimore had caused as much damage as the battlefield.

Help them, Lord.

Before she could even finish the thought, Dr. Mackay came storming toward her. His white collar was soaked with sweat, his shirtsleeves and blue vest already stained.

"Don't just stand there, Nurse! Put down the bucket and follow me!"

She handed it to a nearby woman and hurried after him.

Deep amidst the wounded men an orderly stood holding three skeins of yarn. Dr. Mackay took them from the man and quickly dismissed him. He then handed the skeins to her, along with a pair of scissors.

"Now, do exactly as I say."

Do what? she wondered. *What good is yarn among thirsty and bleeding men? They need water! That is what we always do first!*

"We will take this section here," he said, waving his big hand over the general area where they stood. "Red for immediate care. Green for those to go to Fort McHenry. Blue for the transport steamers north. Understand?"

Of course she didn't understand. She glanced about. No one else had yarn. They were armed with buckets and bandages. "Excuse me?"

Frustration filled his face. That vein at the top of his collar was bulging again. "Tie the appropriate color to the man's left arm, according to what I tell you!"

In her confusion, she said the first thing that came to mind. "What if he has no left arm?"

"Then tie it to the right one! Come!"

He pulled at her sleeve. It was all Emily could do not to recoil from his touch. *What is he about to do? Sort the men into lots? Give the Federal soldiers a red ribbon, permission for care, while tossing the wounded Confederates into carts and hauling them off to prison?*

Emily shuddered. She wouldn't put it past him.

Lord, what should I do?

If she continued to allow him to drag her along she may end up sending Confederate soldiers to their deaths, yet if she challenged him, the berating she'd surely receive would consume any time she could spend caring for the men.

Give me wisdom, she prayed, yet none came.

Dr. Mackay let go of her arm when they reached a pallet of wounded Federal soldiers. "Red yarn," he ordered. "All three of them."

No surprise here.

She did as commanded. He sprinkled powdered morphine directly into their wounds while she knelt to wipe the blood from the first man's face with her apron.

"Bless you, miss," the soldier said.

"No! Follow me!"

Emily was thoroughly confused. "I tie a string to his arm giving permission for care and then I leave him?"

Without any explanation, he went on. She felt she had no choice at that point but to follow.

"These here...red string."

Dr. Mackay had her tie the same color onto three other soldiers in blue and then, much to her surprise, on two Confederate men. However, she was not allowed to touch any of them further. When they reached the pallet of one shoeless soldier, Dr. Mackay said flatly, "This rebel is dead."

He didn't even stop to close the man's eyes. He left him staring heavenward. Emily's heart ached. Red string, red string, blue, blue, green…They continued through the maze of broken, mud-crusted bodies.

Though Emily still thought his actions were ridiculous, she was beginning to see a pattern. Those with superficial injuries, Yankees of course, were tagged for transport north. Confederates able to stand were marked for Fort McHenry. She was surprised at the number of wounded prisoners of both sides who the doctor deemed worthy of the red ribbon. She was horrified, however, at the number who received no marker at all, only a little morphine.

One such man happened to be a Federal sergeant with a gaping hole in his chest. When Dr. Mackay turned away from him, Emily could stand it no longer. She grabbed his arm. He looked back at her, obviously annoyed.

"But he's one of *yours!* Do something, please! Can't you hear him? He's in terrible pain!"

The doctor's face softened slightly. "The powder will help," he said.

"But—"

He bent low to her ear. "There isn't anything to be done. Why the field surgeons sent him here is beyond me." He freed himself from her grasp. "Come…there are still others."

Armed with nothing more than the useless string, Emily continued on. When she reached the last man in their section and tied her last marker, Dr. Mackay turned and said, "Now go back to the ones with the red ribbons. Apply clean dressing to those that have been tended to."

"And when I have finished? What of the ones with no string?"

His jaw twitched. He raked back his hair, which had curled even more in the July humidity. "Aye. Comfort them as best as you are able." He then pointed to a supply wagon. It was filled with baskets of bandages. "Take that with you."

He waded back through the mangled mass of humanity from which they had just come. As she watched him go, Emily noticed for the first time what had been happening behind her.

Jeremiah Wainwright and several volunteers from the commission, including Eliza Henry, were already at work. One gave water to all; another washed away mud; still another was removing soiled bandages.

Two other assistant surgeons as well as Dr. Mackay were now tending to wounds. They were doing so not according to which army the men served, but by the rank of the colored yarn.

It may have been unconventional, but Emily now saw the wisdom in his plan. While other sections were scrambling from one wounded soldier to the next, her portion of the dock was running in an orderly progression.

I misjudged him, she thought. *Forgive me, Lord.*

She snatched the basket of bandages from the wagon and ran after him.

The sun was now high in the sky and the temperature was rising. Emily's head burned.

Of all the days to forget my bonnet, she thought.

But the cries of those around her made her forget her own discomfort.

If these poor soldiers can march through fields and

furrows without complaint, under the baking sun, then so can I.

She continued through the rows, applying bandages, offering prayers and encouraging words. Dr. Mackay moved just a few paces in front of her. He was back to barking orders.

"Steward, move this man to surgery! Clean up this pallet! Fetch me a fresh bucket of water!"

As she dressed the wounds, Emily watched boys in blue, many younger than she, scramble to do his bidding. She felt sorry for them. It seemed even Unionists were terrified of Dr. Mackay.

Abigail's verse drifted through her mind. *Love your enemies. Bless them that curse you.* Knowing that compassion should be shown to surly Yankees as well, Emily set down her basket and went to Eliza Henry.

Going out of my way to show kindness to him might encourage a little on his part. It might ensure better treatment of the wounded men.

"Cup of water for you, dear?" the woman asked when Emily approached her.

"Please."

She drew out a tin cup from the cloth pouch on her shoulder, then scooped up the water.

"Thank you."

"You're welcome, dear."

Emily marched straight to the blistering Scotsman. The man had just finished ordering a Federal nurse to bring him more thread. She looked as though she was about to cry.

"But there isn't any more," she insisted. "We are almost out of iron wire, as well!"

"Then procure some from another section."

"The other surgeons are almost out."

"Then go down to one of the shops and purchase some!"

The woman ran off, apparently to do just that. Emily touched his sweat-drenched sleeve. He turned, practically glaring at her.

Kind words for him in short supply, she had to rely on action alone. Emily handed him the cup. Emptying it in one gulp, he rubbed his glistening forehead with the back of his hand and then returned to work.

There was no thank-you.

"I may know of some available thread," she said.

He pulled a piece of lead as long as her finger from a man's arm. "Then by all means, fetch it!"

Tucking the cup into her skirt pocket, she hurried for the hospital. She was certain she would find Julia inside at her usual post. Her friend always kept a carpetbag with her full of knitting or sewing projects. If anyone had thread, it would be her.

The West's Buildings felt like a furnace. Emily scarcely believed inside could be hotter than the outside under the baking sun, but it was. The heat made her a little light-headed, but she climbed the staircase quickly.

As she had hoped, Julia was seated beside Edward's bed, fanning and reading aloud from the Psalms. He was ignoring her. She turned as Emily approached, then gasped.

"Oh, Em! Your face is as red as a ripe strawberry!"

Emily wasn't surprised. "I forgot my sunbonnet and we have been treating the new wounded outside all morning."

"Then by all means, take mine."

Julia reached for a lovely little green silk bonnet on the table beside her. Emily appreciated her gesture but couldn't be certain it would survive the day.

"That's sweet, but what I really need is thread. Have you any?"

"Of course. Right here." She reached into her bag. "I have two spools...gray and black."

"May I have them both? We are completely out."

"Certainly."

Emily slipped them into her pocket alongside Dr. Mackay's cup. She leaned closer to take a quick peek at Edward, but could tell there was no change.

As she straightened up, Julia set her bonnet on Emily's head and quickly tied a pretty bow.

"Thank you," Emily said, "but I can't promise I'll be able to return it in any condition for you to wear again."

Her friend waved her off. "It is a small price to pay for those caring for our men."

As they walked toward the door, Emily asked about Sally.

"She took the news as well as could be expected," Julia said.

"Poor thing."

"She and her father have gone to the battlefield to look for themselves."

Oh dear, Emily thought. *So the Hastings family has gone to search for Stephen's body, to bring him home for a proper burial.* "If you hear from her, will you let me know?"

"Of course."

Only then, as Emily gave a quick glance around the room, did she notice another soldier now occupied Billy's bed. Her heart immediately squeezed, for she knew what must have happened.

"He died during the night," Julia said, guessing what she was thinking. "Jeremiah said the Scottish doctor took him to surgery, but the poor man didn't survive the operation."

Though civility compelled at least a moment of pause, an acknowledgment of a life that had passed, Emily knew there was not time. Dr. Mackay needed his supplies. Outside was a dock full of soldiers who could still be saved.

Chapter Four

Little Miss Baltimore had returned, sporting a green silk bonnet straight out of the women's fashion magazines. When he had told the army nurse to go to the store and buy supplies, he didn't think this woman would actually seize the opportunity to do some shopping.

But then again, she is a Southern volunteer. I shouldn't expect anything different. She has at least procured two spools of thread.

"Will these do?" she asked, as if concerned that the color of the man's stitches might clash with his ensemble.

He took them from her. "This is no garden party."

She stared at him, eyes wide.

Is she really that dense? "As soon as I finish, bandage him up. Understand?"

"Yes, Doctor."

"And be careful not to spoil that lovely bonnet."

She blinked. Evan couldn't tell if she was still unable to comprehend his comment or if she was simply choosing to ignore him. If it was the latter, then he complimented her. After yesterday's debate over who started this war, at least she was learning to hold her tongue.

He finished suturing, then moved on, patching up every brave boy in blue, every Johnny sporting a red string. The Southern nurse stayed just one step behind him. Evan eyed her repeatedly.

At least she follows my instructions today without argument, without hurling something at me like I am certain she so often wishes to do.

He was no fool. He had seen the disgust, the mistrust in her eyes. She'd thought he was going to sort the wounded into lots by allegiance, treat the loyal and then leave her beloved coconspirators for dead.

He wouldn't do that. He may despise them but he would do his best to save them. He would do his duty, and to do so efficiently, he could not take time to think about the ones, like the reb from last night, who didn't survive.

There was a new school of thought circulating among some doctors in regard to how mass casualties should be treated. Many doubted its effectiveness, but Evan had seen it work firsthand. By sorting the wounded into those who *could* be saved and then in order of urgency of treatment, more could be cared for in a shorter amount of time. He had also learned that assigning a different task to each member of his staff, whether it be cleaning or bandaging, made the process easier.

He glanced about the dock, noting that physicians were scrambling in other sections, while wounded still cried out in pain.

If only they would be willing to embrace new ideas.

Even something as simple as the repeated washing of hands and instruments to help combat the spread of infection was scoffed at by many doctors. Evan cringed every time he saw a surgeon in the field hospital hack off a limb, wipe his saw on his coattails and then move on to the next man.

No wonder so many of our men are dying. For every one the rebs kill, disease takes two.

He continued on, probing, packing, stitching. Mercifully, his thread held until he finished the last of the soldiers marked in red. He walked back through the area, stretching his leg muscles and working the knot from his neck while he checked on his nurse's progress.

She was actually doing quite well, in spite of her ridiculous bonnet.

The supply wagons were unloaded and Evan still continued. In the hospital the ward masters were emptying all beds possible to make space for the new arrivals. He gave orders to the stewards as to which red-tagged men should be moved inside. He also gave instructions for removal of the dead. In this suffocating heat, speed was of the utmost importance. Nearly all of the wounded Evan had left untagged had expired.

Only one remained.

The Pennsylvania sergeant missing most of his chest was still gasping for breath. *She* was with him, holding his hand. As he approached, he overheard their conversation.

"I prayed, ever so hard. Beggin' God to let me see you just once more."

"Hush now," she encouraged. "Save your strength."

"All that's left for me now, girl, is eternity. But, don't you cry...."

Evan watched as she smoothed back the sergeant's hair. The look on his face told him it wouldn't be long now. She must have known it, as well.

"Have you made your peace with God?" she asked gently. "Do you know Christ as your Savior?"

"Now, darlin'," he said, "you know I do. Made that decision a long time ago, I did."

He sputtered. Her shoulders trembled.

"I love you, Anna."

"I love you…."

Regret shot through Evan, a feeling he knew all too well. *No wonder she begged me to save him. But who could have known she would have a sweetheart serving in the United States army?*

He moved closer, knowing there was nothing that could be done, yet wishing there was. His collar grew so tight that he had trouble breathing. Memories washed over him. The little lass was doing what he wished he could have done, what he *should have* done.

Mary…

The rattle began and the man struggled to draw his final breaths. She held on, steady to the end, his hand in hers. When the sergeant died, it was with a smile on his face.

Only then did her unbridled tears fall. Evan stepped forward and closed the soldier's eyes. When she looked up at him, he was pierced by grief.

Despite knowing some rebel shell had caused all this, despite Andrew's death and her being a citizen of this dreadful city, something inside him wished to comfort her. He realized up until now he hadn't even bothered to learn her name.

"I'm sorry, Anna." He stumbled on the words. "I had no idea who he was."

She blinked once, twice, wiped her eyes. "Emily."

"Say again?"

"My name is Emily."

She slowly regained her composure. Evan looked at her, befuddled. "He called you Anna."

"He mistook me for his wife. I didn't have the heart to correct him."

Tears drying, she stood, methodically covering the man with his own bedroll. Evan could feel his anger building. He wasn't certain for whom he felt the emotion, for the poor soldier who'd been mislead or for himself.

He had felt sorry for a rebel.

"You deliberately misrepresented yourself," he said.

"I told him what he wished to hear."

"Aye. I'm certain that came quite easily. You Baltimore women are skilled in the art of treachery."

She flinched. He knew his words had stung.

"He prayed he would see his beloved Anna once more," she said. "Would you have me deny the final wish of a dying man?"

"Are you in the place of God? Have you the power to grant requests as you see fit?"

Her cheeks flushed red. She looked as though she would fire back once again, but he didn't give her the opportunity.

"Go report to Dr. Turner, and for goodness' sake, do your best not to cause any more trouble!"

Without further word, she turned. He went back to work.

I was not trying to cause trouble! Emily swallowed back the words, those and many more, as she stomped away. *There is no point reasoning with a man like him. Arrogant...hardheaded...I don't care how skilled a physician he is! I wish the army would send him on!*

She made her way to Dr. Turner's section of the dock. There a horde of Federal soldiers was keeping guard over the Confederate men lining up for the three-mile march to Fort McHenry. Dr. Turner was treating the last of the superficial wounds.

"Dr. Mackay said I should now report to you," Emily told him.

He tied a bandage around a young soldier's arm. "Wonderful," he said without looking up. "Go and help Miss Elizabeth. I am certain she must be quite tired by now."

"Yes, sir."

If Dr. Mackay had meant for her relocation to be a punishment, it was not. Emily would gladly work under Dr. Turner any day.

She saw Elizabeth at a distance, armed with a drinking gourd and a bucket of water. She was going to each dust-covered man. When Emily caught her eye, she smiled, then motioned to another water bucket nearby. Emily quickly grabbed it.

Thanks to the combination of the altercation with the ill-tempered Scotsman and the blazing sun, Emily's head was now pounding. She wanted to rest but dared not do so. The Federal soldiers had given orders. Already the column of ragtag Confederates was beginning to march. Emily hurried to give a drink to as many of them as possible before they departed.

She offered some to a Virginia man and a Tennessean. A shoeless old man from Alabama tipped his slouch hat but then gave the cup to his exhausted comrade beside him.

"God bless ya, miss."

"God keep you, sir."

The afternoon heat was stifling. Emily's cotton dress clung to her and her petticoats felt more like wet wool than light silk. The column moved faster. Several men in tow struck up the song "Bonnie Blue Flag," but they were stopped by the Federals before they could reach the first *Hurrah!* She ladled out the water as fast as she could, but by now her stomach was rolling. Was it her imagination or was the ground shifting beneath her feet?

"Steady there, girl!" Dr. Turner suddenly tugged her back from the marching men. He felt her cheeks and forehead. "I fear the sun has taken its toll on you. You need to rest. Your face is like a New England lobster!"

Her knees were unsteady, her eyesight fuzzy. Something was terribly wrong. She knew she needed to sit. *But if I take leave, they will be a nurse short. It will mean more work for everyone else, less care for Confederate men.*

"When was the last time you had anything to drink?" Dr. Turner asked.

Elizabeth appeared over his shoulder. She, too, looked concerned.

Emily struggled to put thoughts into words. "I...I..."

"Come now. Let's find you a nice, quiet place—"

"But Dr. Mackay said—"

"I am certain Evan agrees with me. Don't you, young man?"

Oh, no... The heavy bucket slipped out of her hands, water spilling all over the cobblestone. As Emily hurried to right it, her eyes darkened.

A strong pair of arms swept her upward.

She awoke sometime later to the feel of a cool cloth on her forehead. Elizabeth was hovering over her, a palmetto fan in her hand.

"Where am I?" Emily asked when her vision fully cleared. The room was small, relatively quiet. She had never seen it before.

"Dr. Mackay's room."

"What?" Emily ran her fingers over the rough muslin sheet. She was aghast at the thought of occupying *his* cot, mortified when she saw her stockings tossed across a nearby chair.

"It was the only place right now that offered any privacy," Elizabeth insisted. "He deposited you here, then told me how to care for you."

Emily's embarrassment subsided, but only somewhat. "Did he order you to deliver me to Fort McHenry upon my recovery?"

"Whatever for?"

"For my prison term. He calls me a woman of treachery and finds me incompetent at that."

"He must not find you that treacherous. He said I was to do everything in my power to bring about your swift recovery."

Emily blinked and slowly raised up on her elbows. She was still a little light-headed. "He said that?"

Elizabeth removed the cloth, soaked it in the nearby wash basin. She then thrust a cup of cold water under Emily's nose. "Drink," she commanded sweetly.

The water slid down her parched throat. Emily downed the entire contents in two very unladylike gulps.

"He even went to the cook and secured these." Elizabeth handed her two fresh peaches and a slice of hardtack. "He said to eat it all, though I would seriously reconsider the hardtack, especially if you want to keep all of your teeth."

Emily giggled. If anyone knew how to make her laugh, it was Elizabeth, though few people knew that. The girl always played the role of a refined young lady in public.

Rising to a sitting position ever so slowly, she leaned

back against the wall. She started in on the peach. It tasted ever so sweet.

"Have mercy." Her friend chuckled, peering close. "Dr. Turner said your face was as red as a lobster. I believe he was right."

"Wonderful." Emily shuddered to think of what fate she would have met had Julia not given her the bonnet when she did.

Emily offered her friend the second peach but Elizabeth protested.

"Eat it," Emily insisted, "or you may be the next to fall."

They ate the fruit, soaked the hardtack in the water, then nibbled on the soggy remains. While doing so, Emily glanced around Dr. Mackay's room. The space was completely bare. There were no photographs of family or friends, no testaments of faith. There was nothing that revealed any clue to who he was beyond the medical book on the corner desk and the blue army frock coat on the peg behind the door.

She thought what a contradiction he was. One moment he was scolding her for kindness shown to a dying man, the next he was going out of his way to tend to her needs.

She cringed. *He has more important matters to oversee than my needs. There is a dock full of wounded outside. More probably on the way.* Scooting to the edge of the cot, she said to Elizabeth, "Hand me my stockings, will you?"

"Whatever for?"

"I need to get back to work."

"Oh, no you don't! Dr. Mackay gave strict orders that once you regain your strength you are to leave the hospital. Sam and Julia are waiting to escort you home."

Emily leaned back against the wall, air slowly leaking from her lungs. *Now I see...*

The Federal doctor wasn't fussing over her health because he valued her skills as a nurse. She was a "rebel" and he was using the excuse of her frailty to get rid of her.

Now a nurse short and faced with a dock full of army bureaucrats who wouldn't even consider the thought of adapting to new medical procedures, Evan struggled to tend to the battle wounded in sections not his own.

Every lad in blue reminded him of Andrew and every one that he came upon too late made him curse this war and the rebels who had started it all. Were it not for them he would be home in Pennsylvania, back in his little two-room office, stitching up the busted knees of little boys *playing* war.

At the end of the day he would put out the lamps and gallop home. The wheat fields would be ripe for harvest, the sky vast and blue, much like the old country itself. At his doorpost Mary would be waiting. She would seize him, kiss him full on the lips. Then she would take his hand and lead him to the kitchen, where supper would be waiting on the stove. There would be fresh bread, beef stew, peach pie. Afterward they would sit by the fire. She would coax him into reading Burns, and he would promise her shelter and love and that she would always be his queen.

He had failed her on all three promises. For Evan knew if he had truly been a man of his word he would have heeded her warning.

"Forgive, my love. You are actin' out of anger. You seek revenge, you do. Not justice."

He wouldn't listen. The army had to stop the rebellion, had to preserve the Union, and *he* had to do his part. "I must go. This enemy is relentless. More boys will fall."

"Aye," she'd said. "And they will need a competent physician, but tending to them will not ease your heart. It will not bring Andrew back to you."

She was right, but it was too late to do anything about it now.

The man before him, a New Yorker, flinched.

"Hold still now, lad," Evan said to him. "I'll be as quick and as nimble as I can."

"Yes, Doc."

The soldier was sporting a gash from his ear to his chin, courtesy of a rebel bayonet. It had been sutured poorly at the field hospital and the stitches had ripped open. Evan did his best to mend the damage done, to reassure the man.

"Don't worry now. Your lass will view your scar as a mark of bravery and honor."

Or at least he hoped she would. Evan had been telling the same story to every U.S. soldier for the past two years.

Though not a day went by that he didn't regret his decision to leave Mary, he did the best he could to make a difference. He had patched up the Army of the Potomac one battle at a time, cared for men throughout General McClellan's blunders and now George Meade's glory. He knew that his medical skill had served to save lives…but his stubborn insistence on leaving Pennsylvania behind to join in the war had cost him the life he valued above all others.

Evan hoped somehow God would forgive him for his foolishness. *But so far, I continue to pay for my sins…*

He could almost hear Mary's voice in his ear. *For-*

giveness doesn't come by way of earnin' it. It comes by askin'.

But asking and receiving are two different matters, Evan thought. *And God has seen fit to say no or else He would not have sent me to Baltimore.*

The sun finally dipped low in the hazy, midsummer sky. Whatever men could be brought inside were moved. Steamers carried a vast number to points north and a steady stream of rebel prisoners were marched to the makeshift prison pens at Fort McHenry. Of those that still remained on the docks, most of them were rebs. They were guarded by sentinels and looked after by the night nurses, who were now coming on duty.

Bone-weary, skin blistered from all day in the sun, Evan climbed the staircase to his quarters, suddenly recalling the woman he had left in them. He had forgotten the little Southern miss until now. He was pleased to find she no longer occupied the room. He didn't want to look at another person in need. Closing the door solidly behind him, he hoped to shut out the sounds of moaning, the stench of rebellion. He turned for his bed.

There on the cot, atop freshly smoothed sheets, lay a letter addressed to him. The script was precise yet gentle.

I thank you most graciously for your kindness and expertise shown today on my behalf. I apologize for any inconvenience I have caused you. I will adhere to your strict order of two days convalescence at home. Thereafter, I shall return to the hospital, eager to resume any and all duties.

It was signed, "Most appreciatively, Emily E. Davis." Evan crumbled the note and tossed it to the desk. He wondered what her high-society friends would think when they beheld her sun-spotted face, wondered how many cries she would utter over the loss of her flawless white skin when it began to peel.

She'll reconsider her nursing duties when her Southern gentlemen no longer find her attractive. Then the army can fill her position with a loyal volunteer.

Emily couldn't remember the last time she had slept so long or so heavily. It must have been sometime before the war. She woke to find a tray of fresh greens and chicken. Evidently she had missed breakfast all together and Abigail had sent up dinner instead.

The fever from the sun's effects had finally passed, but the skin on her face was now as tight as a drum. Though her stomach was rumbling, she took only small bites. Working her mouth was painful, and yawning, excruciating.

After eating she slipped on a comfortable corded petticoat and wrapper. One look in the mirror confirmed what she had feared; skin so parched and peeling it was hideous to look at. She tried to brush her hair, but her scalp rebelled at the task. Leaving it loose about her shoulders, she headed downstairs.

The house was quiet, but Emily found Abigail in the kitchen, a bushel basket of peaches at her feet and a pot of steaming water on the stove.

"Hello, Abigail," Emily said as she deposited the meal tray on the table.

Her friend took one look at her and gasped. "Law, Emily…"

"I know," she said quickly. "But it is only temporary. Trust me. I have seen much worse on the soldiers."

"I 'magine that, but they used to it…all that marchin'. A lady's skin should be soft, like these here peaches."

She tossed a few into the boiling water, then just as quickly immersed them into cold. The skins slipped easily off, revealing soft flesh.

"Wish I could do that."

"Reckon you do. I got some salve that might help. Want me to fetch it?"

"Not now, but thank you." Emily scooped out the blanched fruit, then as it cooled, began to chop. "You have a whole bushel?"

"There's more than that." Abigail pointed to the corner of the kitchen. Several baskets lined the wall.

"Where did you get them?"

"One of your father's clients."

"That was generous."

"Um-hmm. Don't know what we gonna do with all of 'um though. Only so much jam and cobbler a family can eat."

A thought popped into Emily's head. It must have entered Abigail's mind at the same time, for she laid aside her spoon and said, "Reckon those soldiers at the hospital would care for some pie?"

Emily smiled, though it was painful to do so. "I was just thinking the same. They are all starved for reminders of home, the guards and stewards, as well. Elizabeth says visitors to her ward have brought in food and they were met with great response."

But therein lay the problem. *I do not serve in Elizabeth's ward. What Dr. Turner will welcome, Dr. Mackay more than likely will not.*

"Reckon we ought to fix a special pie for that Yankee doctor of yours?"

"Abigail, you are a wise woman." It may be bribery,

and Dr. Mackay may recognize it as such, but Emily was willing to risk his ire for the possibility of showing kindness to the Confederate men. "What man in his right mind would turn down a homemade pie? Especially one living off of army rations? I'll start on the crust."

Abigail giggled. "Might wanna add plenty-a sugar."

"Splendid idea. Maybe we can sweeten him up a little."

Perhaps then he wouldn't be so eager to be rid of her.

Before the breakfast trays had even been delivered, Evan entered the room to find the prisoners eating. In shock, he stood for a moment and stared. It was peach pie, of all things. In between bites the men were reminiscing out loud about jam, cobbler or any other kitchen delight their wife, sweetheart or mother had ever baked.

Even the rebel major seemed to enjoy his slice. Evan watched as he cast his sister a glance and offered the faintest hint of a smile. He knew he should be pleased to see some sort of progress on the Johnny's part, but he wasn't. The sight of rebels enjoying themselves was too much for him.

He wasn't surprised to find Nurse Emily at the center of it all. Evidently, she'd been quite busy during her time of convalescence—or at least, someone in her household had been.

"What is the meaning of this?" he demanded when she stepped over to meet him.

There was an uncut pie in her hands, a smile pasted on her sunburned face. "Just trying to pass on a little kindness to the men," she said.

No doubt. "They are prescribed three proper meals per day."

"Yes, but a soldier can only stomach beef, beans and

rice for so long. Do not worry. I have followed your orders concerning their diets."

He had noticed that. Those on full diet were hungrily devouring thick slices; those on half, only mashed peaches. Prisoners prescribed low diet had received just a spoonful or two of syrup. He could not argue she had disobeyed his orders. He also realized that not only were the rebels enjoying the treat, his soldiers were, as well. One of the orderlies had crumbs lodged in his beard.

Nurse Emily seemed quite pleased with herself as she then offered up the pie in her hands.

"This one is for you," she said. "I wanted to thank you again for your kindness toward me the other day."

A whiff of the sugar and cinnamon drifted past his nose. His mouth watered. Peach pie was his favorite, and Mary had made it quite often. But it wasn't Mary who had baked this pie. He seriously doubted Nurse Emily had done it, either.

"Did one of your slaves bake that pie?"

Emily lowered her best defense, stunned. *One of my slaves? Why would he think...? Has he seen Joshua? Does he automatically assume that just because I am a Southerner I think men and women should be kept in chains?*

Or, she wondered, *is he one of those Yankees who believe in emancipation but not equality? Does he refuse to eat food prepared by a Negro?*

Emily's face burned, but it was not because of the sun. She was just about to tell the man what she thought of his haughty attitude, but something nudged her inside. *Giving in to anger will solve nothing. It will set another bad example for the wounded and it may just cost me the opportunity to minister to them further.*

She took a deep breath. "*I* made this pie," she said, "with the assistance of my *friend,* Abigail. She is a free woman."

His jaw shifted, but what that meant, Emily had no idea. Once more, she gave her most convincing smile and lifted the dish high.

"We thought perhaps you might enjoy something freshly baked, as a reminder of home."

He did not sniff. He did not show any interest whatsoever. He just stood there, rigid, like the statue atop the city's 1812 war memorial.

And with a heart just as cold, she thought.

Emily tried, goodness knows she did, but beyond what had happened to his brother, she could not feel one ounce of Christian charity toward this man. What she did feel was determination. She would not let him get the best of her. She would not give him an excuse to dismiss her from service.

I will conquer this enemy if it takes me until the end of the war, and I will do it with a smile. "If you do not particularly care for peach," she said, "I understand. By all means, share it with someone else."

She set the pie on the table beside him. She smiled once more, though by now her cheeks were aching. Walking away leisurely, she collected the empty plates and forks. She could feel his eyes upon her.

Jeremiah offered to take away the dirty dishes. Emily handed them over, then went to check on Freddy.

"Are you in any pain?" she asked.

He shook his head. "No, not really." He grinned. "That Yankee is gonna surrender yet—you just wait."

Jimmy leaned over from his bed. "If he don't, can we have the pie?"

"I will bake you another."

Emily had already decided if Dr. Mackay didn't claim the dessert, it would sit on that table come mice or mold. By the time she returned the next morning, however, it was gone.

Victory, she thought, until Mrs. Danforth brought her the empty dish.

"Here you go, dearie, and thank you. The night orderlies said to tell you it was delicious."

Emily blinked. "The night orderlies?"

"Yes. Dr. Mackay insisted they have the pie."

Hmph. So the contest of wills continues, she thought. *We shall see who is the first to yield.*

The summer days were long and despite Emily's best efforts, homesickness and despair were rampant in the wards.

The Federal chaplains were overwhelmed with their own men's spiritual needs, so the commanding officers granted the Christian Commission's request to conduct church services in the hospital.

Reverend Henry was assigned to Emily's section. She couldn't have been more pleased. His kindhearted demeanor garnered respect from everyone around him. Even Dr. Mackay attended the first service, but only to stand at the back wall and glare.

The Confederate men sang the hymns with as much enthusiasm as their tired bodies could manage. A few grew disinterested when the preaching began, but most continued to listen. Many had shown interest in spiritual matters after their experiences on the battlefield. Emily prayed they would comprehend the message of love and forgiveness that Reverend Henry was presenting.

Her heart ached for them. The thought of so many soldiers, both blue and gray, going off to fight and not being prepared for eternity pierced her soul. It was the main reason she did what she did. Repairing broken bodies was important, but leading men to the ultimate healer was essential.

Midway through the sermon, without warning, Dr. Mackay stormed out of the room. Emily watched him go. She supposed the thought of forgiveness extended to "rebels" was simply too much for him to bear.

How sad.

She wondered exactly what he believed. He never spoke of God. He never spoke of anything personal, for that matter. Though weeks had passed since his arrival, Emily knew very little about the man. Had he any family beyond his late brother? Was he married?

Is there anyone who prays for him?

She of course had been doing so, but her requests for thawing his icy spirit were strictly of the utilitarian nature. Emily wanted him to show more kindness to the wounded, that was all. Displaying charity in the midst of such hatred and torment would give the wounded a glimpse of God's Love.

Suddenly she was sickened by her own hypocrisy. As Reverend Henry spoke of repentance and grace, she felt the need for it herself.

Oh Lord, forgive me. I have thought that I am somehow better than Dr. Mackay. But I have viewed him exactly as he does me. As an enemy, good for nothing but injury and trouble, one to be watched, worn down and defeated.

As she surveyed her wounded charges, the ones she believed God's heart ached for, tears filled her eyes. *I have never once considered You have a plan for his life as well. That You love that surly Yankee doctor as much as You love these men.*

Chapter Five

July melted into August. Emily changed dressings, distributed army-approved newspapers and Bibles and did her best to be kind to Dr. Mackay. When he stopped probing wounds long enough to wipe the sweat from his brow, she brought him cups of cold water. She washed the floors when he told her to do so without complaint, although often times the scrubwomen had already seen to the task. Whenever possible, she treated him and the rest of the men in the ward to fresh pie.

It took three tries, but he finally claimed a slice.

"Thank you," he said curtly.

Emily smiled. It was progress.

He still barked orders but at least those directed at her were a little less cutting. For that, she was grateful.

New wounded arrived almost daily, and prisoners the Federal doctors deemed fit for travel were sent on. Jimmy and Freddy were forced to give up their beds, Rob, as well. Edward had mercifully survived the ward master's daily roll calls thus far, but Emily knew his days were numbered. The damage done to his body was healing, but the scars to his mind and spirit were taking much longer.

His family came to sit with him each day. By now it was obvious Julia was expecting a child. Though her face glowed with maternal joy, Emily could tell the worry for her brother weighed heavily upon her.

"How much longer before they send him on?" she asked one afternoon as Emily filled the water pitchers.

"I don't know, but spend as much time with him as possible until then. Keep talking to him. I believe it is making a difference."

"Are they still exchanging prisoners?"

"Yes." Emily did not tell her the rumors she was hearing among the stewards, rumors that the Federal army would stop the exchanges and hold all remaining Confederates until the end of the war.

Trudy and Elizabeth at least had no fear of such for their brother. They had recently received word that George was safe. Emily imagined he was somewhere south of the Potomac, although she did not know for certain. In a city controlled by Northern soldiers, it was better not to know specifics with friends still marching in the Confederate army.

One week later Mrs. Danforth took ill and resigned her post as night matron. Emily was completely surprised when the duty supervisor approached her and asked if she would like the job.

"Would I?"

The offer was considered a promotion, recognition for a job well done. The fact that the U.S. Army was offering *her* a paid position in spite of her suspected loyalties was stunning. There was, after all, the matter of the amended oath she had signed.

When Emily had first come to work at the West's Buildings she had been required to sign an oath of loyalty. The pledges were nothing new in Baltimore. People had been asked, sometimes forced, to sign them since the beginning of the war.

Back then a citizen promised to bear true allegiance to the United States and to support and sustain the Constitution. Emily's family believed wholeheartedly in the document, especially the Tenth Amendment, reserving certain powers to the states. Because of that they originally had no trouble with the agreement. Over time, however, as fear and vengeance spread, the oaths were expanded. Now they included language stating that giving "aid" or "consorting with the enemy" was strictly forbidden. Though Emily had no desire to make war or see it continue, she could not in good conscience sign such a promise.

Her friends, her fellow Marylanders, were this "enemy." If Stephen Hastings, George Martin or Edward Stanton ever showed up on her doorstep hungry, sick or bleeding, she would help them.

"With all due respect, sir," Emily had told the Federal officer that day, "I cannot sign this oath."

"If you cannot sign, then you cannot volunteer in this hospital."

Emily had looked about her. The docks had been full of dying men, Marylanders, Virginians, Pennsylvanians and others who had suffered so terribly at Antietam Creek. She could not turn her back on them, yet she could not lie concerning her convictions. So she'd done the only thing she could think of. Dipping her pen in the ink, she'd found the line forbidding her to comfort the enemy. She'd crossed it out, *then* signed her name. Sally, Trudy and Elizabeth had each done the same.

The Federal officer had looked at them incredulously, but he did not dismiss them. Now, nearly a year later, here she was standing before another officer.

"You have been recommended for this position," he said. "Will you accept it?"

"Yes, sir. Most certainly."

He tipped his kepi and smiled. "Thank you, miss. You will fill a great need. You are to finish out today's duties and then report tomorrow evening at sunset."

"Yes, sir. Thank you."

He started to turn. Emily's curiosity got the better of her.

"If I may ask, sir, who was it that gave you the rec- ommendation?"

She expected him to say it was Dr. Turner or perhaps Reverend Henry. You could have knocked her over with a feather when the answer came.

"By all means, miss. It was Dr. Mackay."

Evan had just stepped out of the dining hall when she came running to meet him. Nurse Emily held her skirts just above the ankles so her petticoats would not catch her feet. He was immediately reminded of Mary, thrashing through the garden, telegram in hand as she hurried to tell him the dreadful news of Andrew's death.

He shoved the memory aside. The Maryland wom- an's eyes were not full of pain, but excitement. He knew exactly why.

"Oh, Dr. Mackay, I must thank you!"

The look on her face was genuine, not that Southern belle simper she had worn since the beginning of his time here. In fact, in the past few weeks he had noted quite a change in her. He wasn't certain what to make of it. The looks she gave were less treacherous and she seemed more willing to accept Federal authority.

At least it appears that way.

He still didn't trust her, but she was arguably the

best nurse in the wards. She worked efficiently. The plaster adhesives and linen bandages he was constantly inspecting testified she was a knowledgeable and capable caregiver.

Like it or not, the Johnnies are taken with her. They follow her instructions and she follows mine. She is fully capable of supervising a ward full of snoring rebs and the guards are competent enough to supervise her.

He needn't worry, yet a nagging voice inside his head told him he should.

She's a Baltimore woman. She'll do anything for the sake of her beloved cause.

"Thank you for recommending me for night nurse," she said. She smiled, blue eyes wide and innocent. It was a look that Evan found almost attractive, until he thought better of it.

"Nurse Emily," he said, leveling a stern gaze. "See to it that you do not make me regret my recommendation."

"I wouldn't even think of doing so, Doctor."

He dismissed her, and she quickly rushed off. Evan wondered if she had indeed spoken truth. He seriously doubted it.

By taking night duty she probably thinks she will be rid of me, that she'll be free to encourage disunion while I am snoring away upstairs in my room, dreaming of whatever we Yankees are supposed to be dreaming of.

He grunted. *Well, she is wrong.*

He had not gotten a decent night's sleep since his arrival in Baltimore. His memory would not allow it. He checked the floors so often he should be claiming the night watchman's pay.

He would be observant, and if he caught her in any secessionist activity, he would immediately report her to hospital command. *Then Little Miss Baltimore will find herself out on Pratt Street, this time without any stones to throw.*

Emily arrived at sunset the following evening. The men lit up with smiles the moment she walked in.

"Miss Emily!" one of them said. "Look, y'all! Miss Emily is back!"

At the far end of the room, Rebekah was just finishing with the medications. Emily went to her.

"Have you been assigned to this section?"

"Yes. Just this morning. Dr. Mackay requested it."

Emily was not surprised. Rebekah gave no doubt to where her loyalties lay. She, like Mrs. Danforth, wore a blue ribbon rosette on her apron.

Two years ago Emily would have balked at this woman in her ward, but not now. Time had softened Rebekah's delivery of political opinions. She no longer referred to Confederate sympathizers as rebel traitors. She simply called them men.

"I am glad you are here," Emily said. "The wounded are in capable hands."

Rebekah smiled, but then her expression darkened. "Julia was here again today. I worry about her. The strain is showing on her face. I can't believe Sam and her father allow her to stay so long."

"I may be to blame for that," Emily said. "I told her to spend as much time as possible with Edward. I fear they will send him on very soon."

"Indeed. Dr. Mackay inferred that just this morning."

Emily sucked in her breath. "Has Edward spoken to you?"

"Not a word. When I brought him his dinner tray,

he only nibbled at it. Dr. Mackay called his condition 'chronic nostalgia.'"

Emily wondered how such a pleasant-sounding term could describe such a dark condition. "Did he suggest any treatments?"

"No, at least not to me. Perhaps you should speak with him."

"Perhaps."

Rebekah gave her an overview of the rest of the men, then bid Emily good-night. Around nine the orderlies came in to turn down the lamps. Emily kept one burning near Private Josiah Bush's bed. The poor boy, only seventeen, was weak and pale, ravaged by dysentery. She set her chair beside him. He seemed to welcome her company.

"That's right nice of you, Miss Emily," he said. "I like it when you are around."

She brushed back the hair from his forehead. His fever was high. "Are you cold?"

"Yes'um."

She found him an extra blanket and tucked it around him tightly.

"Thank you," he said weakly. "Do you have any stories with you?"

"Do I? I brought an entire basketful." Mrs. Danforth had been known to spend evening hours reading newspapers or literature to the men. Emily wished to do the same.

He grinned, though his red-rimmed eyes showed his discomfort. A soldier to his right pushed up on his elbows.

"What did you bring?" he asked.

"Oh, well, let me see…Charles Dickens, a collection of Shakespeare, a few *Harper's Weekly*s…"

"Did you bring a Bible?" Josiah asked. "My mama used to read me stories out of it when I was younger."

Emily was touched. "I do have a Bible. Is there a particular story you would care to hear?"

"I was always partial to Daniel in the lion's den."

She smiled. "I like that one, as well."

Emily pulled the lamp a little closer to her shoulder, then turned to the Old Testament. A few disinterested yawns drifted about her, but by the time God had shut the lion's mouth, every man that could sit upright was doing so. Even Edward appeared to be listening intently.

Lord, please speak to them. May they understand how much You love them.

When she had finished the account, several men thanked her. The rest rolled to their sides and prepared for sleep. Josiah still lay shivering, but a more peaceful expression now filled his face.

"Try to close your eyes," she said. "I will be right here if you need me."

Sleep came but only in snatches. The fever held on. He shivered and clutched his blankets while she sponged his face and gave him what little water he could manage.

The hours dragged on. The role of night nurse was more difficult than Emily had first realized.

Men who she had never once heard complain in the daytime now revealed the depths of their pain. In sleep they groaned over their wounds, tightened their muscles and thrashed restlessly in their beds. Others cursed the enemy.

Emily moved quietly between the rows of iron cots, soothing glistening foreheads, softly singing hymns and whispering many prayers. The cries of pain weighed heavily upon her. She wanted to serve, knew she was desperately needed, but, oh, how she missed the daylight. She missed the other nurses, even Dr. Mackay's constant presence. Tonight she felt so alone.

But I am not alone, she told herself. *God is with me and a sentinel stands guard at the doorway.* Emily glanced at him. He appeared, however, to be getting drowsy.

He must be used to these sounds.

Her eerie vigil continued. Emily paced back and forth, replacing tossed linens and trying to comfort those trapped in their nightmarish worlds. Sometime in the wee hours of the morning, Edward gave a shout.

"Press forward!"

She jumped at the sound of his commanding voice, then recognized what was happening. He was giving orders in his sleep. Before she could cross the room, Edward threw the blankets from his bed. Moving with energy she had not known he possessed, he came charging toward her.

"I don't care what you see, soldier! Move!"

Emily gently touched his shoulder. "Edward, wake up."

Her words failed to penetrate his dream. His wrinkled nightshirt now his honor-bedecked uniform, he waved his right arm wildly as though brandishing a gleaming sword.

"Up the hill! Up the hill!"

Pain gripped her heart as she realized what hill he was so desperately trying to take. It was the one where Stephen had fallen. She tried once more, this time a little louder. "Eddie, wake up!"

"Take cover!" he shouted.

Emily looked over to the guard for help, but the man was asleep. How he and the rest of the ward weren't on their feet, scurrying for safety, was beyond her.

"Eddie, please, lay back down." She gave Edward a gentle tug, hoping to lead him back to his bed.

He grabbed her arm. For a wounded man his grip was like iron.

"Where is Stephen?" he demanded.

His eyes were wide with determined intensity. They frightened her.

"He…he isn't here."

His grip tightened. "What have you done to him? Talk, you dirty Yankee!"

Her heart was pounding.

I must calm him! I must get him settled before he hurts someone!

Emily struggled to free herself but could not.

"Eddie, it's me, Emmy! Let go!"

Footsteps pounded quickly across the boards. She expected the sleeping guard had roused and was coming to her aid. It was Dr. Mackay, however, who pried Edward's fingers from her throbbing arm, yet not before her childhood friend had dug so deeply into her skin that she could not help but cry out in pain. Edward struggled, but the doctor overpowered him.

"Don't hurt him!" Emily begged. "Please don't hurt him!"

"Stephen!" Edward cried.

"Aye. This way, Major. The ground has been taken. Your comrade is accounted for."

With that, Edward instantly relaxed and in a matter of moments, Dr. Mackay had him back in his bed, coaxing him to sleep. She watched, heart in her throat, until she realized how badly she was shaking. The last thing Emily wanted was for Dr. Mackay to see her fear.

He will think me incompetent. He will have me removed.

She moved toward the supply cabinet. The guard was now fully awake, but Emily paid him no mind. Her arm was numb, her chest heaving. She tried desperately to gather her composure but couldn't stop trembling. Edward had been convinced she was the enemy. She shuddered to think what he might have done to her had Dr. Mackay not arrived when he did.

Then an even darker thought pressed her. *Has Dr. Mackay seen Edward do such things before? Is that why he recommended me for this position, so that I might truly see what has become of my friend?*

Emily shook even harder. Her mind was racing, her body torn between running away and simply sinking to the floor in tears.

Get a hold of yourself! she commanded. *Show courage!*

"If this ever happens again, I will see to it that you are court-martialed! Do you understand?"

She turned to see the Northern physician towering over the now-trembling guard. Emily gulped, knowing when he had finished Dr. Mackay would certainly release what was left of his anger on her.

"You are here to protect *her* from *them!*" he said.

Protect me?

Somehow throughout all of it, the ward snored on. She supposed it must be the morphine. When Dr. Mackay finished blasting the guard, he turned and moved toward her. His steps were determined, his forehead furrowed with that disdainful growl. Emily braced herself, but the hard stance eased when he reached her.

"Are you well, lass?"

Lass? Not nurse! Not you little rebel! The man had actually addressed her with a term of endearment, of concern. She was at a loss for words.

"Your dress is torn."

Emily looked down to see that he was right. Her sleeve had been slashed from elbow to wrist. What remained of the cloth was stained by a small trickle of blood.

My own, she thought. *By Eddie's hand.*

"Let me examine it." He didn't wait for her to grant permission. Accustomed to having his orders followed, the Federal doctor simply took her arm in hand and began unfastening the cuff.

Aghast, Emily drew back. The man had no sense of propriety. "That isn't necessary," she said.

She watched as he reddened, but this time it wasn't in anger. "Forgive me," he said, realizing how uncomfortable he had made her. "I am not accustomed to… You are bleeding. The wound should be tended to stave off infection."

Compared to those around her shivering with fever and moaning in pain, her injuries could hardly be considered a wound, but Edward's ragged nails had drawn blood. Dr. Mackay was right. She should not risk infection. She surrendered her arm.

He lifted the fabric. His hands were warm, careful. "Does this hurt?" he asked.

"Not as it did before."

"Good. I do, however, detect swelling."

The pressure of his touch was unnerving. Emily's heart was pounding, and, regrettably, she was still trembling. If he noticed that, though, he did not say.

He reached for a clean cloth from the basket on the table beside them. He carefully blotted the blood. Emily did not know what to make of this gentle side of him, but she hoped it would continue, for her sake and everyone else's.

"Please don't be angry with Ed—" she caught her-self "—the major. He didn't realize what he was doing."

Dr. Mackay's jaw twitched, but his voice remained calm. "They never do."

"I thank you for your handling of the situation. I do not believe I could have settled him on my own."

"No, you wouldn't have," he said, without looking up. "He is much too strong for you."

She cringed. *Why did I say that? Why did I just admit failure? Will he not use it against me?*

"It stings, I know. For that I am sorry."

Sorry? Twice now he had apologized. Emily did not know what to think. Before her was not the angry, ar-rogant Federal doctor she had grown so used to seeing, but a different man entirely.

Have I been wrong about him? Could it be that be-neath that blue wool vest and abrasive personality beats the heart of a good man?

"The major is your friend, is he not?"

Emily answered truthfully. "Yes. We went to school together. His closest friend, Captain Stephen Hastings, was recently killed."

Having cleansed the wound, he reached for a ban-dage. He said nothing more.

Evan's guilt weighed heavily upon him. In reality he knew the tussle with the reb hadn't come to much, but it could have. She recognized that as well, for though she was doing her best to appear brave, she was still trembling.

I should have known better.

He'd been in the army long enough to know the dangers delirious men suffering from chronic nostalgia sometimes posed. He had known for a fact that this particular reb was troubled.

What was I thinking recommending her for this position, knowing what she would face? Look at her, barely five feet tall, mostly petticoats and ribbons at that.

He had told himself that she could handle things like this, that as a nurse she should have expected such and been prepared, but Mary's warning rang through his mind. *Forgive, my love, or the poison of hatred will turn you into the very enemies you so despise.*

Evan hoped Nurse Emily's Southern sympathy hadn't caused him to intentionally place her in danger. *Am I really that cold? No. I can't be.* "I think t'would be better for you if you returned to your daytime tasks."

Her fear was immediately replaced by a different emotion. Her eyes widened in obvious dismay.

"Oh, please, Dr. Mackay, don't do that! Please let me stay on as night nurse."

He was completely surprised. "Given what just happened to you, I should think you would want to leave as quickly as possible."

"But he didn't mean any harm. I know that. The opportunities on night duty are so plentiful."

"Opportunities for what?"

"To read the Bible with the men, to pray for them."

That was hardly what he had expected her to say. Though he supposed if she wished to spread rebel propaganda, she wouldn't be so foolish as to admit that.

"The men are starved for spiritual comfort," she insisted.

At that moment she sounded so much like Mary that his heart ached. Her faith had been of the utmost importance to her, a source of strength. She had longed for others to experience it, as well.

In this case Evan thought Nurse Emily's efforts pointless. Men willing to make war against their own nation would not be interested in the Gospel. Yet there was something compelling about her eagerness to try.

He had to admit, too, that her kindness toward him these past few weeks was making it increasingly difficult to view her as one of those Pratt Street scoundrels.

"Please allow me to stay."

He took a long look at her, the bandaged arm, the torn sleeve and the pleading eyes. Her devotion was misguided but commendable. If she wanted to finish out her duties in this ward, he would let her, but he would be watching.

"Very well then," he said. "Go back to your Bible stories."

Her face literally glowed. "You mean you will let me continue?"

"Aye, but don't be reading them any stories of war, of victory. Best not to encourage them."

"Yes, Doctor."

"And don't be thinking you can handle that major on your own. If he rouses again, you call out for help."

"I will."

She looked at him with those wide blue eyes, appreciative and eager. *She is a pretty little lass,* he thought. *Golden hair and all.*

He quickly shook off the thought. Obviously his lack of sleep was hindering his senses. "Go on now," he told her. "See to that one there shuddering with fever."

She nodded, then scurried off. Watching, he couldn't help but think, *If only everyone in this hospital was as conscientious of duty as she.*

Chapter Six

Emily expected Dr. Mackay to leave, but he did not. Claiming a chair, he took up residence in the far corner of the room. He checked his watch, then, after putting it away, crossed his arms over his chest. The look said he dared any prisoner, guard or nurse to step out of line.

Emily found his vigil unnerving and comforting at the same time. Every time a soldier's cry punctuated the sour air, she twitched. Dr. Mackay evidently had the same trouble. Although he dozed with his chin on his chest from time to time, his head quickly snapped to attention at any threatening sound.

She could tell by the lines on his face that he was exhausted, that he needed real rest. Caution kept her from encouraging him to seek it. If he was there to make certain she was performing her duties in a loyal manner, he might think she was eager to be rid of him. That would only heighten his suspicion of her.

On the other hand, if he had taken up residence for her benefit, as a measure of protection, she would not discourage it, not tonight, at least. She was still shaken.

At present, Edward lay lost in deep sleep. Emily knew he had never consciously meant to harm her, that he would never forgive himself if he knew he had. Still, she had to admit, she was now afraid of him. How could her childhood friend address her as such one moment, then claim she was the enemy in the next? What war raged within him?

She looked over to the now-snoring Federal doctor. *And what war rages inside him?*

For a man so disgusted by Southerners, twice he had come to her aid. This time in doing so he had also shown compassion toward Edward. She still didn't know what Dr. Mackay believed concerning eternity, but she figured there must be some seed of faith within him, some measure of Christ's love.

The room remained relatively quiet as the hours ticked on. Josiah Bush's fever broke just before dawn. Emily breathed a grateful sigh and settled back in her chair as the sun began rising over the harbor. The light of day crept slowly across the wooden floor, yet darkness flittered about her eyes. Sleep was calling. She struggled to resist.

Around six Dr. Mackay awoke, rubbed the knot from his neck and exited the ward. The stewards and day orderlies arrived. Rebekah came on shortly thereafter.

"Did you pass a long night?" she asked Emily.

"A restless one."

She noticed the bandage. "What happened? Are you all right?"

Emily didn't want to make more out of it than it actually was. "Just a scuffle with a sleepwalking soldier," she said.

Rebekah's eyebrow arched. "Which soldier?"

Emily told her, quietly. Rebekah's eyes widened in disbelief.

"Dear me," she gasped. "Edward? You must have been terrified! What if it happens again?"

Emily wouldn't allow herself to think of that. *There will not be a next time.* "I'm fine. Dr. Mackay handled the situation quite well. Edward has slept soundly ever since."

"You should go home and get some rest."

"I intend to." She gave her the report on the other men's conditions, then gathered her books. The breakfast trays had arrived. Already Edward sat nibbling at his. He looked at her as she passed by. The expression on his face told her he had no recollection whatsoever of the previous night.

She offered what she hoped was a pleasant smile as she quickly left the ward. Sam and Julia were in the corridor. Emily immediately covered her torn sleeve with her pinner apron before either of them noticed. There was no use upsetting them. They had enough on their minds already.

"How is he this morning?" Julia immediately asked.

Emily chose her words carefully. "He spent a restless night, but he is awake now and eating."

Julia bit her lip, then looked at her husband.

Something must be wrong, Emily thought.

Sure enough, Sam explained. "We have some news, but we aren't certain we should share it with Edward."

Emily's throat tightened. "What news?"

"Sally sent a telegram. They have found Stephen. They are bringing him home for burial."

Her heart sank. It was good and proper to lay Stephen to rest, but the news of his body being found was like learning of his death all over again.

"Do you think we should tell Edward?" Julia asked.

Emily did not know. What would such knowledge

do to him? She had heard that some doctors advocated telling a soldier everything, that forcing them to relive the moments of the battlefield in someone else's presence actually *helped* them.

But after last night? What if such details bring more grief?

The staircase above them creaked, and Emily turned to see Dr. Mackay making his way toward them. He was wearing a fresh shirt, had shaved and combed his hair. The look in his eyes, however, mirrored Emily's own exhaustion.

"He will know what to do," she said. "We should ask him."

"Ask me what?" Dr. Mackay said gruffly.

"Mr. and Mrs. Ward received word concerning our mutual friend, Captain Hastings."

"The one who died," he said, as if telling her to get to the point.

Not one inkling of sympathy registered on his face. The gentleman who had mended her arm, who'd shown such compassion, was gone. The formidable Federal doctor was back. Emily now hesitated to ask him anything.

"His body has been found and his family is bringing him home for burial."

"And you want to know if you should tell him."

"Yes," Sam and Julia both said.

Dr. Mackay cast them a perturbed glance, then directed those bayonet-gray eyes at her. Emily could feel the chill.

"Is he lucid this morning?"

"Yes."

"Then you should tell him. Put the matter to rest immediately." He looked at Sam and Julia. "Then both of you should leave."

He stormed off, slamming the door to the ward behind him. Emily was horrified. She had come to him for wisdom and he had cast her and her friends aside as if they were yesterday's soiled bandages. She looked at them. Pale and confused, Julia clutched Sam's arm.

"I am so sorry," was all Emily could think to say.

Sam shook his head. "No. He is right. There is no use prolonging the matter. Perhaps burial will bring closure. I'll tell him."

He started forward. Julia followed. Emily tried not to allow fear and suspicion to plague her thoughts, but she could not help it. Was Dr. Mackay acting in Edward's best interest, or was he intentionally trying to cause this family pain? Emily regretted telling him about the day on Pratt Street. What was it he had said? That Sam and Julia were as guilty as sin? Did Dr. Mackay see this as some opportunity to punish them for what had happened to his brother?

Cold chills traveled down her back. *What if Edward becomes enraged? What if in his grief he seeks to harm his sister?*

She had to do something. As her friends stepped into the room, Emily glanced about. Rebekah was busy helping Josiah into a fresh shirt and Jeremiah was at the far end assisting another man. Edward was in his bed, tray still across his lap.

Sam approached him. He had no idea what had happened to Emily last night, and she had no way of telling him now. *He and Julia will be taken by surprise if Edward's battle strength is roused.*

But she would not be taken unawares, at least not this time.

"If I may," she said, quickly approaching. "Allow me."

Sam looked at her. "He spoke with you before, didn't he?"

"Yes. Briefly."

"Then perhaps he will again. By all means…" He made way for her.

Drawing in a quick breath Emily headed toward Edward's bed. Fear raked its icy claws across her arms, making her heart pound. She prayed her emotions weren't showing on her face. *Help me, Lord.*

Edward looked up at her. He handed her the tray with his remaining arm, thinking that was what she had come for. She took it from him and placed it on the small table beside his bed. Julia and Sam were at his feet, but he appeared not to notice them.

"What happened to you, Emmy?"

She didn't know what startled her more, his words or the fact that the torn sleeve and bandage were in full view. She had laid aside her apron without thinking. Edward's face showed his concern.

"It is nothing," she said. "Just a scratch. The doctor has seen to it."

He still stared. "You once bandaged my arm like that," he said.

Her heart was in her throat. He had said more in the past two minutes than he had during his entire stay at the hospital. How could he remember something as insignificant as a childhood injury and not remember what he had done just hours ago?

Emily tried to keep her voice steady. "Yes. I did," she said. "You had trouble climbing my oak tree."

That lost look filled his face. The muscles in his neck twitched. "Stephen was there," he said. "I remember."

Though fear chilled her spine, Emily sat down beside him. "Yes, he was. I remember that, as well."

Edward's eyes were locked on hers. It was as if he was waiting, as if he knew she had something to tell him. Emily whispered a quick prayer.

"Eddie," she said slowly. "They are bringing Stephen home for burial."

He blinked twice as the words sank in. She waited for any sign of anger or desperation. The only look that came was one of resignation.

"When?" he asked.

Her shoulders dropped as she released the breath she'd been holding. She looked at Sam. He came forward.

"Tomorrow afternoon," he said. "Your father and I are going to meet the train."

"Thank you." Edward said matter-of-factly.

Emily breathed once more, this time a little deeper. Julia moved closer as Edward then looked to her.

"Is Sally with her father?" he asked.

"Yes."

Emily gave Julia her place but still remained close.

"Is she well?" Edward asked.

"She is managing."

Their conversation continued. Sensing the danger had passed, Emily faded back. The long night had caught up with her. Her body ached with fatigue. Emotionally she was drained.

Turning, she saw that there, just a few paces in front of her, stood Dr. Mackay. As usual he was watching her. That smug look of confidence was on his face. He had been right, but she hadn't the strength or desire to tell him that. As of now all Emily wanted was a long, cool bath to wash away the dirt and dried blood, then sleep. She hoped such things would remove all thoughts of war from her mind.

Evan watched her leave. Her shoulders were slumped, her steps slow. Few women would have endured the assault she had and begged for the chance to still care for the one who had caused it. She was dedicated, but why she poured so much of her strength into these rebs was beyond him. It had already taken its toll on her once with the sun. If she wasn't careful she would succumb to something far worse.

Naive little lass.

He then turned his attention to her friend, Mrs. Ward. *And there sits another.*

It hadn't escaped his notice that she was with child. He had no idea why that husband of hers didn't insist she remain at home. The man must be a fool, unable to grasp the dangers pregnancy could impose.

Devotion to that Johnny will be her undoing.

He turned on his heel and moved quickly away. He could never look at the young woman for very long without thinking of Mary.

How big had she gotten? How much movement had she felt? Could she yet determine elbows from knees? Guilt raked its icy claws across his chest. He hadn't known of her condition until it was too late. *I should have been there. I never should have left her.*

"Is Miss Emily coming back tonight?"

The frail voice called him from his thoughts. The boy reb, sick with dysentery, was looking up at him.

"I saw she'd done hurt her arm," he said. "She looked mighty poorly this morning."

Evan wasn't going to divulge any details, certainly

not to him. "As far as I know, Nurse Emily will return this evening."

The Johnny looked somewhat relieved. "You tend to her arm?" he asked.

"Aye."

"That's good. I wouldn't want no harm to come to her."

The fire in Evan's belly smoldered. *But you'd let harm come to plenty of others. You'd bring on the death of a thousand innocent women and children if you thought it would secure victory for your cause.*

Movement to his right caught his eye, a flash of yellow silk. Mrs. Ward was on her husband's arm, heading for the door.

At least he's taking her with him this time, Evan thought. *But if they can't recognize the dangers of being here, I'll see to it they have no reason to come at all.* He knew exactly what he would do. *I'll give my recommendation to the ward master. The reb's wounds have healed satisfactorily and now that he is speaking...*

That will settle two issues. Mrs. Ward will remain at home and Nurse Emily can tend to the remaining prisoners without further injury.

A few hours of precious sleep were just what Emily needed. After supper, her parents drove her to the hospital.

"You be careful tonight," her mother insisted. "Don't go near those troubled men without that doctor's assistance."

"I won't," Emily promised.

She had told them of the incident with Edward but did not reveal his name. Emily did not wish to add to their grief. Stephen's impending funeral weighed heavily upon them all.

"Abigail and I will prepare food for after the service tomorrow," Mrs. Davis said. "And the Stantons have offered to open their home."

"That will work well," Emily said. "They have the largest parlor and dining room."

"Indeed."

"We probably won't need it now," her father said.

Emily looked at him. "But Mr. Hastings is acquainted with so many people. Why, those he knew from the city counsel alone—"

"His former counsel members have all expressed their sympathies."

Former. The word still stung. Mr. Hastings had lost his position with the governing body last summer. The issue had been over the effort to raise Federal companies from Baltimore. Sally's father could not support a measure that would form troops to fight against other Maryland men, namely, his own son.

He'd voted no. So had several others. Under pressure from occupying General Wool, he and the other dissenting counsel members had been forced to resign. They were soon replaced by "loyal" men who *would* vote for the measure.

"None of them plan to attend the service tomorrow," her father continued.

Emily sighed disgustedly. "It is a funeral. Can we not dispense with the politics long enough to grieve for a man from Baltimore?"

"Apparently not."

Poor Mr. Hastings, she thought. *Poor Sally.*

Her father pulled the carriage to the hospital's main

entrance. Darkness had just about fallen. Army stewards were lighting the gas lamps at the front door.

"Joshua will be by to collect you in the morning," he said, "as I have business at the fort."

"Will you return in time for the service?" Emily asked.

"I will make certain of it."

Her parents both kissed her goodbye. "God keep you," her mother said. "I will pray for you."

Emily appreciated those prayers greatly, for as eager as she was to keep serving, she was still uneasy. How would Edward fare tonight? In what mood would she find Dr. Mackay?

Navigating the dim corridors, she hurried inside. Rebekah gave her the evening report. Edward had been contemplative but peaceful. Josiah was strengthening. Sergeant Adam Cooper's lungs were worse.

"You may wish to set your chair beside him tonight," she suggested.

Dr. Mackay made his evening rounds. Emily assisted as the morphine powders and other pills were distributed.

"Keep a second oil lamp lit tonight," he told her, for previously she'd left only one burning.

She could not argue with that. She would have clearer vision of whatever may be happening at both ends of the ward. *And perhaps the extra bit of light will keep tonight's sentinel fully awake.*

Emily prepared for a vigil beside Adam, but Dr. Mackay claimed the spot first. Loosening the top buttons on his vest, he looked as though he was going to keep watch for quite a while. She placed her chair once more beside Josiah.

"Have you a story for me again tonight, Miss Emily?"

His innocence warmed her heart. "Indeed I do, Josiah."

"Give us another adventure," the soldier beside him said.

Dr. Mackay's warning concerning scriptures of war was foremost in her mind.

"What about the Apostle Paul and his adventure on the high seas?" she said.

Josiah's eyes widened in delight. "Shipwrecks and snakebites?"

"That's right."

The man to her left, Corporal John Hudson, a Georgia fellow, worked himself into a sitting position. "Snakebites? Be they copperheads?"

"No," Emily said. "But just as deadly."

She turned to the book of Acts and began to read. By the time she got to the part about the snake fastening itself onto Paul's hand, even Dr. Mackay was listening.

"And he just shook it off and went on?" John asked.

"Indeed," Emily said. "Although everyone around expected him to die."

"But he didn't die," Josiah said.

"That's right," she said. "You see, God had a plan for Paul's life and nothing, no shipwreck or serpent, could keep him from it. He has a plan for each of your lives, as well. He loves you so much."

With that, Dr. Mackay came stomping across the floor. "That is enough reading for tonight."

"I like her Bible stories, Doc," Josiah said.

"Hush," he insisted. He stuck his stethoscope in his ears, leaned over the boy.

"I like 'um, as well," John said. "Read us Joshua and the Battle of Jericho. That one where the walls come down."

"Wish these walls would come down," the soldier across from him muttered.

Dr. Mackay pulled his stethoscope from his ears. The look he shot the Confederate man could have snuffed out life. "I said that's enough!" He turned his glare on her. "Put the Bible away."

Emily's heart sank. *No one here is trying to incite rebellion,* she wanted to say. *They simply want to go home!*

Though disappointed, Emily did as she was told. She moved to the table where the water pitchers sat. Claiming one, she then went to each bed. Whether the men were truly thirsty or not, they all drank. Emily did her best to smile, to act as if Dr. Mackay's scolding had not really affected her, but they all knew better. They looked at her with pity.

Inwardly she sighed. She felt like a failure, in every sense of the word. It wasn't that she didn't appreciate their sympathy; she just didn't want to be the focus of their attention.

Lord, I want them to know You. I want them to know Your love, Dr. Mackay included.

"Emmy?" she heard Edward call.

Fear made her muscles twitch, yet compassion tugged her forward. *I have no need to be frightened,* she told herself. *He is fully awake. So is everyone else in the ward.*

"Do you really believe all of that?" he asked.

"Believe what?"

"About God loving you. About Him having a plan for our lives."

Though her insides were still churning, she forced herself to sit down. "Yes, I do."

"Julia says the same. So does Sam."

"They are right."

Edward's eyes held a look of defeat. "Perhaps He loves His purpose more."

"Which purpose is that?"

"Judgment."

Emily's heart squeezed in pain. "Is that what you think is happening?"

"Isn't it? My arm, my friends, my city...I've chosen the wrong side. God isn't with me. The bluecoats and the abolitionists all say so."

She drew in a quick breath. *Lord, give me the right words.* How could she say with certainty what Heaven's purpose was concerning this war? She had seen good and bad on both sides. Edward wasn't personally fighting to keep men in chains any more than every Northern man wished to free them.

"I don't know what to say to that, Eddie, except that we are all sinners. We are all stubborn and selfish, hurting others when we insist upon our own way." She paused. "And you are right. God's holiness demands judgment, but I also know that He grieves for us. In His holiness He provided a way to redeem us, through Jesus."

He was quiet for several moments. Emily simply waited.

"My family didn't want me to join this war," he said.

Julia had once told her that on the first night of the Federal occupation she had begged Edward not to go south.

"I went anyway," he said. "Convinced I was going to throw those Yankees out of town. I wanted to kill as many of them as possible after what they had done to my sister on Pratt Street. And yet I ended up only hurting her and everyone else I care about."

Though the night before he'd torn her flesh in anger,

Emily took his hand in hers. Edward clasped it tightly, but no trace of the vengeful warrior remained.

"I can't even look at Sally," he said. "When I think of what I have done to her..."

She blinked back tears. "She bears you no ill will, Eddie. None of us do. Least of all God. He loves you."

Footsteps crossed the boards, but Emily continued anyway. She would do her best to respect Dr. Mackay's orders, but she would not neglect this moment with Edward. She needed it as much as he, perhaps even more so.

"Our choices," she said, "our failures in life do not change that. God's love is constant."

"Blessed are the peacemakers," Edward quoted. "For they shall be called the Sons of God."

"Peace begins with God," Emily said. "By accepting His forgiveness, letting His love fill our hearts. Only then can we look upon other men, not as our enemies, but as treasures loved also by Him."

Dr. Mackay cleared his throat. Emily looked up. She expected an expression of disdain, but the look in his eyes matched the pain in Edward's.

"I have need of your assistance," he said.

"Yes, of course."

She gave Edward's hand a gentle squeeze, then followed Dr. Mackay across the ward. The look of vulnerability had passed and that determined frown once again creased his forehead. He strode toward Adam's bed. One glance at the man and Emily swallowed back more tears. His fever was high. His face showed pain.

"Hold him while I take a good listen," Dr. Mackay instructed.

Emily carefully claimed the edge of his bed as the Scotsman pushed the poor man from his pillows so that his back was exposed. She cradled the shivering sergeant against her as he moved his stethoscope.

Adam sputtered a weak, kitten-like cry. "So…cold…"

"There now," she said softly. "It will only be for a few moments. Then you can reclaim your pillows."

He coughed raggedly, winced in pain.

"Hold on to me," she encouraged.

He did, but the arms that encircled her were not those of a strong, valiant soldier. They were those of a dying man. Emily looked to Dr. Mackay. She could tell by his distressed expression that the poor sergeant's condition was grave.

God help Dr. Mackay, she prayed. *Help him relieve the suffering.*

He pulled the stethoscope from his ears. "His lungs are completely full."

Disgust filled his eyes, but he gently laid Adam down. Emily quickly covered him. She reached for a nearby sponge to wipe the sergeant's brow.

"Wait here," Dr. Mackay told her as he walked away.

Emily continued to comfort the man as best as she could until he returned. When he finally did come back, he was angry.

"We are completely out of ether," he fumed. "How can one be expected to—" He stopped, stared at her. "You will have to steady him."

She gulped, not liking the sound of that. "What are you going to do?"

"Drain the fluid."

She saw the instruments on his tray, the tube, the packing. She knew what was coming. He was going to cut into the man's chest.

But without ether? Isn't there something else you can do?

With one look at Sergeant Cooper, however, even she knew now was not the time for less invasive measures. While Dr. Mackay readied his tools, Emily pulled back Adam's blanket. She shuddered, knowing what pain the suffering man was about to endure.

"Ready him now," Dr. Mackay said.

She looked into the sergeant's eyes. She saw the fear. She prayed he wouldn't see it in hers, as well.

"I am sorry," she whispered. "You must be absolutely still. This will hurt, but only for a while."

He struggled to speak. "S-sing…"

"Sing?" she said, surprised. "What song?"

"Near…God…"

"'Nearer my God to Thee'?"

He nodded.

Emily had never considered herself musically gifted, but she didn't let that stop her. If it would help the man endure the procedure, she would sing. Softly she began.

"Nearer my God to Thee… Nearer to thee…"

He closed his eyes. Dr. Mackay started in. Blood soon stained his fingers. The poor soldier fainted in a matter of seconds, but Emily continued to softly sing. She hoped the music would be a comfort to those around him, also. They all were watching.

Dr. Mackay inserted the tube, then packed the surrounding area with lint. Emily stroked Adam's hair, kept him from suddenly stirring. By the time she'd reached the hymn's final verse, she could already hear a difference in his breathing.

"It's working," she said.

"Aye, though his lungs may continue to fill."

The sound of snoring soon drifted about them as the other men surrendered to sleep. She and Dr. Mackay kept watch. Vile fluid slowly dripped from the sergeant's chest into a wash basin. Emily emptied it whenever told to do so.

The hours wore on. Sounds of slumber gave way to distress. Battle orders were issued. Cries were interspersed with cursing. Emily wondered how long it would take her to get used to such noises. Mercifully, Edward stayed in his bed.

"You have done well tonight," Dr. Mackay said.

The compliment surprised her. He had never paid her one before.

"So have you," she said. She looked back at Adam, watched his chest rise and fall. "Will he now recover?"

"'Tis difficult to say at this point. Time will tell."

"I hope so. He has a sweetheart waiting for him back home. They are to be married upon his return."

Dr. Mackay evidently did not care to know that. He abruptly changed the subject. "How long have you served here?" he asked.

"Since Antietam."

His left eyebrow arched. He was either impressed or he thought she was lying. "Most women don't last that long."

She tried to take those words as a compliment as well, but she wasn't sure. "I had wanted to go to the battlefield," she said. "But the commission rarely sends women, and those they do are usually the wives of male delegates."

"'Tis for your own protection," he said. "There are a good many things in this world that a lady should not be exposed to. I imagine you have seen enough here already, especially after last night." He paused then added, "They aren't honorable, you know."

Emily bristled but held her tongue. Whether he was referring to Edward directly or the rest of the Confederate army she wasn't certain. She let the insult pass, knowing retaliation would not foster reconciliation.

Give me grace, Lord.

Several seconds of awkward silence passed. "How is your arm?" he then asked.

"It is healing well."

"No further swelling?"

"None whatsoever."

He nodded, then turned his attention back to Adam. His breathing was still labored, but better than previously. Emily watched as Dr. Mackay moved his stethoscope across the sergeant's chest. When he had finished she asked, "Have you served since the beginning of the war?"

He stiffened. Emily realized the inquiry must have triggered some memory surrounding his brother's death. She had not meant to cause him pain. Before she could apologize he answered her.

"I received my commission shortly after the war began."

She nodded. Though curious about a great many things, she did not ask any more questions. Dr. Mackay settled into his chair. Pulling his gold watch from his vest pocket, he studied it for several moments. She took out her volume of Burns. The ward was now quiet.

Somewhere just before sunrise the doctor's head tipped forward as he fell asleep. Emily studied him in the flickering lamplight. Dark brown hair framed his strong, angular face. His usually neatly trimmed side whiskers now blended with the unshaven stubble of his chin.

She thought him a handsome man, at least now when he wasn't scowling. As he stretched out his long legs, a peaceful expression filled his face. *He must be dream-*

ing, she thought. *And those dreams must be carrying him somewhere very far away from this hospital, from this war.*

Emily sighed, realizing he also was a troubled man. Whatever he had witnessed on the battlefields and in the tent hospitals must haunt him, as well. Something drifted through his eyes in brief unguarded moments, much like what she had seen in Edward's when she'd spoken of Culp's Hill. She knew the loss of his brother brought great grief but sensed there was something more.

Perhaps it was the hours spent nursing or simply her women's heart, but despite his gruffness, Emily longed to comfort the man.

Chapter Seven

Evan could hear the ward stirring, but his need for sleep and the pleasantness of Mary's memory kept him from opening his eyes. Caught in that world between slumber and alertness, he could smell the hot coffee, feel her gentle hand on his shoulder.

"Aye, my love. I am awake."

"Dr. Mackay?"

He opened his eyes, not to his wife, but to Nurse Emily. She was the one with the coffee. The cup was on a tray alongside a biscuit. Disappointment rained down on him. All he wanted to do was return to sleep.

"I am sorry to disturb you," she said. "But Dr. Turner is asking for you."

Evan raked back his hair and then rubbed the sleep from his eyes. Duty called. "Aye," he said.

"I thought perhaps you may be hungry."

He stood and stretched, then reached for the coffee. It tasted like mud. It always did, but at least it helped to wake him.

"Sergeant Cooper is breathing much better."

It took a second swallow and a bite of the biscuit she'd given him before his memory served him. *The reb with pneumonia.* He honestly didn't think he would survive the night, but the Almighty had done as He had seen fit.

Once again, Evan thought.

Nurse Emily was still waiting patiently before him. He wondered why, then remembered something about Jacob Turner. "What was it you said?"

"Dr. Turner asked that you speak with him."

Evan downed the last of the coffee.

"Shall I take that for you?" she asked.

He handed her the cup. "Thank you."

He moved toward the door, his gait slowed by his aching muscles and the fog that still clouded his brain. *Another day of drudgery, of probing, patching and piecing them back together. Another day of rotting fish, the stench of rebels and other miserable reminders of this city.*

Evan pressed on. He found Jacob Turner in his ward. His old gray head was bent over some Johnny, one still wearing his kepi and artillery jacket as if he expected General Lee to call roll at any moment.

Jacob stood erect when he caught sight of Evan. "Young man, do you remember Colonel Wiggins?"

"Aye. One of the Potomac Brigades, correct?"

"Indeed."

The colonel was a Maryland man but a true Unionist, brave and inspiring to his men. Evan had treated several of his soldiers following the Antietam campaign.

"The poor chap died of heart trouble," Jacob said. "He's being buried today at Green Mount Cemetery."

Evan felt his shoulders tense. *Another man lost.* True, it was not a rebel bullet that had laid him low, but two years of battling them had surely done the damage to his heart. *His wife is now a widow...his family, his men grieving.*

"Since the wounded are more manageable now," Jacob said, "there are several of us who plan to go this afternoon and pay our respects. Would you care to join us?"

"I would," Evan said. *A loyal soldier should be honored and the more Union blue in view for the citizens of Baltimore, the better.* "What time?"

"Four o'clock."

"I will be there."

"Well said, young man. I will speak to our commanding officer on your behalf. Dr. Warren has already offered to keep an eye on your ward."

Later that afternoon Evan stepped into a pair of freshly polished shoes. He put on his brushed blue coat and tied about his waist the green sash which identified him as a medical officer. He climbed into a waiting carriage with several other doctors and settled into the seat. The men immediately began conversing about this and that. Evan wanted to join in, but as the carriage wobbled along Pratt Street his mind centered upon that angry mob, the ones that had encircled his brother, then later claimed the shots by the Northern men were unprovoked.

He could feel his temperature rising. He tugged at his collar. The wool was uncomfortable, especially in this summer heat. A hazy shade of gray hovered over the city.

How appropriate, he thought.

They arrived at the church. It was crammed full of U.S. soldiers. Women dressed in black silk and crepe cried softly into their handkerchiefs during the eulogy. Wealthy men in stovepipe hats spoke their praise. "The

Star-Spangled Banner" was played and a guard gave a crisp, final salute.

High honors for a man who served his country well.

Throughout the entire event, Evan had his mind on one goal. Victory. His certainty of rebel defeat kept his chin high but at the cemetery, as he stared at the flag-draped coffin, his spirit sank. Memories washed over him. *Red, white, blue, Old Glory.* The same field of colors had draped Andrew's casket. On that day, the April rain had poured down. Mary clutched his arm with one hand and cried into a handkerchief with the other.

I should have comforted her, he thought. *But I just stood there.* Of all the emotions coursing through him that day, the foremost was anger.

He had looked after his brother since their parents' early deaths back in Scotland. Andrew was seven years younger than he. The lad was full of life, of faith and eagerness to defend his new country. Evan respected his choice but did not wish to follow. He was too newly married and too much in love to leave Mary. She, herself a transplanted Highlander, was everything to him.

But I should have gone with him. I may not have been able to stop the mob from attacking, but I could have kept his injury from bleeding his life away.

The minister standing before him now talked of Christ and His resurrection. Evan believed all that. He knew there was a Savior, a sacrifice. One day he would see Andrew and Mary again. He clung to the promise of the bliss of eternity, but it was the here and now that was such agony.

I was a fool and I lost her because of it.

Evan knew what the Scriptures said. He heard what the preachers from the Christian Commission proclaimed, saw how the delegates on the battlefield ministered kindly to the wounded of both armies, yet he could not do the same.

Every time he thought of Andrew, every time he saw another flag-draped casket like this one, his anger toward rebs burned hotter.

This is war. There is no room for kindness, for forgiveness, in times like these.

Before he realized it, the minister was giving the benediction. The mourners began stepping away. Evan stood there, feeling the same shame and emptiness he had felt for the past two years. Jacob Turner came to him.

"The family has invited us all back for a meal," he said.

Evan's stomach was rumbling, but it had nothing to do with hunger. He appreciated the invitation, but he had no desire to attend with the others. He knew he would be forced to make polite table conversation. It just wasn't in him. Yet he had no desire to return to his room at the hospital, either. The loneliness was absolutely suffocating.

"Thank you, but no," he said. "I believe I will take a walk. I'll see you back at the harbor."

Jacob nodded. "Time away from this war will do you well, young man. Go seek some sort of uplifting amusement."

"Aye." He bid him farewell, then walked away.

Evan had no idea where he would go or what he would do next. While the average man had no trouble finding amusement in this town, the choices weren't always uplifting. He had never been given to whiskey or any of the other common vices that so often tempted soldiers. His Christian upbringing and his knowledge as a physician tempered any such foolishness. Probably his only real reckless habit had been racing his stallion across the fields back home.

Mary would chide him every time he saddled up.

"Don't you be ridin' now like some barbarian across the moors," she'd say.

He would rear back on his mount and grin. "Come with me, highland girl."

"No," she'd say firmly, though the brightness shone in her eyes. "And don't you be askin' any other lass to come with you, either."

"I wouldn't dream of it, my love."

Dreams, he thought. Now dreams were the only place he could meet her.

He walked deeper into the cemetery, passed row after row of headstones. It was not an encouraging place, but the trees and grass were a welcome change from the slate sidewalks and stench of the wharf.

Rounding a large oak, he came upon a second funeral party. Evan immediately stopped. There just a few yards before him another set of women were dressed in black silk. The men wore toppers and stovepipes, but there was no honor guard at this service, no blue wool. A Maryland State flag draped the coffin.

He realized exactly what he had stepped into. It was the graveside service of a rebel. Bile filled his mouth. Just as Evan was about to spit and turn on his heel, he recognized one of the women.

Nurse Emily.

She was supporting a grieving woman about her age. Beside them stood an older man. Evan assumed they were the family of the dead Johnny. The man had pinned to his frock coat a Botany Cross, a symbol that he had seen on the rebel uniforms from Maryland.

He looked back at Emily. *You would attend a traitor's burial,* he thought.

But as much as he wanted to feel disgust toward her, he couldn't. He watched as she whispered words to the woman beside her. If she was telling her to curse Yankees and plot revenge, she was doing so with the sweetest, most sympathetic look he had ever seen.

Though his loyalty to Constitution and country commanded him to walk away, he didn't. He scanned the other faces. There were other women from the hospital present, as well, including pregnant Mrs. Ward. Evan now realized whose burial he had come upon. This was the comrade who tormented the rebel major in his sleep.

The women dabbed their cheeks with their handkerchiefs. The men in attendance, those who had wives, sheltered them protectively with their arms. Nurse Emily continued to comfort the dead man's relative until she noticed him.

A look of fright drained the color from her face. At one time Evan would have taken pleasure in the response, but he did not do so now. She was his nurse. She had earned his respect in regard to that.

"What is *he* doing here?" Julia whispered.

"I don't know." Emily tried to keep the fear she felt at the sight of Dr. Mackay from showing in her voice. She was not successful. She could hear the tremble in her words.

Had he come to show sympathy or take pleasure in their grief? Seconds later, she had her answer. Reverend Perry, the man who had been Stephen's minister since childhood, had no sooner spoken the closing prayer than the click clack of boots echoed in her ears. Emily and everyone else turned to see a squad of bluecoats approaching. Sally immediately cried out in fear. Julia did as well the moment the Federal soldiers surrounded the funeral party.

"What is the meaning of this?" Emily's father asked.

A young lieutenant with an upturned nose announced, "We are here to arrest you rebels, that's what, by order of the provost marshal."

Emily's knees went weak but she tried to remain steady for Sally's sake. She was clutching her arm.

"I can assure you, sir," Mr. Davis said, "there are no troublemakers here. Each of these men have signed oaths of loyalty, myself included."

"What about this one?" The lieutenant pointed to Sally's father. "This one bears the mark of treason on his chest."

"The cross belonged to his son. It was all that remained of the boy's personal effects when they found him. And, yes, Mr. Hastings has also signed an oath."

"A recent one?"

Emily's heart was pounding. Her father, Dr. Stanton, Mr. Hastings and Sam had all signed pledges early in the war, yet none of them had signed the current one. When her father failed to immediately answer the question, the lieutenant gave orders.

"Arrest every man but the minister!"

Cries from the women rang out. As the soldiers reached for the men, Emily looked to Dr. Mackay. Her voice failed, but her mind was screaming, *How can you allow this? How can you be so cruel?*

She was stunned when he suddenly stepped forward.

"Lieutenant!" he shouted. "Would you begrudge this family the comfort of a Christian burial simply because the *deceased* was a traitor?"

She held her breath. Apparently so did everyone else

around her. Dr. Mackay met the lieutenant where he stood. His jaw was set tightly. His eyes were sharp. The younger, shorter soldier, however, was not intimidated. Secure in his equal rank with Dr. Mackay, he lifted his chin.

"I have been given the authority by Provost Marshal Colonel William Fish," he announced.

"I realize that," Dr. Mackay said. "But there is no treason being plotted here today. I appeal to your Christian sympathy. Let these people return home."

No treason? I appeal to your Christian sympathy? Her heart continued to pound.

"And just why are you here, Doctor? Should we have reason to suspect *your* loyalty?"

The anger in Dr. Mackay's eyes was unmistakable. Emily thought his voice alone would knock the soldier flat.

"How dare you, Lieutenant! My loyalty is beyond question, as is my service to the Union. I have patched up men like you more times then I care to count!"

No one moved. Even the soldiers stood like stone.

"You are an officer in the United States army," Dr. Mackay said, teeth tightly clenched. "Haven't you more important matters to deal with?"

Chest to chest, the two stared at one another. Emily wondered just how long the battle of wills would last. Finally, the undersize soldier relented. He gave orders for the men to be released but not without stipulation.

"Return to your homes, all of you, immediately. No meal. No wake. No congregating." He then looked back at Dr. Mackay. "You can be certain that I will report this."

The authoritative Scotsman was not threatened in the least. "Go ahead, lad," was all he said.

The soldiers marched off and Emily breathed fully for the first time in minutes. As shock began to abate, the funeral party heeded the command. Dr. Stanton and Sam escorted their shaken wives to their carriages. Emily and Elizabeth walked Sally to hers. They each gave her the basket of food they had prepared for the afterward meal.

Elizabeth defiantly tossed back her red curls. "I don't care what that man said," she whispered to Sally. "I'll be by to visit you later."

Emily wished she could do the same, but she was due at the hospital within the hour. "I'll come in the morning."

Sally hugged them both. "No one could ask for better friends."

When she and her father drove away, Emily turned back for her parents. Dr. Mackay was speaking to them. She cautiously approached. One moment he looked as though he was taking pleasure in their arrest; the next he was coming to their aid. Emily told herself she should be thankful for the latter, but suspicion prickled her skin. Just what was this man up to?

Her father turned to her and smiled.

"I understand this young man knows you," he said.

"Yes, sir," she replied. "I am his nurse."

"Aye, and a fine one at that."

To say she knew not what to make of his cordiality was putting it mildly. She thanked him politely.

"My daughter is on her way to the hospital for night duty," her father said. "But then, you probably already knew that."

"I suspected so."

"Are you on your way there, as well?"

Before Emily knew it, her father was offering to give Dr. Mackay a ride back to the hospital.

Uneasiness rolled through her. This would be no pleasure outing. Emily just knew if Dr. Mackay accepted the invitation, he would find some element of their company unacceptable. *He will reconsider what he has just done and report us all to the provost marshal.*

He seemed to be hesitant about traveling with them, as well. His countenance darkened.

"Come now," her father said. "I insist. It is the least we can do after the kindness you have just shown our family and friends."

Dr. Mackay clearly looked uncomfortable but he thanked him. "I would appreciate that. It is a long walk back to the harbor."

"Wonderful. Just over here..."

Emily gulped. Her mother took her father's arm and they turned for the carriage. Dr. Mackay offered his. Anxiety pulsed through her as she slid her fingers around his blue wool. Even with her leather glove serving as barrier between them, his uniform was rough and scratchy.

Just like his temperament, she thought.

"Do you often take walks through this part of town?" she asked, doing her best to make polite conversation. What she wouldn't give right now for a basket of bandages to roll or some other menial medical task to perform.

"No," he said. "I was attending the service of a respected army officer."

The word *respected* was not lost on her. No matter what he may have said to the zealous Federal lieutenant, he was letting her know, in no uncertain terms, he hadn't come to honor Stephen.

She responded kindly anyway, reminding herself that he had just come from a graveside service, as well. "I am sorry to hear that. My condolences. You knew the man well?"

"Not really." And that was the end of that.

They passed silently through the rows of granite and marble. Upon reaching the carriage, she promptly let go of his sleeve. Joshua was seated in the driver's box and he nodded when her father introduced their guest. Dr. Mackay nodded back and much to Emily's surprise, reached up and shook Joshua's hand.

So he does believe in equality, she thought. *At least when it comes to former slaves.*

Mr. Davis helped his wife into the carriage, then turned to assist his daughter. Emily had just enough time to adjust her hoop and smooth out her skirt before Dr. Mackay claimed the seat beside her. His broad shoulders and long-legged frame left little room between them. Fire burned her cheeks. She wasn't certain if it was the August heat or the Federal doctor's close proximity.

Evan settled back into the seat but did not relax in his state of mind. What had he gotten himself into? What had he been thinking? Thinking of the past, no doubt. His impulsive need to rectify a wrong had driven him to make another.

When the lieutenant and his squad had interrupted the funeral, he'd first thought they must have good reason. However, when he saw Mrs. Ward, wide with child, turn pale and clutch her husband's arm, he was compelled to intervene. He would not allow trouble to come to that woman, not if he could help it. Before he knew it, he was defending the lot of them.

Now he was riding in the rebel lawyer's carriage. The man mistakenly believed Evan was lax concerning loyalty.

"It is unthinkable," he said. "I spend the majority of my time advocating for men who have been denied due process of law."

Evan's anger was rising. Under no circumstances would he feel pity for the so-called innocent citizens of Baltimore who had been imprisoned at Fort McHenry.

The man continued. "They arrest our citizens without probable cause. There are those that say in times of war security is all that matters… But I say, at what cost? What good is peace if it is purchased at the price of chains?"

Evan's blood was boiling. *Without probable cause?* This city's history and the way that the local newspapers continued printing pro-Southern garbage was all the cause needed for him. He was just about to tell the rebel lawyer what he thought when the wife intervened.

"Dr. Mackay, my daughter tells me you are from Pennsylvania."

So I have been discussed at home. Evan turned to look at Emily. Her cheeks were pink. Was it because she knew her father's speech wasn't winning any converts to the Cause? Or because she was embarrassed to admit that he'd been a topic of discussion for the Davis family?

"I am," he said to her mother, doing his best to keep his tone civil.

"Are you from Philadelphia?"

"No, ma'am. From a very small town, a farming community. Though it is not far from the city."

Emily now joined in, obviously trying to keep the conversation from returning to the subject of war. "I am told that is a beautiful part of the country, though I have never been."

He nodded. "The countryside rolls from one low hill to another, and in the summertime the wheat fields move like waves upon the ocean."

She smiled, her expression genuine. "That sounds lovely."

"It is."

"I suppose this time spent in the city must be dreadful."

Evan could feel the darkness creeping in. "I manage."

"Have you a family up in Pennsylvania?" Emily's father asked.

Pain shot through him as though the rebel lawyer had fired a derringer at his chest. "No," Evan said. "I have no family."

He heard Emily draw in a sharp breath, but he did not turn to her. It was bad enough that her mother was now looking at him as though he were a stray puppy in need of a home.

"Well, Doctor," she said. "As long as you are here in Baltimore, consider yourself part of our family. You have an open invitation for supper anytime."

"Indeed," her husband insisted. "Our home is yours. Our church, as well. We would be pleased to have you attend services with us."

The invitation struck Evan as odd to say the least. What was this? He was a stranger and a Northern man at that. Was this simply Christian charity or some Southern plot to weaken a Federal man? If that were the case he would not play into their hands. "Thank you but I would not wish to impose. Besides, my duties at the hospital keep me very busy."

"You sound like my daughter," the woman said. "I

keep telling her duty is commendable, but it isn't good to be constantly surrounded by the effects of war."

Anywhere in this city I am surrounded by the effects of war, he thought.

"Someone must deal with the damage," he heard Emily say. "There are so many, on both sides, in need of healing."

He looked at her.

The expression on her face was one of fidelity, of quiet strength. Clearly she was not the prissy little socialite he had first thought. She ministered to loyal men as tenderly as her beloved rebs and he had to admit, he admired the fact that this wealthy Southern family treated former slaves as equals. Evan had never understood what supposed difference a man's skin, ancestry or title made. Nobility was defined by character, not birthright.

Nurse Emily seemed to understand that.

As he continued to hold her gaze, her cheeks darkened to a deeper shade of crimson. Even in her black mourning dress, Evan thought her pretty.

The carriage came to a stop at the hospital's main entrance. The American flag stood tall and numerous sentinels with muskets on their shoulders were stationed about. He breathed a silent sigh. He was glad to be back on familiar ground, yet he thanked the family for their kindness before exiting.

"You are quite welcome, Doctor," the lawyer said.

Emily moved to step out, as well, her silk fabric rustling. Evan offered his hand to her. As she clasped it he took notice of how good she smelled. Lilac water, freshly washed hair, he would take those fragrances over the odors of the hospital any day.

"Thank you, Dr. Mackay."

"Evan," he said, although he wasn't certain why.

She let go of his hand the moment her feet touched the ground, but for some reason he wished she had waited just a little longer.

Chapter Eight

The moment Dr. Mackay had escorted her into the building, he disappeared with barely a good-evening. Emily should not have been surprised. It was his nature to play the part of a gentleman one moment and an ogre the next. She found the man who had offered his arm and spoken so poetically concerning his home in Pennsylvania much more to her liking, but he never stayed around for very long.

She made her way to the women's washroom, where she promptly traded her black silk for simple cotton. She stashed her carpetbag in a secure nook and stepped into the ward just as the evening bell sounded. Rebekah came to her immediately.

"How was the funeral?"

Emily told her the brief details. Even Rebekah, Unionist to the core, was horrified to know the Federal soldiers had disrupted the graveside service.

"Oh! How dreadful! Thank goodness that Dr. Mackay was with you."

Emily could feel a tingle in her cheeks as the scene replayed through her mind, particularly the carriage ride. Why the memory provoked such a response, she was not sure. It wasn't as though the Northern doctor stirred some romantic notion in her. *Gracious, no. A Federal soldier? I would never think that way about him!*

She may wish for the war to end, may agree with Lincoln's proclamation granting freedom to slaves, but she detested the thought of her city being occupied. The Federal government had instituted martial law in Baltimore and many a citizen, including her and her friends, had been terrorized by the soldiers.

Today's funeral was only one such example. Emily found Dr. Mackay's involvement entirely disturbing. How had those soldiers known about the service? Did he send them? If so, what made him change his mind?

"Sergeant Cooper is much improved," she heard Rebekah say. "Dr. Warren removed the tube to his lungs."

Emily focused her thoughts on her duty. "Good."

"Private Bush is taking solid food."

"Wonderful. It will help him to regain his strength."

"But Edward…" Rebekah paused, then discreetly nodded in his direction. "He hasn't eaten a bite today."

Emily looked to see him propped up in his bed, staring off into the distance. Once more, that lost look was on his face. Her shoulders fell with a tired sigh. Already they were aching and she had a full twelve hours to go.

"More than likely he's thinking of Stephen. He knows the service was set for today."

"Perhaps you should tell him about it."

"Perhaps…" Emily would wait to see for herself how Edward was tonight. If she did give any details, she would leave out the part about the men in blue.

Rebekah bid her a good-night, then gathered up her basket and bonnet. Emily started across the ward. Edward saw her approaching and waved her over. She whispered a quick prayer. *Give me wisdom, Lord. I don't want to do or say anything that will hurt him.*

"Did you attend?" he asked straightaway.

The decision had been made for her. She drew up a chair. "Yes. Stephen was laid to rest honorably. Sam and your father placed a Maryland Flag over his casket, and Reverend Perry gave the most beautiful eulogy."

Edward nodded his approval, but his eyes showed grief. Emily's heart ached.

"Did many attend?"

She told him who had come, minus the soldiers. After a long pause he then asked, "How is Sally?"

"As well as can be expected, but it will do her good to know that you asked about her." *She loves you,* Emily wanted to add. *And I believe she always will.*

He was quiet again. She waited to see what, if anything, he would say next. A man from across the room, one who had been wounded in the leg, was trying out a pair of crutches. Emily watched him silently and offered an encouraging nod when he looked her way.

"Will you do something for me?" Edward asked her.

"Of course."

"Keep Julia away. I grow tired of her."

A hint of brotherly teasing showed on his face. Emily tried to coax more. Laughter would be good for him.

"Do you realize what you are asking? She will fight me tooth and nail. You know how stubborn she is."

He smiled, but then his look darkened.

"They are about to send me on to prison."

Emily felt her muscles tense even further. She knew now where Edward's concerns truly were. This was the real reason he wanted his sister to stay away. Julia would have difficulty with his transfer. "Has the ward master been by?" she asked.

"Today. Not long before your arrival. I don't want my sister to be here when they come for me."

He was concerned for her health, especially now that her visits were getting shorter. Julia still came each morning but only for a few moments with Sam at her side. Her time of confinement was drawing near.

"I understand, Eddie. But try not to think of any of that. Just think about that little niece or nephew of yours that will soon enter this world."

"I hope he's smart enough not to make the same mistakes I have."

Not knowing what to say to that, Emily simply squeezed his hand. When the orderlies came in to turn down the lamps, Edward rolled to his side. She stood and glanced about the room. Her heart was heavy. She wondered why Rebekah had not mentioned the ward master's presence this evening. She supposed she had been so busy with the evening medications that she failed to notice him.

Emily wondered how many of the men before her now would make the march to Fort McHenry tomorrow. *What will conditions be like when they reach the prison camps?*

She was well aware that the convalescing men had to move on. The field hospitals in Gettysburg were full of wounded still awaiting transport to the general facilities. Conditions here were better than there. She wanted the waiting men to receive proper care, but she shuddered at the thought of any of her current charges, especially Edward, being marched to prison.

Lord, give them each the strength to bear the transfer when the time comes. Give me the strength, as well.

When Josiah asked for his evening Bible story, Emily felt compelled to read the account of Christ's crucifixion. She began with the time Jesus spent in the garden. She read on through the trial, the beatings at the hands of the Roman soldiers. When she reached the forced march to Calvary, a hush fell over the room. It took all she had within her to keep her voice steady. She could see it in their faces. They each grasped the relevance of the story in their own lives.

"That's worse than Yankee soldiers," John said. "And Jesus didn't fight back. He could have, but He didn't."

"No, He didn't," Emily said. "He forgave them. Just like He forgives each one of us."

"It's them Yankees that need the forgivin'," a man at the far end of the ward insisted. "They're the ones who wouldn't leave well enough alone. They brought about war."

Her heart sank like a stone to the bottom of the Baltimore harbor. Before she could even whisper a prayer on the man's behalf, John spoke again. "Them Yankees is just like us," he said. "I didn't used to think so, but I do now. As I lay in the pouring rain up yonder in Pennsylvania, do you know who the first person was to come to my aid?"

"Who?" the first man asked.

"A Yankee." The corporal then looked at Emily. "It was a man from the Christian Commission, but he weren't from Maryland. He was from Massachusetts."

"I met one from Chicago," another soldier said. "He walked for miles just to bring me some soda crackers and a little bread. I hadn't had nothin' to eat for four days."

"A man from Rhode Island did the same for me," another one said.

"But didn't he first give you what for?" the disgruntled soldier asked. "Didn't he tell you that you was to blame for all the sufferin'? That *his cause* was the right one?"

"No. He just treated me like I was his brother. Sure was hard to think of that Northern man as an enemy. Made me wish I'd never fought in the first place."

Emily listened, tears in her eyes. That which she prayed for most for this nation was reconciliation. Apparently God was answering those prayers, one man at a time. He was using the delegates of the Christian Commission to do so.

Like rain-soaked wool blankets on the battlefield, silence covered them all. Finally, Emily dared to speak. "It doesn't matter where you are from or what you may have done in the past. God loves you. He waits for you to come to Him, just like your fathers, mothers and sweethearts back home."

John nodded. So did Josiah. Emily prayed the others would understand in time. But the person she thought of most at that moment was not even in the room.

Where is Dr. Mackay tonight? Has he been called to some emergency, or is he leaving me to fend for myself? She figured it was the latter, for the anger had been quite visible on his face when her father had spoken of Baltimoreans being arrested without probable cause. Yet she had also seen an almost affable expression when he'd offered her his hand. Emily could not help but wonder which side was the true man.

He watched her through the crack in the door. There she sat, Bible on her lap, between the rows of iron cots. The woman held obvious sympathy for rebs, and yet every officer, every doctor in this hospital, thought well of her.

Even me, he thought. *Too well, in fact.*

She was drawing him in with all her talk of love and forgiveness. Evan told himself to be careful. That carriage ride had been enough to show him the danger. He wouldn't deny the fact that he thought her a pretty little lass. Any man would, but she made him think of things he shouldn't be thinking. Guilt had stabbed him the moment he'd taken her hand.

Mary is my love. She always will be.

Still, he continued to covertly watch. His protective nature told him to take up residence in the room, especially when he saw how close she was to the rebel major. *But I am through with rescuing her.* The guard on duty tonight was a trustworthy man. He'd be awake all night. If there was any trouble, *he* could come to her aid.

And the major will be gone on the morrow, he reminded himself.

The Georgia corporal was now saying something. She was nodding and smiling. Evan couldn't hear what they were discussing but considering the Scripture and the look on her face, he was fairly certain mercy and pardon were part of it.

A rock lodged in his throat. He tried to swallow it back. *Would it be that it was all that simple,* he thought. *You cannot undo what sins have been done. I know that better than anyone.*

He turned from the door. Another night of restlessness and regret lay before him.

Emily was anxious about being alone that night but thankfully the hours passed peacefully. The men snored heavily as the terrors of the battlefield were forgotten, at least for a time. She spent the evening walking quietly among the beds, straightening covers and swatting away flies.

The sun rose over the harbor, and the inky, black water lightened to a shade of bluish gray. Emily watched from a window as the wharf stirred to life. Ships were loaded, anchors drawn.

"Do you like the sea?" she heard Adam ask. His voice was still fragile but stronger than it had been.

"Not particularly," she said, going to him. "I have always preferred green fields or mountains."

He coughed. "I love the sea. Was raised by it. Lookin' forward to returning."

"I am certain you are."

She smiled at him. His eyes showed weakness, but he managed to give her one in return.

"I haven't thanked you for what you did for me."

"There is no need. I am pleased to see you are improving."

"Thank that Yankee doc for what he done."

"I will, but you can tell him yourself. He will be by directly to examine you."

And he was. Evan's neatly trimmed side whiskers and newly laundered shirt gave him a fresh appearance but his cutting looks and particularly sharp tone soured the morning rounds.

"Change this bandage before you go," he ordered. "And bring me a bucket of water!"

Exhausted as she was, Emily did her best to respond pleasantly. She carried out his instructions, then told him, "Sergeant Cooper spoke with me at length this morning. He wishes to thank you."

A grunt was all she got in return.

"I wish to thank you, as well. You are a gifted physician, Dr. Mackay. I feel it is my privilege to serve under you."

His eyes widened in disbelief. She wondered if her

look was the same. *My privilege to serve under you?* Where had those words come from?

"'Twas God that saved him," he said. "Not me."

Emily blinked, still in shock over her own words, now further with his. *So he does acknowledge where healing comes from.* "That is true, but He used *you* to do so." She decided to take the opportunity to thank him for his intervention at the funeral. "My family, my friends, we are all very grateful."

He crossed his arms over his chest as if he wanted her to be certain he held no Southern sympathies.

Do not worry, she was tempted to say. *I know where you stand.*

"I did so because of Mrs. Ward," he said.

Emily blinked again. "For Julia?"

"In her condition she shouldn't see her husband carted off to jail."

So that was it. If he had sent those soldiers, this explained why he had changed his mind. She tried to be gracious. "Thank you. I, too, was concerned. Her brother is, as well."

Dr. Mackay's jaw twitched. Something passed across his face that Emily could not interpret. He reached for her elbow, tugged her a little closer. Her stomach fluttered when he bent low to her ear.

"He is on the list," he said. "The ward master will call for him within the hour."

She gulped back her emotions. *So Edward's suspicions proved true.* "He knows," she said. "He told me so last night. He asked me to keep his sister from the room."

A look of compassion shone on his face. Emily was so struck by it that all she could do was stare.

"Make certain she doesn't enter the room when they

are being called," he told her. "Have that husband of hers promptly escort her home, though hopefully, the major will be gone before she arrives."

For the first time, she believed his orders were truly out of concern, not politically motivated. He was still holding on to her elbow. He must have realized it, for he suddenly let go.

"If there is any trouble, alert me immediately."

"I will."

He looked past her. "Go on now," he said. "The ward master has arrived."

Emily turned. An older, overweight Federal officer stood in the doorway. He had his list in hand. A hush fell over the room as soon as the Confederate men noticed him.

"The following persons are hereby removed to Fort McHenry," the man said. "Gather your personal items quickly."

She held her breath, hoping against certainty. The first name was announced.

"Major Edward R. Stanton…"

Emily had still an hour before Julia would arrive. Biting back her grief, she went to assist him. Edward wished to wear his uniform, so she helped him into it. The coat now practically swallowed him, particularly the empty left sleeve. She fastened what remained of the buttons.

"I will keep you in my prayers, Eddie."

He leaned forward and kissed her cheek. "Farewell, Emmy."

John and Josiah were called, as well. Dr. Mackay was quickly administering the last of the medication. Rebekah had arrived and was assisting the others. In a matter of moments the selected men fell into a line.

Some were on crutches, some on the arms of their comrades. They each touched their caps and offered thanks to Emily as she moved among them.

She blinked back tears, wished each one of them well. Surrounded by armed guards, they prepared to march. When a Federal soldier pulled back the door, Emily glanced down the corridor. To her horror, Sam and Julia were approaching.

They are early!

She hurried for them but was too late. Julia and Sam took one look at the mixture of freshly pressed bluecoats among rags and knew exactly what was happening. She immediately went pale.

"No! Samuel, please! Not Edward!"

Emily stepped in, moving to block her friend's view of the men preparing to march. "Let Sam see to him, Julia. It's better for Edward that way. Come with me."

Sam transferred his wife's hand to hers. "Go with Emily, sweetheart."

Shaking, Julia broke down completely. "Tell him I love him...."

"I will."

He hurried for the ward. Emily led her friend in the opposite direction.

"Oh, Em, what if Edward can't make the march? It's three miles!"

"There will be stewards attending them. If there is any trouble, the physicians at the fort will see to him." She tried her best to sound calm, but in truth Emily was just as upset as Julia. It always pained her to see men transferred, but today was especially hard.

Tears streamed down Julia's cheeks. One of the supply rooms was unlocked, so Emily took her there. A table and two chairs offered a place to sit. Some of the commission volunteers must have been rolling bandages, for the table was full of them. She settled her friend in a seat and offered her a clean handkerchief. Julia wiped her eyes. She was trying to bring her emotions under control, but Emily knew the task was difficult. Fear laced her voice.

"First they took my father. Then they took Samuel. Now they are taking my brother."

Both Dr. Stanton and Sam had spent time at the fort during the beginning of the war because the Federal army had suspected them of disloyalty.

"But they came home, Julia," Emily gently reminded her. "God took care of them. He will take care of Edward, as well."

"I want to believe that...." She cried into her handkerchief.

"I know it is difficult. I am sorry. I wish it didn't have to be this way."

"I hope he is paroled soon."

"We'll pray for that."

Julia arched her back and winced. She shifted for a more comfortable position. Emily knew the pregnancy weighed heavily upon her. She tried to think of something to ease her mind.

"Edward and I spoke last night at length."

"What about?"

She offered her a smile. "You. About how tenacious you are."

Julia gave a quick laugh. Emily considered it a victory.

"No more than he," Julia said.

"Oh, I am certain about that. I remember well the arguments between you both growing up."

Julia shifted once more. She bit her lip and wiped her

eyes. Her hands were still shaking, even harder now it seemed. Her color did not look good.

"Can I fetch you something?" Emily asked. "Anything?"

"No, but thank you. I do hope Sam will be able to speak with him."

"I'm sure he will."

The moments passed. Julia grew tired of sitting, of waiting. She began pacing the tiny room. Her own heart aching, Emily started placing the bandage rolls in a basket on the shelf. They could hear the thump, thump, thump of boots on boards. They knew the wards were emptying.

How many are being transferred today? How many will claim their beds?

All of a sudden, Julia's cry pierced the air. "Oh! Oh, Em!"

Turning, Emily gasped in horror as her friend lifted her skirt from the floor. Julia's petticoats were stained with a rush of water and blood.

Oh, dear Lord, no!

"It's too early!" Julia gasped. "It's too early!"

Panic seized her, but Emily did her best not to let it show. "Sit down!" she told her. Just then Rebekah walked in. Thankfully, Sam was with her.

"Emily, we thought we would—" She stopped, eyes widening as she recognized their friend's distress. "Oh! What should we do?"

Sam immediately rushed to his wife's side, but Emily had no idea what course to take. They had spent the last year nursing wounded men, not studying midwifery.

"Stay with her, both of you," she commanded. "I'll fetch help."

She tore off as fast as she could in search of the one

person in the hospital she believed would know what to do. Skirts flying, she raced back through the corridor. The Confederate men were making their way toward the main entrance. Evan was shouting orders to the guards at the front of the line.

"Get the carts for the weakest of them!"

"Dr. Mackay!"

He turned immediately, as if he already knew what was wrong. Emily had never before seen fear in his eyes, but she saw it then. "Where is she?" he demanded.

"The supply room!"

He took off, legs so long and fast that she could not keep up with him. By the time Emily reached the room, Rebekah had cleared the table. She had gathered blankets and the other necessary supplies and instruments. Sam was holding Julia's hand, promising her that everything would be all right.

"Take him outside!" Dr. Mackay shouted at Emily. "And stay with him!"

No! She is my friend! I'll not leave her alone!

One glance at Sam told her he was thinking the same. Before either of them could protest, Rebekah pushed them toward the door.

"Go," she urged. "He knows what he is doing."

The door shut solidly in front of them. Sam blinked, then took to pacing the narrow corridor. Emily felt the weight of fear and exhaustion as they came crashing down upon her. She sank back against the wall. Her mind was screaming.

I can't do this anymore! I don't want to do this anymore! The countless wounded! Stephen...Sally...Edward...now this!

At that moment Emily wanted to get as far away from this hospital, from this terrible war, as possible.

She wanted a place of happiness, of frivolity, one where choosing a new ball gown or which volume of poetry to read was her biggest concern.

But as Sam paced about, systematically destroying the topper in his hands by twisting the brim, as Julia's cries interspersed with Confederate footsteps from the hall, she knew she was exactly where God wanted her to be.

Emily pushed to her feet. Dr. Mackay's commands to Rebekah could be heard from beyond the door.

"Put pressure here! Hold fast!"

When Julia let out a particularly sharp cry, Sam dashed for the door. Emily stopped him.

"Sam, the Good Lord is with her."

He raked back his hair. She could see the fear in his eyes. "Of all places...a Federal hospital?"

She tried to reassure him. "Dr. Mackay is the best physician I know."

His left eyebrow arched. "Do you trust him?"

Their past history raced through her mind, the scowls, the abrasive, unyielding personality. *He is a Yankee, a Federal soldier! One who makes it quite obvious what he thinks of all of us. Get your wife, Sam,* she was tempted to say. *We will take her to our own kind.*

Faith, however, won out over fear. Dr. Mackay had expressed concern for Julia before and time and again Emily had witnessed his medical skill. Perhaps God had allowed these circumstances for a specific reason, for Julia's benefit. "Do I trust him? In matters such as these...yes. I know he will do everything he can."

Sam's mouth shifted with emotion. "I love her, Em."

"I know you do. And she knows that, as well."

He sighed.

"Come on. Let's pray for her."

After doing so, they continued to wait. Both realized they should notify Julia's parents concerning what was happening, yet neither of them wanted to leave.

The solution presented itself when Trudy and Elizabeth rounded the corner. Unaware of the emergency, they had come, baskets in hand, to restock their supplies.

"Em!" Elizabeth said. "What is going on?"

She quickly explained and Elizabeth offered to fetch Dr. Stanton.

"Joshua is waiting for me outside," Emily said, remembering. "Ask him to drive you."

The sisters wasted no time. They scurried off. When they had gone, Emily and Sam continued to wait. He paced while she prayed.

Give Dr. Mackay wisdom, Lord. Give him success.

Just when they both thought they could stand it no longer, a baby's cry filled their ears. Sam's face lit up and he quickly hugged Emily. Sometime later, Rebekah opened the door.

"Samuel Ward," she said with a smile. "You have a beautiful baby girl."

He gave a shout. "And Julia?"

"She must remain confined for several days, but she is well. You may see her now."

The proud father rushed in. As relieved as Emily was, Rebekah's words tempered her joy.

"Confined?" She whispered. "What happened? Is the baby strong enough?"

"The baby is quite strong. According to Dr. Mackay, she isn't that early. Julia must have miscalculated the time."

"But what about the blood?"

Rebekah shivered slightly. "I have never seen so much, even with the wounded. It was something to do with the afterbirth tearing inside, but Dr. Mackay managed it. He was able to stop the bleeding."

Oh thank You, Lord.

"Come in and see her," Rebekah insisted, her brightness returning. "She is precious."

Emily stepped inside. Julia was pale, weak-eyed and wrapped in U.S. Army blankets, but she was smiling. Her beautiful newborn daughter was in her arms. The child was dark-haired and perfectly pink in the face.

"Oh!" Emily gasped. "She is something!"

"Indeed," Sam said grinning with pride. "Just like her mother."

Emily returned his smile; then her eyes drifted to the corner of the room. Dr. Mackay's tall form was bent over a washbasin. His shirt was soaked with sweat, his blue wool trousers speckled with dust and blood, but at that moment all she wanted to do was kiss him. She wanted to fall upon his neck and shower him with appreciation for what he had done.

What joy he must feel knowing that God granted him success, that a beautiful and healthy new life will now brighten this dark world.

But as he turned, Emily was shocked to see the sorrow in his eyes, the hard set of his mouth. He looked as though death had triumphed instead of life.

Chapter Nine

Evan's chest was so tight that he could not breathe. The heat was unbearable, yet he was chilled. His hands, only moments ago steady and dependable, now shook uncontrollably. Well-wishers cooed over the child. All he wanted to do was get out of this room.

Nurse Emily caught his eye and, with a look of grave concern, quickly assessed his condition. He strode past her before she could speak. A thousand thoughts fired through his mind as he hastily stepped into the corridor and turned right.

The path ahead was clogged, blue subduing gray. His fellow physicians and army personnel were doing their duty, managing the last of the departing enemy soldiers, yet Evan was in full retreat. He was searching for refuge, for relief, but there was none to be had. Everywhere were legless, armless scoundrels with that dash of rebel pride in their eyes. They were weakened by defeat, yet still strong enough to remind him of what they had done to Andrew, what he in turn had done to Mary.

God forgive me.

He snaked his way through, rounded a corner and pushed past a gaggle of cackling army nurses and orderlies. He needed air. His lungs desperately craved it, but he knew that the outside docks would offer no privacy. Away from the immediate commotion, he came upon an empty room. He quickly commandeered it. It was not much wider than a buckboard wagon, just a nook where the scrubwomen left their buckets and brushes to dry. Shutting the rickety door behind him, he fell to his knees.

His legs were useless, his chest heaving. So ashamed of himself he was, for he hadn't tasted the salt of his own tears since he was a child. He had shed not one for Andrew or Mary. Now he struggled to bring his emotions under command. He would not allow himself to come to this. He wouldn't allow those rebs to bring him to such weakness. He must remain strong. After all, he was an officer in the U.S. Army.

But Evan knew full well he had lost the battle. He had been beaten by a Baltimore woman and her child. Now her friend, the little rebel sympathizer herself, came to finish him off. Skirts folding to the dirty floor, she knelt beside him. That look was on her face.

"Go away!" he ordered, but she did not obey. The next thing he knew her hand was on his shoulder. Her touch burned like hot lead through his flesh.

"What is it, Evan? What troubles you so?"

How dare she address him by his given name! This was an army hospital. She was his subordinate and a *Southerner* at that. He opened his mouth to scold her, yet the words would not come. A groan rose from deep within and all that he did not wish to reveal came pouring out.

"I didn't save her. I could have. God, forgive me...I know I could have...."

"You did wonderfully. The baby is healthy and Julia will heal in time."

He shook his head, could feel his heart ripping in two. "No. *Mary*. I didn't save *Mary*."

"Who is Mary?"

"My wife."

The revelation so stunned her that she started to draw back. *He is a married man?* Then she realized, *Was. He was a married man.*

His shoulders were shaking. This formidable Federal soldier was literally trembling in her arms.

"I shouldn't have gone."

"Gone where?" she asked.

"To join the army. I immediately requested commission following Andrew's death. I wanted to make certain more men like him wouldn't die needlessly from their wounds. Wounds from which they could be saved...but I ended up losing her, as well."

Pain stabbed her heart as a regiment of questions marched through her mind. How had he lost her? Had it been sickness? Some dreadful accident? An unscrupulous raiding party? Was that why he hated Southerners so?

"Oh, Evan, I am so very sorry. So sorry indeed. May I ask what happened?"

"She miscarried a child. My daughter."

Oh, gracious, Emily thought. *No wonder he was so protective of Julia.*

"The bleeding wouldn't stop. They both died." His voice was ragged, broken. "I didn't know she was with child. If I had, I never would have left her."

"Of course you wouldn't have."

"I should have known. She begged me not to go. Told

me vengeance was what I sought...." His face showed his grief. "Aye. Vengeance is what I received. God has heaped it upon me each day since her death."

He was on his knees in the dust of a former cotton warehouse but it might as well have been biblical sackcloth and ashes, for Emily had never heard a more lonely, desperate cry. "Oh, God, forgive me."

"He already has," she said softly. "He already has. God loves you, Evan."

He shook his head. "He may have saved my soul from torment eternal, but each day here on earth He exacts payment for my sins."

"What makes you say that?"

"Her voice haunts me in my sleep. The memory of her pleading, begging me not to go."

"You are grieving. You loved her very deeply...and that is a fine and honorable thing. In time, the pain will lessen."

The tears were drying. Emily could feel his shoulders tensing.

"He sent me *here*. Of all the hospitals, of all the cities, God sends me to Baltimore. To view each morning the very street on which my brother died, to unknowingly pass the traitors who clustered around his train car." Bitterness laced his words. His hands shook, but now in anger. "I have probably patched up the very ones who threw the stones! If that's not punishment, I don't know what is...."

"Evan—"

He pulled away from her, making it clearly known that her comfort, her presence, was no longer wanted. She, however, did not retreat. Emily remained exactly where she was, on her knees beside him. She grieved for him, for the family he had lost, for the life, the blessings, he was missing now.

"Perhaps God sent you here to make peace."

He cut her with a devastating look, eyes sharp as a sword. "Peace? With rebel traitors?"

"With yourself and with your enemies."

That vein near his collar was bulging as he pushed to his feet. Emily remained on the floor, looking up at him. He may tower over her, may wound her with his words, but she was not afraid of him. She was armed with the truth.

"God does love you," she said quietly. "But you can't feel His love, His presence, because you won't let go of your hate."

"And what would you know of that?" He sneered. "You're a—"

"Rebel? Yes. Dr. Mackay, I suppose based on your definition, I am. Do you think I enjoy living under martial law? Do you think it's easy for me to watch my childhood friends, my fellow Marylanders, being rounded up and sent to prison?" She stood, slowly brushing the dust from her dress. "I have watched you blister and bully everyone in our ward, but I came to *you* for the sake of my dearest friend."

"Why did you?"

Even at her tallest, she came only to his chest, yet she locked eyes with him and maintained, "Because I believe God has His hand upon you. You are the most gifted physician in this hospital. You are skilled at treating wounds, but, oh, what healing you could bring if only you would allow God to do so for you."

His eyes flashed fire. Jaw twitching, he looked as though he would blast her with his anger. Instead, to her surprise, he turned on his heel and stormed toward the door. Just short of reaching it, he stopped.

Don't go, Emily silently pleaded. *I do not wish to be at war with you.*

Evan raked his fingers through his nut-brown hair. He looked back over his shoulder and his breathing seemed to slow.

"I trust you will keep what happened here today to yourself," he said.

That vein had disappeared and a hint of vulnerability showed on his face.

Emily breathed. "Your secret, Dr. Mackay, is safe with me."

It was two weeks before Julia was given permission to return home. Even then Dr. Mackay insisted that her father keep a close eye on her. Precious little Rachael Anne was thriving. The innocent baby girl helped lift the sadness the women felt over Edward and the other men's departure.

It helped the wounded left behind, as well. Word spread quickly of the birth of Major Stanton's niece, and even the most grizzled prisoners and ill-tempered guards inquired of the child when they spoke to Emily, wishing health to her and her family. One of the chief surgeons, a man who had a particular affinity for whittling, carved her a wooden lamb.

"That way she'll know what a special little lamb we think she is," he said.

Undoubtedly men on both sides were thinking of their own families, wishing for home. Emily thought often in those days of Evan. The news of his wife's death explained quite a bit of his behavior, but she couldn't help but wonder, *Who was Mary Mackay?* What kind of woman could capture the love of such an unyielding man and still hold his heart prisoner two years after her death? From Evan's confession that day among the scrub brushes, she guessed his wife had been a woman of faith.

She begged me not to go; said vengeance was what I sought.

Had Mary Mackay prayed each night for her husband's heart to soften? Had she begged God to have His way in his life? More and more, Emily found herself praying such things.

On the morning when Julia and Rachael left for home, Emily worked to return the supply room back to its original purpose. Rebekah had already overseen the orderlies removing the iron cot Julia had occupied following delivery. It had belonged to Dr. Mackay.

Beds being at a shortage, he had given up his own, insisting he didn't fit in it anyway. He had tended to Julia with the utmost care and respect. Emily knew exactly why. He was trying to make up for not being there for Mary.

Despite him being at war with her neighbors and friends, she believed what she had told him. God had given him the gift of healing. What a difference he could make in this fractured nation if only he would allow the Savior to heal *his* wounds.

And when that happens, I want to be there, working beside him....

The moment the thought crossed her mind, Emily felt the fire in her cheeks. *What kind of ridiculous notion is this?* she wondered. *Yes, I am committed to nursing. I want to continue service in some way even after this dreadful war, but why on earth would I wish to do so with him?*

She could not deny the fact that she had learned much from Dr. Mackay. She would not dismiss the admiration she felt in such moments as Julia's delivery or how he had skillfully tended to Adam Cooper. Emily had studied Evan's handsome features in the lamplight that night, and thought him a remarkable man.

But Julia and the others had brothers serving in the Confederate army. What would her friends think if they knew she had taken an interest in a haughty Northerner?

No! she quickly told herself. *I do not have romantic feelings for Dr. Mackay. He may have a few admirable qualities but he is not the kind of man I wish to marry! He is wounded, both in spirit and mind. I simply wish to nurse him.*

Emily replaced the chairs around the supply table. She stocked the shelves with the fresh blankets and bandage rolls that the commission had just delivered moments ago. She worked with expediency, almost with a fury, repeatedly telling herself it was her Christian compassion which drew her to Evan Mackay, and not her woman's heart.

Evan listened for it, the gossip, the tales he was certain Nurse Emily would spread amongst her rebel allies.

He was reduced to tears, on his knees, begging for forgiveness!

How could he have been so foolish? Why did he say those things, especially to her? Soon everyone in Baltimore would know. They would view him weak. They would challenge his and all Federal authority.

He paid close attention to the scrubwomen's whispering when they moved through the wards. He watched for any change in the Johnnies' eyes as he made his rounds each morning. He was just waiting for one of them to make some impudent remark. Yet a fortnight passed and he had heard nothing, saw no change in the way the prisoners looked at him.

Either they are all skillful conspirators, he thought, *or she didn't reveal a thing.*

If the latter was true, Evan did not know what to think. Why would Nurse Emily keep his confidence? Why would she not seek some recompense for the countless hours he had balked at her kindness and bullied her men?

Since the birth of Mrs. Ward's child, he had gone out of his way to distance himself from her. When long hours of sleeplessness came, he wandered every ward but his own. He did not want to be alone with her. He did not want to risk speaking again of what he had stupidly revealed.

When their paths did cross, he made sure the interactions were short. He would order her to gather supplies or to move to another section of the hospital for some menial task. Yet she did not give up. That look of compassion in her eyes remained. Daily she brought him coffee, fresh water or some baked good from home.

Never once did she mention the departure of her beloved rebel major or the ill effects it had had on his sister. On the contrary, she had repeatedly thanked him for his assistance in delivering the baby and tending to the mother. When she gave him reports concerning the child, her blue eyes were wide with joy.

"She grasped my finger today. She is growing so strong!"

Evan was completely baffled. Why did she, a Baltimore woman, insist on speaking to him as though he were her friend? Did she really wish to include him in her happiness, or was she trying to cut out what little remained of his heart, reminding him of the child he had never held?

She is either the most cunning, calculating rebel I have ever met, or she genuinely cares for me as much as her beloved Johnnies.

He wrestled with that thought. *No. That cannot be. She cannot care for me. She may be a Christian and talk of love and forgiveness but this is still Baltimore. I am still her enemy.*

The wards were shuffled once more as another round of rebs arrived the first week of September. Evan wondered if they would ever stop coming.

Because of the load, many of the convalescing prisoners were assigned as "nurses" to assist in the care of their own. Rebel or loyal, Evan didn't like wounded serving as caregivers. They were often still too weak to lift their comrades or too ignorant to follow instructions properly. He grumbled when one such "nurse" was assigned to his ward.

He was a tall Florida boy. He had been shot in the wrist, and the commanding officers now deemed him capable enough of lending assistance. The reb was competent among his fellow prisoners. He followed orders well enough, but like the rest of his kind, Evan did not trust him.

Something in the Southern boy's eyes told him to expect trouble.

More wounded, more hands. At least the latter was a blessing. As the newly arrived Confederate prisoners were settled into wards, extra volunteers were assigned to the hospital. Emily was grateful for a second night nurse, Maggie Branson. It was good to have someone else to talk to when the soldiers' cries grew loud. Maggie possessed obvious compassion for the wounded men. She treated them with respect. Emily took an immediate liking to her.

It was quite apparent, however, that Dr. Mackay did not think much of her. Then again, he didn't think much of any woman from Baltimore. Maggie's family owned a boardinghouse in town.

"For goodness' sake, Emily," she said one night shortly after her arrival. "Does that doctor ever offer a kind word?"

He had blown through like a tornado on his evening rounds, barking orders and scolding Maggie for wrapping a bandage in the wrong direction. Emily did not reveal that she knew the true reason for Evan's stormy temper. She would carry that secret to her grave.

"He is a busy man," she said simply. "And he has quite a bit on his mind."

More often than not, Emily found herself defending him. She did so subtly, of course, but consistently. Though she tried to pin the feelings on Christian compassion alone, she was becoming increasingly aware that Evan Mackay stirred more inside her than her sympathy.

But this cannot be, she told herself. *I cannot take an interest in a man like him. He believes I am nothing more than a dissident bent on destruction. He despises me.*

She knew he was avoiding her. He had gone out of his way to do so ever since that day she had learned of Mary. Though reason told her she should be thankful for the limited contact, Emily often caught herself glancing over her shoulder at night, staring toward the corridor door, hoping for just a glimpse of his face.

"Would that be all right?"

She blinked, realizing Maggie had asked her a question. "I'm sorry. What did you say?"

Maggie smiled sweetly. "Lewis asked if he may read to some of the men who are having difficulty sleeping."

Lewis Thornton Powell was a Confederate convalescent not much older than Maggie. He had come from Gettysburg, and his nursing skills had so impressed the officers there that they suggested he assist in Baltimore. Dr. Mackay was against his presence of course, but he had been assigned to the ward anyway.

Emily was thankful for his help. Lewis was both strong and perceptive enough to steer sleepwalking soldiers back to their beds. He was generally quiet and for the most part pleasant. Maggie was evidently a bit taken with him. Emily had noticed the smiles she gave him.

"As long as he doesn't read anything pertaining to war," she told Maggie, remembering Evan's warning.

"Oh no," she said. "Nothing like that. It's *Oliver Twist*."

"That's fine."

Maggie rushed off to tell Lewis, a wide smile on her face. He nodded his thanks to Emily and opened his book.

Summer was nearing its end, but so far September provided little relief from the heat. Emily moved silently about the room that night, fanning the sleeping and keeping the flies from pestering her charges.

With each new man she came upon, she couldn't help but think of those who had previously occupied the same bed. Freddy and Jimmy, Billy, Josiah, John, Adam, Edward. Only one Maryland man was left in this lot. His name was Private Benjamin Reed. He was among the sleepless tonight. Emily watched him for a moment. He was propped upon his pillows, listening as Lewis read. She hoped the story would provide him enjoyment.

Maggie waved to her. "Come," she said. "See what Oliver does next."

Emily had already read that particular Charles Dickens story twice, but she thanked her anyway. "I brought a book of poetry. I'll keep watch on the ones sleeping at this end."

Maggie nodded and grinned, then scooted her chair a little closer to Lewis.

Yes. She is quite taken with him.

Emily chose a seat at the opposite side of the ward. The young Alabama man who now occupied Edward's bed was recovering from typhoid fever. Emily checked his forehead, then straightened his linens. Afterward she opened Robert Burns. She started where she had last left off. The title of the poem jumped out. "Bruce's March to Bannockburn."

She blushed. It was a Scottish cry for freedom, a call to war. *Oh, Evan would love this one. Get caught reading it and I'll be citing insurrection for certain.*

She turned to another page. She did not wish to think of him tonight.

"Highland Mary."

Emily flipped a few more. "Mary Morrison."

Sighing, she shut the book and slid it into her pocket. *Clearly, there will be no escape by reading tonight.*

The entire area was awash in snoring. Lewis had retired to his bed, and Maggie had taken up post not two feet from him. Embroidery work on her lap, her head bobbed gently in rhythm with her needle.

Emily walked through the rows of iron cots. Ben still lay awake, but he did not indicate that he wished for any assistance or company. She checked the tables. Rebekah had cleaned the basins before going home, but the fresh water was running low. Longing to keep busy, Emily snatched the buckets and started for the door.

But for a guard stationed every so often, the corridors were deserted. The entire hospital seemed to be asleep tonight.

I hope they are having pleasant dreams, she thought.

She filled the buckets, then made her way back through the halls. Oil lamps cast shadows across the floor. The guards stared blankly at them. A year ago, traveling unescorted through the U.S. Army hospital would have terrified her. Now she had grown accustomed to it. She didn't bother the soldiers. They didn't bother her. Her reputation for treating all men with equal respect, regardless of the uniform, had earned theirs.

All but one, she thought. She knew she did not need Dr. Mackay's approval to do her duty, but she longed to have it.

If only he could see that regardless of our beginning, I bear him no ill will. I do not seek an opportunity to exploit his weaknesses nor do I chafe under his authority. If only he could understand how much I care for him.

"No!" she said out loud, only to have the fire fill her cheeks once more. *I am talking to myself!*

Embarrassed, she turned to look behind her. If the guard had heard, he paid her no mind. Emily drew in a deep breath, but her inner argument continued.

I do not care for him! I respect his skills as a physician. Yet she knew that explanation was hollow. She respected Dr. Turner as well, but she did not run to him whenever there was trouble.

Sighing, she spun back around and nearly screamed. There he stood. His collar was loosened, his hair slightly askew. Emily nearly spilled the water all over his brogans.

"I was on the staircase," he said. "I heard you call out. Are you well?"

He scanned her as though he was searching for some obvious wound. Her ears began to thud. It was as if a battery of artillery was firing in her brain. If he knew the true reason she had called out, she would die of shame.

"It was nothing," she managed. Emily took a half step back, as if greater distance between them would quell the cannonade. It did not.

His gaze swept the corridor behind her, then the floor. "Is this yours?" he asked.

She realized her volume of Burns was lying on the boards. It must have fallen out of her pocket. "Yes."

He knelt to pick it up, then examined it curiously. Just a hint of a smile cracked his lips. "Robert Burns."

He opened to the page she had marked. Emily had no idea where she had stuck the ribbon. She prayed it wasn't on the war poem, for surely he'd consider that as volatile as stolen battle plans or Confederate dispatches.

"My luve is like a red, red rose…"

As the words rolled off his tongue in the dialect in which they had been written, her ears thudded even louder. Evan's smile broadened. His features warmed.

"Is this your favorite?" he asked.

"One of them."

"I had a copy myself, sometime ago."

To say she was shocked was putting it mildly. She had imagined that he never read anything beyond medical texts or military reports. But as usual, this man was full of surprises. "You may borrow it if you wish."

He handed the book back to her, taking instead the

first water bucket and then the other. A look of sadness replaced the smile. "I have no use for such frivolities now." He started to turn.

Emily then understood. "Did Mary enjoy poetry?"

Evan glanced back now with a look of fond remembrance. "She did. 'O Wert Thou in the Cauld Blast' was her favorite."

Emily knew the poem well. It was a man's promise to protect the woman he loved. Surely Mary Mackay had seen him as her strong guardian. "Beautiful words," she said.

"Aye. Fit for a beautiful girl."

He set down the buckets and reached into his vest pocket. He pulled out the watch she so often saw him studying. Tucked inside was the image of a young woman. Her dark hair was not bound by pins or combs. Instead, it hung long and loose about her shoulders, in an unconventional, almost wild sort of way.

A Highland princess, Emily imagined. She smiled. In doing so, she garnered one from him. She couldn't help but think how handsome he was.

"She is lovely. How long were you married?"

"Not quite two years."

His face darkened. He had loved his wife so, and still did. Emily found his continued devotion all the more winsome.

Remember your duty, her mind scolded. *Think of who you are and who he is. You are a nurse. You are here to tend to wounded bodies and souls. He is your superior, a Federal officer! He is not your potential suitor.*

Flustered by her thoughts, Emily bit her lip and stared at the book in her hands. She no longer dared look him in the face. Dr. Mackay must have sensed her discomfort or felt his own. He quickly put away the watch, then picked up the buckets and turned for the ward. She followed.

Maggie's chair was even closer to Lewis's cot than it had been previously. The two were exchanging whispers. They broke apart the moment Evan and Emily stepped into the room. Lewis rolled to his opposite side and Maggie returned to her embroidery.

"What is going on there?" Evan asked Emily.

"I believe she is taken with him, and he with her."

He set the buckets on the table. His tone had changed entirely. "'Tis improper," he said flatly.

He is right. Although there was nothing wrong with the two swapping stories when the workload was light, Lewis and Maggie's relationship was definitely more than that.

"Indeed," Emily agreed, her own conscience pricked. *Nor is it proper that I have been thinking of you.* "I'll speak to Nurse Branson."

"Do more than that. Keep your eye on them both. I don't trust either of them."

Uneasiness smothered the emotions she had previously felt and proved her point. Propriety *was* of utmost importance, but Emily didn't like what he was asking her to do. He wanted her to spy. If Lewis Powell wished to express his belief in States Rights and Maggie Branson to inquire of soldiers still serving in the Confederate army, Emily would not stop them. How could she? She had done the same.

"I need not remind you what this city is capable of," Dr. Mackay said. "The women here serve the South. They will do anything to aid their men, their precious cause."

Those gray eyes were locked on hers, and for a moment Emily felt as though he could see right through her. "Why are you telling me this?" she asked.

"Because in these past two weeks I have come to believe that you are different."

"Different?"

"Aye."

Emily didn't know what to say to that. More than anything, she hoped he would see her for the woman she was. She was heartbroken over this war. She wanted to ease the suffering. She wanted to do so with him.

But he saw none of that. All he saw was a potential Unionist, a lost sheep who had realized the error of her ways and was trying to make her way back to the Federal fold. Tears clouded her eyes. Emily turned so he would not see.

"Thank you for your assistance," she said.

She filled a cup, intent on carrying it to the first soldier she found awake. Dr. Mackay thought the water was for him. His long fingers brushed hers as he took it from her hand. Emily felt a shiver travel straight up her arm.

"Thank you," he said. "You have always been very kind."

The artillery barrage began again. Which fired first, her ears or her heart, she wasn't sure.

"I know I haven't been the easiest physician to work with."

Her mouth felt as though it was stuffed full of lint packing. Swallowing hard, she dared to look at him. "You are grieving," she said. "It is understandable."

Evan's broad shoulders rose, then fell with a sharp breath, almost as if he hoped no one in the room had heard what she had just said.

Emily could not understand. *Why does he think his pain will be viewed as a sign of weakness?*

"Aye," he admitted. "So I am. I appreciate your… forbearance."

Something significant passed between them in that moment. So much so that Emily once again had difficulty breathing. She felt as though the real Evan Mackay was standing before her, the one Mary must have fallen in love with, the honorable, gifted physician who had served God and humanity before distrust and disgust had darkened his heart.

Though she feared her eyes were revealing much more than she wished to make known, she did not break his gaze. "I am praying for you, Evan."

He gave her hand a quick yet gentle squeeze; then he moved for the door. Emily felt the warmth of his touch long after he had exited the ward.

Evan made his way up the narrow staircase to the officers' quarters. The night watchman tipped his kepi as he passed by. The man had apparently grown so accustomed to Evan's wanderings that he no longer inquired if everything was well. He was not well, of course. Memories of Mary drifted through his mind and Andrew's death remained constant in his thoughts.

He was empty inside, but he was functioning. He had to admit, knowing Nurse Emily cared enough to speak to God on his behalf was a comfort. Her words whispered through his mind.

I am praying for you, Evan.

I am. Which he took to mean, *I have been* and *I will continue to do so.* How long had she been praying for him? Today? This week? Since that day in the scrub closet? He knew Mary had prayed for him each day of their life together. He knew because he could feel the difference when those prayers stopped. He felt the barrier, that wall between him and God.

You can't feel God's love, His presence, because you won't let go of your hate.

He had been a believer long enough to know Emily's words were true. But how could he let go when every day in this city was a constant reminder of what had happened to his family? How could he forgive when he knew each reb he tended would fire upon U.S. soldiers again if given the opportunity?

Perhaps if all the rebs were like Nurse Emily, I could manage it.

He reached his room. He didn't even bother lighting a candle. Laying his watch on the table and tossing his vest aside, he sat down on his cot. Jacob Turner's snoring was heard beyond the wall and on the floor below a Johnnie trapped in a nightmare was giving orders that no one would obey.

Evan's mind returned to the night the rebel major had assaulted Emily. He'd been convinced she was his enemy. He would never forget the emotions in her eyes—shock, fear, but beyond that, compassion. She showed grace to the scoundrel in spite of what he had done.

He saw the same emotions on her face when she looked at *him.* That day when Evan had poured out his secrets, confessed his faults, her eyes had been full of love. His starving spirit craved her words of encouragement.

You are the most gifted physician in this hospital.... Oh what healing you could bring if only you would allow God to do so for you.

Evan lay in the darkness. The silver moon shone through the cracked windowpane above his bed as his thoughts continued to churn. He wanted God's healing. He wanted to be rid of the anger, the guilt and the grief he had carried for the past two years. His heart told him to pray, yet still he resisted.

What could he say to the Creator of the universe? Where would he even begin?

Chapter Ten

Emily waited for a moment when she was certain Lewis and the other men were asleep. Sometime after midnight Maggie came to fetch herself a drink of water. Emily seized the opportunity to broach the subject.

"May I speak with you? It concerns Lewis."

The girl flashed an innocent smile and with a giggle whispered, "Isn't he just the most handsome man?"

The poor soldier had been kicked in the face by the family donkey when he was thirteen. He had told Emily the story the day he arrived. His jaw had been broken and, as a result, the left side of his face was more prominent then the right. Emily thought his lines odd, his expressions cold at times, but Maggie saw differently.

"I realize you have eyes for one another. Far be it from me to tell you who you should court…"

Maggie's smile faded. A look of embarrassment took its place.

"But it isn't proper for you to be sitting so close to his cot, nor exchanging whispers like you do."

"Did that Federal doctor take issue?" she asked.

Emily was honest. The girl was probably only five or six years younger than she, but she felt it necessary to mother her. "Yes. He did, but I am concerned for you, as well. All I am saying is be careful, not only concerning your reputation as a lady but as a nurse. Remember, this is an army hospital and Lewis is a prisoner of war."

Maggie blanched, seeing where Emily was leading. "And if anyone thinks we are spreading secessionist ideals, it could make things very difficult for him."

"Yes, it could, but it could also be difficult for you. They could ask you to leave, or even worse."

Emily didn't need to say anything more. Only three women had been held at Fort McHenry thus far, but Maggie obviously did not wish to be the fourth. She nodded gravely.

"I understand."

"Good. You are a fine nurse, Maggie. Don't let anything jeopardize that."

"I won't. I promise."

Emily offered her a gentle smile. She could sympathize with the girl's predicament. She also knew what it was like for a man to become a distraction during duty.

Maggie returned to her chair, although she did move it several feet away from Lewis's bed. Satisfied, Emily went back to work. The night continued quietly, the men sleeping soundly. Even Ben managed to capture a few hours.

Sunrise came, and Evan returned to the ward. Emily took one look at the dark circles under his eyes and knew sleep had evaded him. Before leaving for home she went down to the kitchen. The staff was busy preparing the morning meal, but one of the cook's assistants secured a warm biscuit and a fresh cup of coffee for her. She promptly took them to Evan.

"Thank you, lass."

She loved it when he called her that. The smile he

gave her sent her heart fluttering. Emily had to draw in several deep breaths to slow it to a normal rhythm.

He downed a mouthful of coffee just as Rebekah stepped up to join them. Emily wasn't even aware that she had arrived until she wished them both a good morning.

Disappointment filled her chest for she did not wish to leave. Knowing, however, it would be conspicuous if she delayed any longer, Emily delivered the morning report. She then gathered up her belongings and started for the door.

The Johnny convalescent from Florida followed orders well enough. He immediately carried out whatever task he had been assigned. He even scrubbed floors without complaint.

Old General Lee must have taught cleanliness was next to Godliness because the reb had every speck of dust, blood and vomit removed by the time Evan returned from the midday meal. Seeing that, he had him start on the windows. They were filthy, as well.

"That be all, sir?" the prisoner asked when finished.

Evan stared into his eyes. The boy played the part of a hardworking, obedient minister's son, but Evan was certain something else was there.

You would slice my throat or any other Unionist if given the opportunity. Evan would be glad to be rid of him. *Let the officers at Fort McHenry see to him.* He hoped parole for this particular reb would be denied. That way, Lewis Powell would spend the rest of the war in chains.

"Empty the chamber pots so Nurse Rebekah doesn't have to do so," he told him. "She must attend to more important matters."

"Yes, sir. Right away."

Powell hurried off. Evan watched him go. He wondered if the little rebel miss who had been caught whispering with him had been spoken to as of yet. He hoped so or he would see to the matter himself. Nurse Emily innocently believed the Branson girl was simply taken with the boy, but Evan suspected there was much more going on than that.

They are planning something. I am convinced of it. And when I catch them, those two rebs will be sorry they ever crossed the United States army.

The afternoon passed slowly. Finally the dinner bell sounded. Evan picked at his meal, while others around him engaged in banter and periodically tried to draw him in. He endured the conversation for a few moments, then left the table. Emily would be arriving shortly. He wanted to speak with her.

She was already in the ward when he returned. Having arrived early, she was restocking the supply cabinet. He approached her.

"Did you reprimand Nurse Branson?"

Bandage roll suspended in midair, she turned to look at him. Evan caught just a hint of lilac water. The scent was lovely, but he did his best to ignore it.

"I spoke with her last night," she said.

"And?"

"She assured me that she would think twice concerning her actions, lest they be misinterpreted."

"Oh, there is no misinterpreting them."

The look in her eyes at that moment caused him to think he had wounded her in some way. *What did I say? We discussed the Branson girl's infatuation with the Florida reb just last night. You agreed with my assessment.*

Her pink mouth shifted slightly. Evan stared at it for longer than he should have. "Was there anything else that you wanted?" she asked.

"No," he said quickly. "Nothing further. Just keep an eye on them both and fetch me if there is any trouble. I am going to get some sleep."

Fetch me if there is trouble? What kind of trouble was he expecting? Did he think Maggie was planning some sinister revenge for making Lewis empty chamber pots and scrub windows? Or did he think the man would dash from his bed, wield a knife and slay all supporters of Lincoln before sunrise?

Emily sighed. *Will he ever see beyond the uniforms to the people beneath?*

The night was a long one, the air humid and stale. She moved about, reading requested passages from the Psalms. Most of the men were then able to sleep. Ben, however, continued to toss and turn. Emily asked if he would like to talk or if there was anyone to whom he would like to write. He shook his head no and rolled to his side.

Maggie had taken her post by a North Carolina man who'd developed wound fever. Emily sponged the forehead of another man sick with the same. Evan passed through the room twice that night, once with a sour glance for Maggie, the second with a cold reminder to her.

"Keep your eye on them both," he whispered.

Whatever evil plot he thought would unfold did not happen. When Emily left the hospital the following morning, her shoulders sagged. A beautiful sunrise colored the horizon, but she found no joy in the coming day.

Joshua and Abigail were waiting on Pratt Street.

"You look tired," Abigail immediately said.

"I am." Emily climbed into the seat beside her. Joshua gave the reins a click. They rolled from the hospital.

"How's that Yankee doctor?"

Abigail's inquiry sparked a flurry of feelings, none of which Emily knew how to respond to. Her friend then clicked her tongue, smiled mischievously.

"What?" Emily asked.

"You. Trying to hide it. You don't think I know?"

"Know what?"

Abigail gave her a look. "You've got your cap set for him."

Embarrassment flooded Emily's face. "I do not. It is nothing like that."

"What is it then?"

She couldn't say exactly—or rather, *wouldn't*. The fact was Emily did have feelings for Evan, strong ones, at that. And if Abigail had noticed, had the rest of the girls, as well?

"He's a Federal soldier, Abigail," Emily insisted.

"And I'm a freeman's bride. You my friend, ain't ya?"

"Yes…but that's different."

"Don't see how." Abigail chuckled once more. "People are people. Don't matter what skin they have or what clothes they wear."

Deep down, she knew Abigail was right. There was more to Evan than that dreadful uniform and military bearing. She had seen glimpses of whom she believed to be the true man. But she knew full well any silly notion of some grand, romantic adventure while healing the wounds of humanity was ridiculous. He would not let go of his hate.

She told Abigail about how he treated Lewis and

Maggie, how he still often spoke to her. She even told her about his brother.

"Sounds like you need to pray for him."

"I have been."

"But?"

"Well, he's like the wounded soldiers, the ones who end up losing their arms and legs because of infection."

"What do you mean?"

Emily's throat tightened as tears threatened in her eyes. "Unforgiveness is slowly eating him up inside. I fear it will ultimately destroy him."

Abigail slid her arm around her. "Don't give up hope. Love is more powerful than hate. You just gotta keep believing that."

When Emily returned to the hospital the following night, she tried to keep Abigail's words in mind. Love could soften hearts, foster forgiveness. All things were possible with God's grace.

Her faith, however, was severely tested that night. The heat was stifling and nearly every guard, prisoner and doctor was in a sour mood. Emily moved through the ward with a bucket of fresh water. Evan's face held a particular scowl as she brought him a drink.

"I wish I had lemonade or cold tea to offer you," she said, hoping to coax a smile.

He wiped the sweat from his forehead with the back of his hand and grunted. "That would be too good for them."

Hiding her disappointment, Emily quietly walked away. She returned to her wounded charges.

Lewis and Maggie seemed to be the only cheerful people that night. She hummed a happy tune as she changed bandages. He fanned patients until the heat took its toll on him as well. His nightshirt was soaked

and his body exhausted. Emily convinced him to return to his own cot.

"But they need me, Miss Emily," he insisted.

"You won't be able to help them if you become ill
yourself. Get some sleep. I will wake you if need be."

He was out in five minutes. Eventually the rest of the
ward was snoring as well, all except Ben. He wrestled
and punched his pillow for hours. Emily went to him.
Tonight he seemed to welcome her company.

"What did you do before all of this?" he asked her.

She offered him a slight smile. "The same as other
girls."

He grinned. "I'll bet you had a beau come calling
every evening."

Emily swatted the fly circling his bed. "Hardly," she
said. "What did you do before the fighting?"

"I worked the docks."

"What, here?"

"Yes."

"I didn't know that you were a Baltimorean."

"Oh yes. Born and raised. My brother, Jake, and I
worked the wharf since we were fourteen. Then came
the war."

"Did Jake go with you?"

He shook his head. Sadness filled his eyes. "He died
the day of the riot."

Emily's heart squeezed. "I'm sorry to hear that."

"I was back in one of the warehouses, seein' to some
bales of cotton. I didn't know the trouble had started.
Didn't know then that the soldiers had fired upon our
men." He winced. "My brother died on the cobblestones."

Tears clouded her eyes as she continued to listen.

"I enlisted the day we buried him," Ben said. "Went

to Virginia just like a lot of other fellas from around here."

It was a story she had heard time and again, yet it never failed to bring a quiver to her chin. Little did anyone in this city realize then what far-reaching effects that dreadful riot would bring. Men like Ben Reed, like Edward and Stephen, donned gray and butternut. Men like Evan Mackay put on blue.

Two years had passed and the war still raged. The color of the uniforms made no difference when it came to the scars. Each side carried them.

Ben's thoughts then moved from his brother to his comrades. "A lot of good fellas have given their lives, yet my state's still occupied by bluecoats."

The thought crossed her mind that Evan would not like this conversation, but Emily decided to let Ben speak. Doing so had helped Edward. She hoped the same would be true for this man.

"Do you know that song they sing 'bout Maryland?" he asked.

"I do. The one set to 'O Tannenbaum'?"

"That's the one."

Just days after the Pratt Street Riot a poem began circulating among the Southern newspapers. A Maryland man, living then in Louisiana, had heard of the bloodshed. Outraged, he had written words to express his feelings. Rumor told he was a literature teacher named James Ryder Randall, although his name appeared on none of the copies of the poem, nor the song sheets, as it was later set to music.

Her father had once shown Emily a copy of the score but then burned it, saying he was certain anyone caught with the lyrics would be arrested. He was right. Newspaper editors who had published the poem soon found themselves in the custody of the provost marshal, but the battle cry would not die.

"The fellas and me in my regiment used to sing it as we marched," Ben said with a fond smile. "Wonder if I'll ever see them again."

"This war must end eventually."

He nodded slowly. "Well when it does, I know what I'll be singing...." He started in, "'The despot's heel is on thy shore, Maryland, my Maryland!'"

Emily stiffened. His singing was barely a whisper, but Confederate music was against hospital rules.

"'His torch is at thy temple door...'"

She knew she should stop him, but Ben's face was so proud, so happy. She didn't have the heart to take the song from him.

Emily cast a quick glance in the sentinel's direction. He was far enough away that the music could not be heard. She was further relieved to see the man was dozing. He was the same guard who had nodded off the night Edward had attacked her.

I'll wake him as soon as I finish speaking with Ben. Perhaps a little nap will put him in a better disposition, as well.

Ben continued. "'Avenge the Patriotic gore that flecked the streets, of Baltimore and be the battle queen of yore, Maryland! My Maryland!'"

Emily glanced at Maggie. She appeared to be dozing, as well.

"This here's my favorite verse," Ben said. "Sing it with me. 'Dear Mother! Burst thy tyrant's chain, Maryland! My Maryland! Virginia should not call in vain, Maryland! My Maryland!'"

Emily thought of those soldiers who had interrupted Stephen's funeral, how they had terrified her and everyone in her midst. As she then thought of her neighbors imprisoned unjustly, she was drawn into state patriotism. She joined him. "'She meets her sisters on the plain—"Sic simper!" 'Tis the proud refrain—'"

"How *dare* you!"

The breath was ripped from her lungs. Hot coals of condemnation rained down on her the instant she heard Evan's voice.

Heart pounding, Emily turned. "Dr. Mackay, I—"

"Get outside!" he ordered. "Immediately!"

Ben lay as pale and still as a corpse. The guard at the door was now fully awake. Emily knew they would be the next to incur the doctor's wrath.

I should have stopped this when I had the chance, she thought.

She stepped into the hall. The light was dim but Emily didn't need a lamp to see how angry Evan was. His face was as crimson as blood. That vein in his neck was bulging.

"What were you thinking?"

"Please let me explain—"

"There is no explanation which can possibly justify what you have done! A rebel battle song? You may as well have handed him a musket!"

"Please! It isn't like that."

"I heard you singing."

"Yes, I joined in the song. I shouldn't have, I know, but it isn't what you think."

He crossed his arms over his chest. "Then tell me what it is."

Her mind was churning, her knees now trembling. *I told Maggie not to do anything to jeopardize her position as a nurse and yet I have done exactly that.* Emily desperately sought the words. She didn't know what was worse, knowing she had indeed broken hospital rules or the disappointment she saw in his eyes. It cut her to the core.

"The man was troubled. He couldn't sleep. He was remembering his fellow soldiers, how they used to sing—"

"And so you'd encourage continued sedition with a treasonous song?"

"No…it wasn't like that, honestly."

"Honesty? 'Tis a fine time for that. I *trusted* you!"

"Evan, please!"

"My name is Dr. Mackay. You would do well to remember that, Nurse Emily."

She was desperate to make him understand. "He lost his brother in the Pratt Street Riot! He joined up just like you!"

His eyes burned with fire. Emily had never seen such a look of hatred before.

"That Johnny is nothing like *me*."

Without further word, he snatched her arm. His grip was as tight as Edward's, yet it hurt so much more for Evan was fully aware of what he was doing. She was no longer his nurse, his confidant. She was *his enemy* and would be treated accordingly.

He marched her through Dr. Turner's wing. Heart in her throat, Emily feared she was going to be sick. Evan pushed through the doors and led her down another corridor. Ahead, four sentinels stood guard with muskets on their shoulders. They eyed her incredulously as Evan deposited her in front of them.

"Don't let this woman out of your sight until I return."

Shocked but obedient, the guards surrounded her. Evan stormed off. Emily then looked to the small window above one of her captor's heads. The sun was rising, a new day dawning over Baltimore, but darkness had fallen over her. Her service as a nurse was over and any hope she had of knowing Evan Mackay's love was gone.

He marched back toward the direction of his room. He needed to fetch his coat and kepi before appearing in front of his superior officers. He also needed a moment for his anger to subside. If he went in there ranting and raving they would think him a fool.

Yet that is exactly what I am. I am a fool for ever trusting her.

He told himself he should have known all along she was nothing more than a rebel. Her smiles, her cups of coffee and the secrets she carried for him were just a ploy to gain his confidence.

No telling what she was planning while weaving her web of feminine charm.

Yet as angry as he was, his thoughts betrayed him. He couldn't help but think of the tears in her eyes, the sincerity of her voice when she'd tried to apologize, to explain. She'd admitted to breaking hospital rules and insisted she had only done so out of compassion, to ease a troubled man.

He couldn't sleep. He lost his brother. He is just like you!

He had been run through with those words for he knew she had spoken truth. He was no different than that Johnny she had sung to. He also longed for someone to ease his pain.

Evan pushed his fingers through his unruly hair. Anger retreated as guilt charged forward. *I shouldn't have handled her that way, marching her to the guards. What she did was wrong, but does it really warrant bringing it to the attention of my commanding officers? Has any real harm been done?*

As long as she doesn't do something like that again... As long as that reb knows his music will not be tolerated....

He pushed open the door to his ward and glanced about. The Johnny in question was stone-still in his bed. In fact, they all were. The presence of Nurse Rebekah and several scrutinizing guards had put fear into them all.

His heart slowed. That was good enough for him.

I'll go back and tell the guards it was a misunderstanding. I won't report her. I'll warn her to never do anything so foolish again.

Just before he turned, Nurse Rebekah called out, "Dr. Mackay, a prisoner has escaped!"

The bottom dropped out of his stomach. His mouth soured as all charity toward Emily Davis drowned in a sea of hate. Evan looked to the bed of the Johnny convalescent. Lewis Thornton Powell was gone.

Chapter Eleven

A great commotion seized the hospital. Federal officers were shouting orders through the halls, although Emily could not fully hear what they said. Their commands came in snippets as they passed from room to room, floor to floor.

"Look sharp!"

"...effective immediately!"

"Make certain..."

"...and be quick about it!"

Armed soldiers scurried about, their brogans heavy on the boards. Only two guards now remained with her. The others had been pulled for other duties by a foul-mouthed major, cursing rebels from the Mississippi to the Mason-Dixon line. He glared hatefully at Emily and then clomped away.

Her shame great, she shuddered. What trouble her song had brought. *Surely every Confederate prisoner in this hospital will now bear the scourge of my indiscretion.*

Just when she thought she couldn't feel any worse, the click clack of boots signaled the arrival of more guards. To her horror, Trudy and Elizabeth had been rounded up, as well. Both of her friends were wide-eyed with fear.

"Emily!" Trudy quickly gasped. "What is happening?"

"We were pulled from our wards without a word of explanation!" Elizabeth exclaimed. "Even Dr. Turner didn't know the cause."

Just as Emily tried to explain, Evan's booming voice filled the corridor. "Sergeant, escort the women this way!"

She spun around before a guard could lay a hand on her and hurried toward him.

"Don't do this!" she begged. "I am the one who broke the rules! They did nothing wrong!"

He was dressed in full uniform, blue frock coat, sash, vest, kepi, gloves. There was no doubt which side he represented. His chest stood out, much like that pompous young lieutenant at the cemetery.

"Don't feign innocence," he said. "You may have been the canary, but I know all of you are in on this."

"In on what? I have no idea what you are talking about."

His eyes were dark, narrow slits. "Where is that Branson girl?"

Emily blinked. *Maggie?* The last thing she knew the other nurse had been asleep in her chair. She told him so.

"She isn't asleep now," Evan said. "In fact, she isn't anywhere to be found."

Well, that wasn't so surprising. By now the day nurses had come on duty—that was evident by Trudy and Elizabeth's presence. "Then I suppose she has already left the building."

"Aye. 'Tis convenient, isn't it? I suppose you would have fled as well had I not come upon you when I did."

Why on earth would he think she would leave her post before her duty was done? And why did he act as though her foolish song was equal to an assassination attempt on the president or one of his cabinet?

"It was *only* music!"

He crossed his arms. "Move them on, Sergeant."

Emily was shuffled into the pack and marched toward the part of the hospital where the military leaders issued commands. A portly soldier with a scowl on his face opened a door. She, Trudy and Elizabeth soon found themselves in front of a panel of officers. Their faces were grim.

Emily gulped. She told herself there was nothing to fear, that they were just ordinary men. *They are simply husbands, fathers, brothers from cities and states not unlike my own.* But she was afraid, very afraid. Would she and her friends be the next women to occupy a holding cell at Fort McHenry? Would her father be able to come to their aid?

Evan stepped to the panel, exchanged words with the officers, then claimed a place at the wall, in perfect view of her. The look he gave was one of absolute disgust. Emily bit back tears. *Why won't you listen? Why can't you forgive?*

The man at the center of the table introduced himself as Colonel Ezra Cole. Emily had seen him in passing around the hospital but had never spoken to him before. "Do you ladies understand why you are here?" he asked.

Trudy and Elizabeth glanced quickly at one another. "No, sir," they said in unison.

Colonel Cole cleared his throat. "A rebel prisoner, a Florida man named Lewis Powell, has escaped."

Cold dread washed over Emily. Regret coursed through her veins. Now she realized what Evan was accusing her of. It was far worse than a Confederate song. *He believed Lewis was planning something, yet I dismissed his concern. I trusted Lewis. I thought he would comply with present authority and await his exchange like the others.*

Elizabeth leaned toward her. "Are they speaking of the convalescent in your ward?" she whispered.

"Yes."

Trudy had no idea what anyone was talking about. Lewis had only been at the hospital for one week. She had never even met him.

Emily chanced a glance at Evan. *You were right. I should have listened to you.*

If he read her expression, he offered no grace. *You are my enemy,* his stance said. *You will be defeated.*

Heartbroken, yet determined, she squared her shoulders. He may seek punishment for her. She may even deserve such, but she would not allow it for her friends.

"Sir," Emily said to the colonel. "May I speak?"

"Of course."

Her stomach was rolling, but she took a deep breath. "None of us had any knowledge of this man's escape until this moment. In fact, Nurse Trudy has never even met him."

Colonel Cole leaned back in his chair, his eyes focused on her. "The prisoner was assigned to your ward?"

"Yes, sir. He was."

"Then perhaps you would care to enlighten us. Where is he now?"

"I do not know, sir. The last I saw him he was asleep in his bed."

"And when was that?"

She couldn't remember exactly, but she thought it was sometime when she was sitting with Ben Reed.

I remember glancing about.... The guard was asleep.
Emily winced, realizing yet another mistake. *I should
have woken him then! If I had, none of this would be
happening.*

She spilled the entire story to the colonel, holding
nothing back. The man listened intently, making notes
every so often on the paper in front of him.

"So you are saying that to the best of your recollection, the prisoner left the room sometime between the
start of the song and Dr. Mackay's arrival."

"Yes, sir. It was only a matter of a few minutes."

Colonel Cole looked to Evan. "Was the prisoner still
in his bed when you arrived?"

Evan blinked as though he was surprised. "I did not
think to look for him, sir. When I saw the blatant display of rebel pride, my only thought was to squelch it."

"Indeed," the colonel said dryly. "No doubt your ire
was raised."

Emily blushed on Evan's behalf. His fiery temper
must have been well-known to his superiors.

"And you ladies…" the colonel said as he looked to
Elizabeth and Trudy.

"Sir," Elizabeth said. "Neither I nor my sister had yet
arrived at the hospital in the time of question."

"Is that true?" he said to Trudy.

"Yes, sir."

At that moment, Reverend Henry and Dr. Turner entered the room.

"Colonel," Dr. Turner said. "If I may be so bold, I
believe you are questioning the wrong girl."

"And how is that, Doctor?"

"I would be looking for the Branson girl. It was quite
obvious to anyone with eyes that she was sweet on the
boy."

Colonel Cole looked at Emily. "And where was she during your song?"

"Just across the room, sir. She was asleep in her chair."

He grunted. "Or so you thought." He looked again at Evan. "I suppose you didn't notice her, either?"

The Scotsman's face reddened as he admitted that no, he had not. In his anger toward *her* indiscretion, he had committed one of his own. Evan had failed to notice what was happening in his own ward.

Oh, Lord, Emily thought, *please don't let this bring trouble on him.*

Colonel Cole motioned to the guard standing beside Emily. "Go and see about Nurse Branson," he said. "Although I suspect if she is part of this, she is long gone by now."

There was a pause. Emily held her breath while Colonel Cole fingered his mustache.

"Now, ladies," he said slowly. "I am afraid we still have a problem."

Emily had a feeling she knew what it was, for there on the table before him were several sheets of familiar paper.

"The three of you began your work here following the battle of Antietam. Correct?"

"Yes, sir," the women each said.

"And each of you altered your oaths of loyalty." The man smiled slightly, but Emily couldn't tell if it was a look of satisfaction or pity.

"Yes, sir," Elizabeth said. "We crossed out the line which said we could not give aid or comfort to the enemy."

"And why, may I ask, did you do this?"

"We are nurses, sir," Trudy said.

He stared at them. Emily knew he was waiting for a different answer.

"Sir," Evan said, "each of these women has friends or family serving in the rebel army." He cast her a cutting glance. He may as well have run her through with a sword.

Despite her pain, Emily agreed. "What Dr. Mackay says is true, sir. We each know someone serving in the Confederate army. We have nursed men on both sides of this conflict with equal compassion."

"But you would give aid to rebel men directly if given the opportunity?"

She gulped before answering and looked at her friends. They nodded.

"Yes, sir, we would. We would not turn them away."

The colonel leaned back in his chair. He sighed as if not knowing what to do.

Reverend Henry stepped forward. "Sir, I know and trust each of these women. They are fine nurses and have proved this time and again. Don't punish them for their mercy."

"I agree," Dr. Turner said. "They are not responsible for the choices of others. They only wish to show compassion to all."

"I am not punishing them for their mercy," Colonel Cole insisted. "But they have each confessed rebel sympathy. And this one—" he gestured to Emily "—is filling the wards with illegal music."

"Sir," Emily said. "It was wrong of me to do so. I dare not ask you to forgive my transgression, but please do not punish my friends because of it."

He sighed once more. "I do not wish to punish any of you. Your reputation for care is well known throughout this hospital." He stared straight at her. "You say you acted out of compassion for the troubled man."

"Yes, sir."

"Given the fact that you were previously attacked by a rebel, it is understandable that you thought it necessary to use any means to keep him calm."

Emily blinked. How did he know that? Had Evan reported such?

"However," Colonel Cole then said, "we cannot have the loyalty of our nurses in question. Therefore, this is what we will do."

He motioned to his right. The officer beside him straightened the stack of paper; he readied an inkwell and pen. Emily's heart sank. She knew what was coming. Decision time was at hand.

"You will each sign a new oath. A *complete* one. *And* you will cut off *all* contact with your rebel men."

A lump filled her throat. "Sir," Emily said. "I appreciate your understanding. I wish to remain a nurse in this hospital but—"

He leaned forward. "But?"

"I cannot sign your oath as it is written."

A look of incredulity filled his face. "Come now," he said. "We are not barbarians. No one is asking you to deny care to a bleeding family member who comes to your doorstep. Only that you remain loyal to our Constitution, that you report such persons to the proper authorities."

Her future as a nurse depended upon what she did next. *Be reasonable,* her mind told her. *Sign the paper. The army need not know what you really think. You can still tend to the wounded. Just give them what they want.*

She looked at Evan. His face had softened to a look of concern. He was watching her intently, waiting to see what she would do. Emily's heart squeezed. If she signed, she could remain. She could prove to him that she was not the stone-throwing rebel he thought she was.

But then she remembered Lewis and Maggie. They had each displayed a face of submission while secretly harboring an ulterior plan.

Emily realized if she signed Colonel Cole's oath, she would be doing the exact same thing. She would never aid in the escape of a Confederate prisoner, but she would also never give information that would lead to the arrest of one of her friends. To sign an oath pledging to do so would be a lie.

In her heart, the decision was made. She knew full well what it was going to cost. She swallowed hard, tried to sound brave.

"Sir, I cannot speak for my fellow nurses...only for myself."

Emily could feel Evan's eyes upon her, but she dared not look to him. The colonel nodded. Heart pounding, the lawyer's daughter gave her best defense.

"I eagerly support the United States Constitution, and I wish nothing more than to see this nation reconciled, with a true balance of power achieved. But until then, I cannot deny support for my state, or for the men who have chosen to take up arms in her defense. Therefore, I cannot sign your oath."

Elizabeth reached over, squeezed her hand. "Nor I, sir."

"That goes for me as well, sir," Trudy said.

Colonel Cole looked at them in disbelief. So did the officers beside him.

"Then you leave me with no choice," he said. "You will hereby be escorted from this facility immediately, never to return."

He motioned to the guards at the back of the room. They stepped forward. Emily chanced one last glance at Evan before the Federal soldiers led her away.

He refused to even look at her.

They were gone within a matter of minutes. The guards marched the Baltimore women to Pratt Street. Reverend Henry took charge of the two sisters and Nurse Emily's coachman was waiting to collect her. Evan watched from the second floor window as she rolled away.

Good riddance, he thought, and told himself he meant it. He turned back for the ward.

Men were still patrolling the halls, but by now everyone knew the Johnny and his treasonous nurse were long gone. Evan hoped his commanding officer would send a squad to the Branson boardinghouse to arrest the girl, *if* she was foolish enough to be there. If she wasn't, they could arrest the rest of her family for all he cared.

Loyal Nurse Rebekah was hard at work as usual, maintaining an orderly and disciplined presence in the room. The remaining rebs in the beds all wore faces of uncertainty. There was no talk. They simply looked at him, fearfully.

You should be afraid, he thought. *You will lose this war. You will pay for what you have done.*

Evan went through the motions of the day. Around noon Jacob Turner called for his assistance with an amputation. The air in the surgical room was rancid, the heat oppressive. Both men worked in relative silence, eager to finish quickly.

But as the flap of skin was closed over the stump and the bone saw returned to its case, Turner became chatty.

"I must admit, I admire their honesty."

"Whose?" Evan asked.

"Those young ladies."

Evan held his needle mid-suture. "They refused to pledge loyalty to the Union."

"They did sign an oath."

"An altered one."

"You don't think Colonel Cole knew that?"

Evan blinked. "What are you talking about?"

"Young man, the colonel knew *exactly* what they had done. This is a border state. Of course there will be sympathy for rebels here, but we *need* nurses."

He could feel the fire in his chest. No wonder this war was taking so long to win. No wonder so many men had died. The army needed officers who would put the rebels in their place, not coddle them.

"So he allowed Southern sympathizers free rein of the wards?"

"Hardly," Jacob insisted. "He had them watched. They each earned his trust, his respect. He would not have dismissed them had *you* not forced his hand."

Evan couldn't believe what he was hearing. This was not *his* fault. He was protecting this hospital. He was for the Union. "She sang a rebel battle song."

"Tell me, have you never before made a mistake?"

The old man's words were like a knife to his soul.

"Did you see the look on her face?" Jacob asked. "Nurse Emily was devastated. Not because she was being dismissed but because she had disappointed all of us."

Evan didn't care how remorseful Emily Davis had appeared. It didn't change what she had done. "She and her friends unashamedly declared support for traitors."

"They could have lied, but they didn't. Would it be that everyone took their oath so seriously."

"They are Maryland rebels. I am still certain *she* had a hand in the escape."

Jacob looked at him like a father disappointed with his son. "Come now, would a woman who refused to lie even to save her position really help a prisoner escape from this hospital? You may not agree with her politics, young man, but don't besmirch her honor." He shut his instrument case. "I, for one, will miss her."

Evan grunted as he finished up his task. *I won't give her or her rebel friends another thought.*

Providence willed that Emily's parents should both be at home when she arrived. Through a veil of tears she told them what had happened. Though troubled by the dismissal, her mother hugged her immediately. Her father looked almost pleased.

"You did the right thing, dear," he said. "You told the truth. You stood fast on what you believe and I am proud of you."

She appreciated his words but wished none of it had happened. She had lost her opportunity to minister to the wounded and anything else she had hoped for. "I should have listened to Evan."

His eyebrow arched. *"Evan?"*

Emily caught herself. "Dr. Mackay. He knew Lewis wasn't honorable, but I didn't believe him. Now I have lost my opportunity to do good in this city."

"You have worked very hard for a long time," her mother said. "You have served unselfishly, but now it is time for you to look to your future."

She knew what future her mother wished for her: marriage to a wealthy gentleman, far removed from the reach of war. Emily wished to please but the only life

she wanted was with that stubborn, hard-hearted Scotsman. Tears filled her eyes.

"Please excuse me," she said.

"Of course, dear."

Emily quickly moved for the staircase, but she overheard her mother's surprise.

"You don't think she—?"

"I do indeed," her father said. "Question is, what does
the good doctor think?"

Emily's embarrassment stung as badly as the truth.
She had fallen in love with a Federal soldier, but the man
thought of her as nothing more than a stone-throwing
rebel.

The midday meal was late in being served. The
hospital-wide search for the missing reb had disrupted
the cook's schedule. Evan sat in the dining hall with his
fellow doctors and picked at his beans and ham. The
meat tasted like shoe leather. The beans were as tough
as hardtack.

What I wouldn't give for a slice of peach pie.

He quickly shoved the thought away. He had told
Jacob Turner that he wouldn't give Emily Davis a second thought. He'd meant it. He settled for stewed apples,
but they weren't nearly as good.

Evan then returned to duty. The afternoon passed
long and laboriously. He went about his tasks while the
rebs stared at him and whispered about *her.* He was determined to ignore them, yet one had the audacity to
address him.

"You didn't dismiss her did you, doc? You didn't
really send her away, did you?"

Stubborn lass, he thought. *She did that herself.* "No.

I didn't dismiss her, but she will not return to this hospital."

The Johnny's face was crestfallen, as were all the rest within earshot. None, however, looked more disturbed then Private "Maryland, My Maryland."

That's right. She's gone, Evan wanted to say. *Was your song worth it?*

The reb reached under his pillow. Evan quickly moved, ready to confiscate whatever the traitor was fetching. He froze when he recognized the item. It was *her* poetry book.

"Nurse Emily left this behind," the reb said. "Will you see she gets it back?"

For a moment Evan's thoughts returned to that night in the corridor, the light in her eyes, the sweetness in her voice. When his hand had brushed hers, he'd actually had trouble breathing.

He pushed the memory aside and took the book from the reb. "Aye. I'll see she gets it."

He would give it to Nurse Rebekah. He knew they were acquainted with one another. Before he could turn to do so, the Johnny drained pale.

"Something wrong?" Evan asked, though he really wasn't inquiring out of concern.

Sweat began to bead upon his lip. "She didn't want to do it, Doc…. She didn't mean to cause no trouble. I talked her into it."

Evan's pulse quickened. He stepped closer, glared at him. "You talked her into what?"

"Singing."

He grunted. He didn't believe it. "You are covering for her because you are taken with her. You all are."

The man shook his head. "I knew Lewis was planning something. I heard him and that other girl whispering one night when I couldn't sleep."

That got Evan's attention.

"Miss Emily was just trying to help me, like she always did. She let me talk about my brother. She let me sing."

"And?" he said, growing impatient.

"When I noticed the guard had fallen asleep and Lewis was creepin' from his bed, I talked her into singin' with me. I kept her from noticing what was going on. I knew she would try to stop Lewis, but, well, he seemed like a determined fella to me. I didn't want her to get hurt."

Blood boiling, Evan was ready to explode. "Sergeant!"

A sentinel came running.

If the reb hoped his confession would ease his inner pain, he was sorely mistaken. Evan would see he paid his debt in full.

"See to it that this man is removed from the ward," he commanded. "It was he who aided the escaped prisoner!" He eyed the guilty Johnny. "Did you think I would commend you for your honesty?"

"No, sir. I just wanted you to know Nurse Emily did nothing wrong."

Evan wanted to spit on the man's gentlemanly concern but kept himself under control. As soldiers in blue surrounded the bed, he turned for the door. Colonel Cole would be pleased to know Powell and Branson's unknown accomplice had confessed to his crime.

By the time he returned, the Maryland reb was gone. The bed linens were changed and the space occupied by another prisoner. The new man was pale and quiet. Evan shot him a look as he passed by.

Don't even think of stepping out of line.

Though he was relieved to know Emily had not actively participated in the escape, her unwilling involvement proved his point. Her compassion for rebs was dangerous. Only nurses of impeccable loyalty could be trusted. He was a fool to think any differently.

Night came and his ward was staffed with orderlies to fill her position until a suitable replacement could be secured. Exhausted as usual, Evan climbed the staircase. He realized he had forgotten to give Nurse Rebekah the poetry book before her departure. Grumbling, he pulled it from his pocket and tossed it to his cot. Then he sat down.

The September heat burned and already the nightmares down below had begun. Evan raked his hands through his hair. He hated this place. There were nights when he felt as though he was locked in an asylum.

He knew full well that he could leave. Other physicians did it all the time. They sought temporary reprieve from the madness by a night at the theater or supper in a loyal home. If he had any sense, he would do the same.

But where would I go?

Baltimore held no comfort for him. The only place he wished to be did not exist. Pennsylvania had repulsed the rebel invasion, but Mary no longer tended the home fires, awaiting his return. Evan had sold his home to another, along with every stick of furniture, every reminder except those that would fit in an army trunk. Tugging it from beneath the bed, he sifted through what little remained of his previous life.

There was a tintype of him and Andrew, taken just before the war, an embroidered handkerchief with Evan's initials. Mary had stitched it when they'd wed. He still had her Bible, but he had not opened it since her death. He did so now, but only because of his emptiness.

A scattering of hand-tatted bookmarks and scraps of paper bearing her tiny, precise script fluttered to his lap. They were like knives to his soul. Unable to view them, he quickly scooped them up and placed them back into the Bible. He then laid the Holy Book inside the trunk and closed the lid.

He wasn't worthy to touch it, let alone read it. Shame filled his soul and guilt cut him as sharply as the cries from beneath the boards sliced his ears.

I should have listened to her. If I had, I would not be here.

But he was here. Short of desertion, of escaping like that dirty Johnny, here was where he would remain.

Chapter Twelve

Although two weeks had passed since the incident at the hospital, it still seemed strange to be donning silk when she had grown so accustomed to cotton. Emily fastened the hooks and eyes of her rose-colored tea bodice. She pinned a silver broach to her collar.

My best dress. My nicest jewelry. I need not be concerned about bloodstains or vermin at the prayer meeting.

She tried to summon some measure of enthusiasm concerning where she was headed. It wasn't that she didn't enjoy the gatherings on Charles Street, where a daily prayer meeting held at her church had begun shortly after the start of the war.

She loved the hymns and welcomed the occasion to pray with her friends and neighbors. Emily had often attended the event with her family before taking her post at the hospital.

It was in a pew one day in September of 1862 that she had first felt impressed to serve as a nurse. Now she was returning, a little more than a year later, with no position, no certain future. She did not want her nursing duties to come to an end, and, despite her mother's efforts, she certainly did not wish to become the wife of some young lawyer or city politician. Evan Mackay remained constantly in her thoughts.

Reason told her to be angry that she should scorn him and all Yankees intent on trampling upon the Constitution. In the past few weeks Federal control had tightened even further. A rash of newspaper closings had occurred. Journalists were jailed and their presses suspended. The latest victim was the editor of the *Baltimore Republican*. The man had been taken into custody for printing a poem entitled "The Southern Cross."

Emily sighed. *The Federal army certainly keeps my father in business.* Still, she could not look upon the men in blue as enemies, not when she had seen firsthand their suffering.

When she had finished dressing, she joined her parents in the dining room. Abigail had prepared a scrumptious breakfast of eggs and ham. Emily's father said the blessing; then they started in.

"Will you visit Julia after the service today?" her mother asked.

"Yes. I would like to stay all afternoon. That is, of course, unless you have need of me?"

Her father smiled. "Your mother has her own circle and I have business as well. You should spend time with your friends. It will be good for you."

For the first time in over a year the sewing circle was scheduled to meet. Emily was looking forward to seeing baby Rachael and her other friends. She wondered, however, if they felt as low as she for being dismissed from service.

At least Rebekah is still there, she thought. *I know she will care for the wounded.*

As hard as she tried to keep the thought away, she couldn't help but wonder what Evan was doing at that moment.

"Two days leave?" Evan said. "Whatever for?"

He looked at Jacob Turner through sleep-filled eyes. He had been roused from what precious little he'd been able to capture.

"Because you need it, young man. You have grumbled around this hospital long enough."

"But—"

"No arguments. You are coming with me. Pack your bag."

Turner was already dressed in full uniform, every hair in place. His gloves were tucked in at the waist as though he were ready to attend a society ball.

"Pack my bag?" Evan said with hopeful curiosity. "Where are we going? Philadelphia?"

"The Barnum Hotel."

His shoulders sank in disappointment. Why would Turner bother with a Baltimore establishment, let alone one probably overrun by rebels? "Why waste our pay on a bed there when we can sleep just fine here?"

Jacob's gray eyebrows rose. It was obvious to him that Evan never slept "just fine" at the hospital. "We aren't lodging there," he said. "We are dining with a local businessman—a Unionist—and, I might add, his daughter."

Evan groaned. He saw where this was going. Turner evidently thought he needed the company of a lady to lift his spirits.

"Come, man, it's only a meal. It won't kill you. Afterward, Reverend and Mrs. Henry have invited us to stay with them."

Evan knew the minister and his wife made a practice of inviting officers into their home for a respite from duty. All who had attended spoke well of the time spent with the older couple. The reverend owned an extensive library and he allowed his visitors to enjoy it. His wife was not given to fussiness over manners. If a soldier wished to bury his nose in a book and shut out the rest of the world for a few hours, she did not interfere.

The thought of that made the prospect of dinner at the Barnum bearable.

"That explains this evening," Evan said. "But what about this afternoon?"

"We'll take in the culture of the city."

Evan huffed. That was the last thing he wanted to do. Turner must have realized.

"They aren't all stone throwers, young man. Come. I'll show you."

Jacob ordered Evan to meet him at the main entrance within the hour; then he shut the door. Reluctantly, Evan shaved, brushed his coat and fastened his brass buttons. By the time he was finished he looked every bit the respectable, dutiful representative of the U.S. Army, but he wasn't happy about the assignment he must now undertake. The only thing more detestable then patching up wounded rebs was having to come up with gracious words for them.

He met Turner at the entrance. The old man had secured a carriage. The moment Evan climbed into the vehicle he took off, chattering all the way.

"Certain sections of this city remind me of Boston," he said. "The ships, the architecture…"

As they traveled up Pratt Street, Evan did his best to focus on what the man was saying about the wharf, yet all he could think of was what had taken place here previously. They were traveling the exact route Andrew had taken two years earlier.

Jacob chatted on.

"Lovely woman down at the intersection of Pratt and Light. She has the sweetest disposition and the best charlotte russe I have ever eaten."

Evan couldn't fathom it. What was wrong with the man? He was a Bostonian, for goodness' sake. Men from his own state had been attacked by that blood-thirsty mob.

But at least they had the satisfaction of firing back, he then thought. *They had their weapons. Andrew did not.*

Fear then snaked its way up his neck. Here Evan sat in an open carriage, in full uniform. *How many rebs are lurking among the storefronts, the alleyways, ready to take a shot at us? Is that Johnny convalescent among them?* He wondered where the boy was now. Who had he met up with? What destruction was he planning?

They continued throughout the city. For three hours, Evan listened as Jacob Turner talked of food and Baltimore architecture. Finally the old man pulled the carriage in front of a church and set the brake. At first, Evan thought this was simply another stop on the tour. There was nothing significant, however, about the building in front of him. It was just an ordinary facade, an average steeple. People were milling about, and it looked as though a service was about to begin.

"Why are we stopping here?" he asked.

Jacob looked surprised. "For the prayer meeting."

"Prayer meeting?"

With the exception of Colonel Wiggins's funeral, Evan had not stepped inside a house of God since Mary's death.

"Come," the old man said. "You will enjoy it. I promise."

"I don't think so—"

"They'll feed you. There's always a table with water and some baked goods manned by the local parishioners. There are ladies here who make the best bread and cookies in all of the South. I know one who…"

Evan climbed from the carriage only to shorten Jacob's narrative. Did the man know every woman in Baltimore who offered fresh bread or pies? He did not question the doctor's loyalty, but he did question his judgment.

We don't know these people. This city is capable of anything.

Evan held back, although Jacob secured a sampling of sweets from the nearby refreshment table. He chatted for a moment with the hostess, then a gentleman in a stovepipe hat. When he returned, he was still prattling away. Now he spoke of the preacher, the singing and the number of Unionists who attended the meeting.

At least that is something, Evan thought.

"Well, it looks as though the service is about to begin," Jacob said.

Evan reluctantly followed him toward the front door. Uneasiness nipped his heels. He removed his kepi as he stepped across the threshold, though he sensed the act of respect did little to impress the master of this house.

"The altar or the balcony?" Jacob asked.

He froze. "You go on ahead. I'll wait outside."

Jacob looked disappointed if not outright concerned. "It's only an hour. Not much different than the colonel's funeral."

A funeral was one thing, a prayer meeting quite another. "I'll wait outside," Evan said again, and he turned on his heel.

Rather than return to the carriage, he took up post beneath a nearby maple tree. Crossing his arms, he surveyed the area. He wondered just how many of the businessmen entering the building were secessionists.

His eyes then scoured the refreshment table. His stance relaxed just a bit as he noticed a particular boy in blue. The brave soldier had an empty coat sleeve. A woman in a pink silk dress was speaking to him, her back turned toward Evan. Whatever she was saying must have been an encouragement to the boy, for he was smiling.

At least there is one good loyal woman here, he thought.

The soldier's comrades joined him and he introduced them to the lady. She turned. Evan caught sight of her face. *Emily.*

He watched as she spoke to the men, seemingly with ease. Evan couldn't grasp it. She had watched as her rebel friends arrived at the hospital, bloodied and butchered. She had witnessed their march to prison time and again, yet she spoke to soldiers of the opposing army with respect and compassion.

And I was one of them.

It was no secret to him why the past two weeks had been so unbearable. He *missed* her. Emily Davis had been a light in the dark dungeon of wards, a spirit of kindness and gentleness. Whether he wanted to believe it or not, the Baltimore woman had been a comfort to him in his grief.

And I had her removed from the hospital.

He remembered what Jacob had said to him that day

in surgery. Evan was forced to concede the man was right.

I forced Colonel Cole's hand. She acted foolishly by singing that song, but had I reprimanded her privately, I doubt she would have done so again.

He remembered the tears in her eyes. Even in that moment, her concern was not for herself, but for her friends.

Do not punish them for my indiscretion.

Yet that was exactly what he had done. Mary's words drifted through his mind. *You must forgive, my love, or your hatred for your enemies will lead you to act just as they.*

She was right. He had become just that. Evan hadn't used a paving stone or a musket, but in his anger he had punished three young nurses simply because they were determined to show compassion to the rebels he so despised.

Emily listened as the prayers rose around her, silently adding her own. She prayed for the protection of Trudy and Elizabeth's brother, George Martin, and for the rest of the Maryland men still fighting. She prayed for Edward and all the others who were now prisoners of war.

Then she thought of the young soldiers like the ones she had spoken to just before the service, those who were disfigured, discouraged and worried that their wives and sweethearts would no longer think of them as men.

Bless them, Lord, and give their loved ones the courage to face whatever difficulties lay ahead.

Emily then remembered Joshua and Abigail and all the other former slaves now trying to make the most of their newfound freedom. She prayed also for those who still lived in bondage.

May they soon have the opportunity for a better life.

But most of all she prayed for Evan. Her heart ached. *Please Lord, open his eyes. Let him see how his unforgiving nature is destroying him.*

When the closing hymn was sung, the congregation began to depart. Emily's mother turned to her.

"We must speak with Reverend and Mrs. Perry for a few moments, and then we will drive you to Julia's house."

"Thank you," Emily said. "I'll wait for you outside."

She gathered her Bible and fan, then moved for the aisle. On the front steps she met up with Sergeant Malone, a Northern man who was having difficulty with his cane. Emily had spoken with him several times before. His wounded knee gave him great pain.

"Ah, Miss Emily," he said, smile wide when she took hold of his arm. "You're always around when I need you. I can't seem to navigate these steps without you."

"You will master them soon enough, Sergeant. I have no doubt."

She helped him toward a wagon where a fellow soldier had just pulled in from the street. He hopped off, ready to collect his friend.

"Sorry, Davy," he said. "They held me at post. Got here as quick as I could."

"That's all right. Miss Emily took good care of me."

She smiled at Sergeant Malone, then the other man. He tipped his kepi. "Bless ya, miss," he said.

The sergeant looked back at her. "I suppose this is the last time we will meet," he said. "I'll be returning to New York tomorrow."

"Oh, that's wonderful! Will you please give my regards to your family?"

"I'll do that, as long as you promise me one thing."

"What is that?"

"Continue to look after the rest of our wounded boys."

A lump filled her throat. Emily wanted nothing more than to do so. She reminded herself that letting a soldier lean on her as he hobbled down the church steps was just as important as working at the hospital. *I can still show kindness. Perhaps by doing so they, in turn, will show compassion to each other, blue or gray.*

"I would be honored to do so, Sergeant. You look after yourself now, you hear?"

"Oh, I intend to, miss."

She watched as his comrade helped him into the wagon. With a final wave, they drove off. Emily then turned back toward the church. Her heart flip-flopped. There just a few feet in front of her was the one man she'd never expected to see again.

Evan had watched her assist the wounded sergeant, her face pretty and bright. The moment she saw him, however, the look faded. An unreadable expression now masked her features. Would she flee or scorn him? He did not know.

He was surprised that she spoke first.

"Dr. Mackay…I—I was not aware that you were here."

Her manner was cordial but guarded. She offered him a smile, but it was not as steady as the one she had given the sergeant. He understood exactly why.

His head told him to leave, that no woman in her right mind would even give him the decency of a listening ear. But Evan felt compelled to try. "I came with Dr. Turner," he said. "May I speak with you for a moment?"

She hesitated but then nodded. People brushed past on all sides. What he had to say was not for public ears, so he motioned toward the tree. "If you would be so kind," he said.

Slowly, she stepped beneath a canopy of leaves that had already begun to turn gold. When she looked up at him, Evan was cut by his guilt. In her eyes he saw only innocence. She was no stone thrower, no rebel spy. She was simply a young woman who had the audacity to treat wounded men of opposing armies with equal respect.

He shifted his kepi from one hand to the other. His mouth felt as though it was full of cotton. "I wish to… apologize."

Surprise flooded her face. Evan took solace in the fact that at least it wasn't anger.

"Apologize?"

"Aye. For my part in your dismissal. I know now you were telling the truth. You did not have anything to do with the prisoner's escape. That rebel private confessed."

She blinked. "Which private? Private Reed?"

He returned his kepi to the other hand. Why did he feel so anxious? "Aye."

"What exactly did he confess?"

"He told me he had you sing because he knew Powell and Branson were planning something. He wanted to keep you occupied so you would not interfere."

A look of hurt, of immense disappointment filled her face. She pressed her lips together for a moment. Evan wondered if it was to keep them from quivering. Emily was finally learning the hard lesson that despite what she thought, those rebs were not honorable.

He felt sorry for her, nonetheless.

"I believed I was comforting a troubled man," she whispered.

"I know that. I should have believed you when you said so. You do not lie. You have made that point clearly enough."

She looked up at him, and her expression tugged at his heart. He shifted his kepi back to the other hand. *Have out with all of it,* he told himself and cleared his throat.

"My anger over the escape blinded my judgment. That was why I brought your oath into question before Colonel Cole."

He told her what Jacob had said, how the colonel had already been aware of what she and the other nurses had done. "Had I not publicly forced his hand, you and your fellow nurses could have remained at the hospital."

He expected her to stiffen, to fire back harsh words in revenge. Instead only a look of pain shone in her eyes. Evan's guilt was heavy. He hated himself for disrupting the duty she so loved.

"I have no right to ask for your forgiveness," he said, "but I want you to know that I am truly sorry for what I have done."

That look of hurt changed to the one he had seen so many times before. "Evan, of course I forgive you. How could I not?"

Evan. Not Dr. Mackay. And of course I forgive you? He was completely baffled. "I am your enemy."

She shook her head, her golden curls swaying ever so slightly. "You are not my enemy."

"I accused you of treason. I had you removed from the hospital."

"You did what you thought was necessary at the time." The corners of her mouth lifted with the slightest smile. "We all rush to judgment. We all make mistakes. If we were perfect creatures, then Christ need not have died."

The weight of her words, of her gaze, was like a cannon crushing his chest. His shoulders sagged. His lungs begged for air.

"Aye, but some of us have made more mistakes than others."

He lowered his eyes. The ruffled hem of her skirt pulled a memory from his mind. Mary had one just like that. She had been buried in it. Inwardly he groaned. His life was one long series of regrets.

"I know it must be difficult for you to be here in Baltimore," he heard her say.

Evan looked up. The little lass could read him like a book. She knew he was thinking of the past. "I never should have come," he said.

Her expression was gentle, and tenderness marked her voice. "Yet had you not, how many more would have died? Think of all the Federal soldiers you care for whenever those trains pull into the station. Those men are alive today because you tended to them. And what about Sergeant Cooper or Julia? Or little Rachael?"

"What are you saying? That God accepts my sin? That he excuses my pride, my hard-heartedness?" He knew that couldn't be the case. He had been raised on the Scriptures.

"No," Emily said. "Your hatred has indeed cost you dearly. It has cost you the time you could have spent with Mary and the life you may have had after her passing." She moved a little closer. His heart beat faster.

"But God's love is great, and His grace is greater than our sins. He has used you for His purpose, despite what you have done."

How could she look at him like that? How could she speak with such compassion, such confidence that it made him want to fall upon his face and seek his Creator? His eyes began to cloud.

"Let go of your hatred, your guilt, Evan. God has so much more for you."

"Emily..." His tongue felt thick. Try as he might, the words would not come.

"I say!" Jacob Turner suddenly called from the front steps. "Miss Emily! What a lovely surprise!"

As she turned to smile at the old man, Evan snapped back to attention. Emily Davis had done it again. She had reduced him to weakness and confusion. What was it about her that disarmed him so?

Chapter Thirteen

Before her emotions could become obvious, Emily bid both physicians a good day, then hurried to her father's carriage. Her thoughts were all aflutter and her hands were trembling.

You do not lie. You have made that point clearly enough.

He had come to the meeting. He had sought her out. His declaration filled her with joy for she had been vindicated, at least in his eyes. That, however, which truly gripped Emily's heart was the look on his face, just before Dr. Turner arrived. When she'd told Evan she'd forgiven him, it became clear that he could not comprehend such a notion.

Her father gave the reins a click. The carriage rolled up Charles Street. "I noticed Dr. Mackay was at the prayer meeting today," he said.

"Yes," Emily said. "Did he speak with you?"

"No, but I see he spoke with you."

Emily could feel heat creeping into her face. There was an explanation expected. She could hear it in her father's voice. Her parents knew she had taken an interest in Evan. Undoubtedly they could give her a list of Baltimore gentlemen far more suitable for the title of husband.

"Dr. Mackay came to apologize," Emily told them. "He said he had allowed his anger to cloud his judgment. He said he knew I was not involved in Lewis Powell's escape. Another man confessed to assisting by distracting me."

Her father nodded contemplatively, his stovepipe hat shifting slightly. "Good," he said. "A wise man admits when he is wrong."

Her mother cast her a glance but said nothing. The carriage came to a stop in front of Julia's house. Eager to end this conversation, Emily gathered her sewing supplies and quickly climbed out.

"We will be by to collect you at four o'clock," her mother said. "Don't forget we are to attend the Moffits' autumn gala tonight. It will be a lovely evening. I am certain you will enjoy it."

Emily inwardly groaned. A night in high society was the last thing she wanted, but she promised her mother, "I will be ready."

She hurried through the garden gate. Sally met her at the front door. She was holding little Rachael. The baby's pink gown stood out in stark contrast against Sally's black taffeta.

Emily greeted them warmly. Sally, struggling to smile, walked her to the parlor. Julia was on the settee, knitting needles in her lap. Emily was pleased to see her color was improving.

"How was the prayer meeting?" Julia asked.

"Very well," Emily told her. "Everyone is asking about you both. They are eager for your return."

Sally didn't say anything, but Julia smiled. "Father says I may attend soon, but I cannot serve at the bread table for at least several more weeks." She chuckled. "And if Samuel has his way I will never work another day in my life."

Emily smiled. She knew confinement was getting to her friend. Julia had always been a busy bee and it was surely torture not to be baking bread and serving it at the prayer meetings.

"Rest will make you stronger in the end," she told her.

Julia rolled her eyes at Sally. "Spoken like a true nurse."

Sally smiled, though the look was still heavy. She then handed Rachael to her mother. "I'll fetch us some tea."

When she had gone, Emily whispered to Julia. "How is she?"

"It is difficult for her. She has been by my side day and night. I tell her she need not do so much, that she should rest herself, but she says she would rather be here than at home."

"Surrounded by Stephen's memories."

"Yes."

Emily crossed the space between them, reached for Rachael. The dark-haired beauty wiggled happily. "Have you heard from Edward?"

Julia frowned slightly. "No, but hopefully soon." She held up her yarn. "I am making him a pair of socks."

"That's a fine idea."

Emily claimed the nearby rocking chair and settled Rachael in her arms. The baby stared up at her, eyes wide. Emily couldn't help but remember that Evan had been the first to hold her.

"Has there been any change?" Julia asked. "Any hope of returning to the hospital?"

She shook her head, doing her best to keep her emotions in check. Despite Evan's apology she knew she would never return to her nursing duties here in Baltimore. Something as simple as packing crates at Apollo Hall was also doubtful. In order to have access to the Union camps and hospitals, the Christian Commission had to be absolutely certain of the loyalty of their volunteers.

While Reverend Henry would grant her exemption, Mr. Goldsborough Griffith, president of the Maryland chapter, would not. Emily couldn't blame him. He had the reputation of the entire organization to protect. There had already been instances of commission wagons being used illegally to transport goods to the Confederate army, accusations of spying as well. They could not run the risk of further scandal.

"I am sorry," Julia said. "I know it pains you deeply."

Sally came back into the room, a tray of tea cakes in her hand. "I for one don't know how you could stand it, Em. They all began to look like Stephen to me. I never want to step foot inside a hospital again."

"That is understandable."

Rising, Emily took the tray, giving Sally the baby instead. She snuggled Rachael close as she glanced at the tintype of Edward on the mantel. Emily knew despite her grief for her brother, Sally looked to the future. She longed for what Julia had now, a husband, a child of her own to love.

Sally placed Rachael in the cradle. "Well," she said. "We had best finish our quilt for this little lady before she grows too big to use it."

"Indeed," Julia said.

They rolled out what they had started. Emily claimed a corner, then from her basket fished out her needle and thread. Trudy and Elizabeth soon arrived.

"Just like old times, isn't it?" Trudy said.

Everyone smiled and did their best to think of positive topics to discuss. Sally shared a recipe for canning tomatoes. Trudy had one for pickles. War-relevant subjects, however, soon invaded.

"How are your efforts on behalf of Elijah and Elisha coming along?" Elizabeth asked Julia.

She and Sam had befriended two young slave boys back when they had worked the refreshment table at the prayer meeting. Over the past few months, they had tried repeatedly to ransom the pair.

"Not well at all," Julia said sadly. "The dry goods merchant who holds their papers will not let them go."

Listening, Emily's heart sank a little deeper in her chest.

"I thought at first the man was being greedy," Julia said, "but we have offered more than what he has asked for, time and again. I think he is simply being cruel."

"He knows you and Sam care for the children," Trudy said.

"Yes. Samuel says the man must realize that we are abolitionists."

"And so he will not budge," said Elizabeth.

Julia nodded sadly.

"What will you do now?" Emily asked.

"Keep trying, I suppose. Keep praying. I know the boys are in God's hands."

Her words caused Emily to think of Evan. All her prayers on his behalf were at best only partially successful. He may no longer view *her* as a stone thrower, but unforgiveness still poisoned his heart. Even today, as he had come to apologize, the hardness in his eyes was there. Emily knew she could not continue to pine for a man filled with such hate. There could be no future between them.

Biting back her pain, she focused on the stitches in the fabric before her.

I don't know why You allowed our paths to cross, Lord but I trust that You had a purpose. I leave him in Your hands and I ask You...please heal my heart.

Jacob talked all the way to the Barnum Hotel, scarcely taking a breath. He was speaking of new medical techniques in the Boston hospitals. That was one subject Evan was interested in. He did his best to listen, yet Emily Davis's words kept interfering.

I forgive you. How could I not?

He had accused her of aiding in the escape of a rebel prisoner. He had brought about her dismissal from the hospital. Yet still, she extended grace.

Even after I have made it perfectly clear what I think of those Johnnies, she forgives me. She tells me I have been used by God.

Evan could not reconcile her charity with his actions. He could not.

"Come on, young man," he heard Jacob say. "We mustn't keep Mr. Collins waiting."

"Mr. who?"

"Mr. Collins and his daughter, Louisa. He owns several cotton mills here in town. He makes tents for the army. Remember? I told you."

Evan didn't remember any such details concerning the man's loyalties to government and country. In fact he hadn't even realized they had reached the hotel until then. He hopped from the carriage, although he wasn't exactly eager to dine. "Aye. Sorry."

He followed after the old man. Just inside the lobby,

beneath a cut crystal chandelier, an obviously well-to-do businessman was waiting. His daughter, a dark-haired, dark-eyed copy of himself, was on his arm. Jacob made the introductions.

"Dr. Evan Mackay, may I present Mr. Jefferson Collins and his daughter, Louisa."

Evan nodded. "Sir… Miss."

The cotton man responded in kind. The girl did, as well, although she looked about as happy to be there as Evan felt.

"Shall we, gentlemen?" Mr. Collins said, and they entered the dining room.

Water glasses clinked and the pleasant hum of civilized conversation swirled about them as they walked to a reserved table. Collins assisted Louisa with her chair; then they all sat down. Unsurprisingly, Evan had been placed next to her.

While the waiter took their orders, Evan scanned the room. Just across the way he spied Emily's father. The gray-headed Southern lawyer must have been informally arguing in defense of some reb. His table companion, a known officer attached to the provost marshal's department, did not look pleased.

He's pressing some constitutional point, no doubt, Evan thought. *That must be where she gets it from.* Once more he remembered her words. *Of course I forgive you. You are not my enemy.*

How in a time of war could she not consider him the enemy? Sides had been taken. He would stand on what was right. She would foolishly adhere to her convictions.

His chest burned. *She cannot look upon all men as equals. We are not equal. Traitors and renegades are not the same as those who hold to the Union.*

Her words drifted again through his mind. *If we were perfect creatures, then Christ need not have died....*

"Louisa is interested in nursing," he heard Collins say.

Evan turned his attention to the man, then to his daughter. He tried to sound attentive, yet he was still distracted by a woman not even in the room. "Is that so?" he asked. "Do you wish to serve in one of the hospitals?"

Louisa's lips pulled into a thin line. "Perhaps," she said. "I have not really decided as of yet."

"Good nurses are always in demand," Jacob said.

"Yes. I suppose they are."

The turtle soup arrived. Evan was glad to be occupied, for it was obvious what was going on here. This was an introduction, and it had nothing to do with Louisa's interest in nursing. It was a father's attempt to marry his daughter off to a respectable, loyal man.

Probably because his own reputation is in question in some way, Evan thought. *Collins may have contracts with the army, but he is a Baltimore man. One wonders where his devotion truly lies.* There was only one Baltimore native who Evan trusted to be honest, and it was not the man facing him or the woman seated at his side.

He twisted the napkin in his lap when Jacob then pointed out Louisa's supposed skill at the piano. *The man should mind his own affairs. I will tell him so at first opportunity. A wife, especially a Southern one, is not what I need.*

He glanced at Louisa. She sat ramrod-straight, lifting her spoon to her mouth. Although he would rather leave the table immediately, he tried for the sake of manners, for the uniform he wore, to act like a gentleman.

"How long have you studied piano?" he asked her.

She lowered her spoon, looked straight at him. Her voice was soft enough that her father did not hear, yet Evan understood perfectly.

"You needn't bother, Dr. Mackay. I wish to be here no more than you."

He was taken aback by her abruptness, but she would get no argument from him.

"Very well, miss. Enjoy your soup."

"I intend to, sir."

While her father did his best from time to time to encourage conversation, she remained tight-lipped. Meanwhile, Evan spent a good bit of his meal covertly eyeing the lawyer's table.

The tension on the Northern soldier's face had eased somewhat. By the time they had finished their coffee, both the rebel and the U.S. Army officer were laughing.

How can that be? he wondered. *One is keeping law and order, the other seeking freedom for those who break it.*

Of course I forgive you. You are not my enemy.

Evan shook his head in disbelief. Emily Davis and her family, even the provost marshal's office itself, may be able to forgive what had happened in this city, but he could not. He *would not*. The honor of his country and the future of the Union depended upon it.

"Well, that was a colossal waste of time," Jacob remarked with a laugh as they returned to the carriage.

"Indeed it was," Evan said, climbing into the seat. "What gives you the right to orchestrate an evening like that? Especially with a Baltimore woman?"

"There are a lot of good people in Baltimore," he said. "I meant no harm. Simply a diversion, as all of today has been."

Jacob gave the reins a click. The horse stepped out.

"You work too hard, young man, and you take this war much too personally."

"Personally?" Evan said with a look of disbelief.

"Yes." The old doctor cast him a concerned glance. "I know about your brother. We all do, in fact."

An icy chill wrapped itself around him, threatened to steal his breath. How did Jacob know of Andrew? There was only one way he could think of. Emily had betrayed his confidence, perhaps not to the rebels, but to his own kind.

"I know from some of the boys in 'The Washington Brigade,'" Jacob said as if he knew what Evan was thinking. "We crossed paths with them about a year ago." He glanced at him again. "Don't you remember?"

Evan didn't remember seeing anybody from Andrew's regiment since the funeral, but Turner was insistent.

"I know about Mary, as well," he then said.

He felt the blood literally drain from his face. Evan wondered if the man also knew how he had treated his wife. Did he know he'd left her crying?

"I was assigned to cover your duties at the field hospital while you were on leave."

"I didn't know that."

"No need. You returned after the funeral. I could tell you wanted to be left to yourself, so I respected your privacy. Respected it too long, I see now."

The horse clip-clopped over the cobblestones. The carriage moved from lamplight to darkness and back again repeatedly. Evan felt it was a metaphor for his existence, brief moments of life quickly swallowed up by the blackness of death. Emptiness consumed him.

"Let it go, son," Jacob said. "What happened to your

brother, to your wife, was terrible, but you can't blame it on every citizen of Baltimore."

Deep down, Evan knew he was right. *Especially not Emily. It isn't her fault.*

"Have you a family, Jacob? I have never asked."

The man displayed a proud smile. "I do. I have a beautiful wife, an equally beautiful unmarried daughter and two lovely daughters-in-law."

"And your sons?"

The man's jaw shifted and his voice lost its brightness. "Killed," he said. "One at Antietam, the other at Fredericksburg."

"I'm sorry," was all he could think to say. Evan wondered if he had unknowingly come across the man's sons. He had worked the field hospitals following both battles. "I am certain they fought valiantly."

The gray-headed father nodded appreciatively. "I know they did, but it doesn't make their loss any easier to bear."

"No, it doesn't."

They were quiet for a moment. Jacob then spoke. "You see, my boy, I understand the anger you feel, but it will serve you no good purpose. You can't go back in time and stop those stones from striking your brother. You will only end up killing yourself. Hatred is a poison to one's veins. Let God cleanse you of it."

He could feel that poison coursing through him even now. The thought of Andrew, of Jacob's sons cut down in the prime of life, made his mouth sour, his muscles tense. He wanted justice. He wanted those rebs to die.

A battle raged inside him. He didn't want to be filled with anger and hatred, but he could not stop what he was feeling. Sighing, he stared upward, past the flick-

ering gas lamps to the inky black sky. It stretched vast,
limitlessly above him.

God has so much more for you.

Is that true? he wondered. Would the Almighty
welcome him back, or had Evan exceeded his limit of
grace?

The pale, pastel gowns of marriageable young
women shimmered in the candlelight. Music and
laughter drifted about the ballroom. Were it not for the
sprinkling of blue frock coats among the guests, no one
would believe the country was at war.

All Baltimore society had turned out for the Moffit family's autumn gala. Emily found the witty banter
and social maneuvering shallow and uninteresting but
nevertheless, she smiled. She curtsied. She made polite
conversation with each man who requested a dance. Yet
as Emily moved about the floor, she wished with all
her heart that she were back at the hospital. Even when
faced with the worst—fevers and nightmares beyond
her power to soothe—she had never felt half so useless
there as she did here.

The only partner Emily truly enjoyed that evening
was a Federal captain who repeatedly spoke of his home
and sweetheart back in Maine.

"She has blue eyes just like yours," he insisted. "And
curls the color of gold."

Her heart went out to him. He was so homesick. "And
when are you to be married?"

"As soon as I get leave."

"Then I hope your papers come quickly."

"As do I."

The orchestra finished the song. He bowed to her. "I
thank you, miss."

She honored him with a smile. "God keep you, Captain."

The dance caller announced another waltz and the eldest Moffit son, David, came to claim her. Emily endured the dance. His polished phrases hinted at an interest in courtship, but thankfully she need not worry. The Moffits were slaveholders. David was one society man that her parents would not consider.

The music faded, and before he could offer her punch or chocolate, Emily excused herself and left the room. The orchestra was taking its final break. She stepped out on the veranda.

"There you are."

Hearing her father's voice, she turned happily. He had arrived late because of an impromptu meeting at the Barnum.

"Did your supper go well?" she asked.

"Yes. The provost marshal's office saw reason." He kissed her forehead, then frowned slightly. "The prettiest girl at the dance should not be the saddest. What is wrong?"

Emily tried to smile. She had been making quite the effort to do so all night. She did not want anyone, especially her parents, to think she was sulking.

"I was watching you just now," he said. "You were doing quite fine convincing Mr. Moffit that you are enjoying yourself. But I am your father. I know the truth. Tell me. What is it?"

She slowly sighed. How could she tell him she did not wish for this kind of life? There were so many other things she thought more important. She looked down at her newly crafted ball gown. The lace, the ribbons and the intricate beading were beautiful. Her parents had insisted she have the new dress for this event. She knew they only had her best interest at heart. They wanted to make certain she secured a good match.

"I do not wish to sound ungrateful…"

"My dear, I would never think that of you." He smiled, waited.

"It's just when I think of my dress, my new slippers, I can't help but wonder what price they would fetch."

He blinked. "What price?"

"How many crates for the Christian Commission could be filled? How many pounds of potatoes could be purchased and distributed among the prison camps and hospitals?"

Her father chuckled. "If that is the case, then by all means, sell the items tomorrow. I will match your sum with a donation of my own."

She looked up at him. "Truly?"

"Of course."

He had always been unfailingly generous and had endured quite a bit of criticism over the years because of it. Some of his business associates still thought it obscene that he actually *paid* Joshua and Abigail to work for him.

"I should have known you would turn out this way," he said. "I should have realized such the day you came home from church and announced you wished to travel to Indian territory. Do you remember that?"

"Yes. I was twelve. I wanted to deliver medical supplies and foodstuffs."

"But the mission society wouldn't take you because you were too young."

"And female."

He smiled. "Well, times are changing. There are more opportunities for women to serve."

His expression then turned serious. Emily wondered where this conversation was leading.

"My dear, your mother and I would like nothing better than to see you settled here in Baltimore with a fine husband and a passel of children." He paused. "But if you truly believe God is calling you to a different form of service, we will not stand in your way."

For a moment all she could do was blink. Had he really just said what she thought?

Her father grinned. "Yes, you heard correctly."

Emily was completely overwhelmed. Tears filled her eyes. She hugged her father tightly.

"Oh, thank you! Thank you!"

She still had no indication what she was supposed to do next, but the freedom he was granting her was a gift as precious as a service opportunity itself.

Her father kissed the top of her head. "I will make some inquiries," he promised. "See which missionary organizations are open to taking young women. But you must promise me this." He raised her chin, looked into her eyes. "You will accept no commission without first giving the entire matter much thought and prayer."

"I promise."

The look he gave her at that moment almost made Emily want to settle in Baltimore and provide him and her mother with the grandchildren they so desired. For one quick second Evan Mackay passed through her mind but she pushed the thought away. No matter what feelings that man stirred within her, she would not pine.

Wherever You lead, Lord. And if I am to one day know a husband's love, may he be a man after Your own heart. May he love others as much as he loves You.

"How many more dances have yet to be claimed?" her father asked.

Emily glanced at the card on her wrist. "Four."

"Then by all means," he said, motioning toward the ballroom. "Finish them so we may return home."

Emily laughed and hugged him once more. "Yes, sir."

Jacob said not another word until they reached Reverend Henry's home. Upon entering, the minister and his wife greeted them warmly. They offered them coffee and apple pie in the parlor.

The couple was kind, trustworthy and likable in every sense of the word. Yet as usual, Evan was having a difficult time keeping focused on the conversation. Mrs. Henry must have sensed his mind was full.

"Perhaps Dr. Mackay would like to use the library," she said to her husband.

"Why, yes," the reverend said as he turned to Evan. "Would you?"

Solitude *was* what he wished for. After all that had happened today, all that was still spinning in his brain, Evan needed time to think. "Indeed, Reverend. Thank you."

The same invitation was extended to Jacob, but he declined. "No. Thank you, anyway, but I *would* prefer another slice of pie."

"By all means," Mrs. Henry said with a smile.

Reverend Henry led Evan to a room at the back of the house. "I think you will find this to your liking. It is very quiet. I have written some of my best sermons here."

"Quiet is good," Evan said. "Not much of that in an army hospital."

"No, there isn't."

He opened the door. The room was already lit by lamps and a small fire warmed the hearth. From floor to ceiling, books lined the shelves. Evan perused them. There were works of theology, literature and history.

"My home is yours, Dr. Mackay. Please, if there is anything you have need for, do not hesitate to ask."

"Thank you, Reverend."

The man nodded and shut the door. Evan stood for a moment in the stillness, breathed in the silence. There were no reminders of battle, no orders to issue, no cries from the wounded. For the first time in two years, Evan was left completely alone with his thoughts.

It was a dreadful, frightening thing.

The war had left him with nightmares and scars. He knew the person he had once been, the townspeople's physician, the churchgoing man, the one Mary had fallen in love with. He knew what he had become— angry, bitter, paranoid, alone.

He raked his fingers through his hair.

Let go of your hatred, Evan. God has so much more for you.

On the shelf before him, staring him straight in the face, was a Bible. Before his guilt, his fear of God's rejection could stop him from doing so, he reached for it. Opening it at random, his eyes fell upon a passage in Ephesians.

"And be ye kind one to another, tenderhearted, forgiving one another, even as God for Christ's sake hath forgiven you."

Evan sucked in his breath. He knew it was no accident that he had turned to this page. His hands began to tremble as the words leaped out. *Even as God for Christ's sake hath forgiven you.*

The warmth of God's love, of grace, covered him like a blanket. He sank to his knees, felt as though he had returned home.

Oh, Father in Heaven, You are so merciful, so merciful.

And in the light of that mercy, Evan knew what he must do. It was what Mary had told him from the beginning, what Emily had displayed time and again.

Help me to forgive the rebs, Lord, and the people of Baltimore. I cannot do it on my own.

Chapter Fourteen

The fire had long since died and the collar of his now-rumpled frock coat was itching his chin. Evan woke with a start, surprised that morning had come. The Bible was still in his lap. How long he had read, he did not know, but his spirit had craved the Word like a starving man craves bread. Although he had spent the night in a chair, he had not slept so well in years. He felt refreshed, renewed.

The scent of bacon and eggs now filled his nose. A plate was on the table beside him, along with a cup of coffee. Mrs. Henry must have set the items there. Stomach rumbling, he reached for them. For the first time since he'd left Pennsylvania, he bowed his head and gave thanks for the food.

When he had finished eating, he stood, straightened his uniform as best as he could and brushed back his hair. The house was quiet. He wondered where Jacob and the reverend were. He found Mrs. Henry in the kitchen. She was up to her elbows in a bowl of bread dough.

"Doctor," she said with a bright smile. "Did you sleep well?"

"I did indeed. Thank you for breakfast. It was delicious." He put the plate and cup in the sink.

"It was my pleasure."

It was then that he noticed the clock on the wall above her head. *Ten-thirty!* When had he ever slept so long? "I apologize for the lateness of the hour," he said quickly. "I did not mean to inconvenience you."

She chuckled softly as she wiped the flour from her hands with her apron. "It was no inconvenience. I am pleased that you rested well. However, Dr. Turner and my husband have already gone out. They left early for the prayer meeting."

Evan's interest was sparked. "The one on Charles Street?"

"Why, yes. Did you wish to join them? There is fresh water and some clean linens for you in the guest room."

Evan scratched his scraggly chin. Time was short, but if he hastened he could manage a shave. "Thank you. I believe I will join them. Please excuse me."

"By all means, Dr. Mackay."

He hurried upstairs. When he had put himself in order, he started off. Sunlight poured from the sky and the city held a certain charm that morning. Chrysanthemums bloomed in the gardens along Charles Street and the trees were painted in various shades of green, gold and burgundy. Evan viewed the sights as though scales had been removed from his eyes. He felt so alive.

Anticipation coursed through his veins. It had been so long since he had attended a church service. He was eager to worship, eager to do so with Jacob and Reverend Henry. The person he most wanted to see, though, was Emily.

He hoped she would be there. He wanted to thank her for her prayers. She had carried on where Mary had left off. She had displayed Heaven's grace, gently insisting that God had not given up on him.

Evan knew the days ahead would still be difficult. Upon returning to the hospital, and with each subsequent battle, his attitude of forgiveness would be tested. He wondered just what he would feel the next time he came face to face with a Maryland reb. He wondered what he would think. He knew he would never agree with their politics, their course of action, but he prayed that the peace he felt in his heart this morning would remain.

When he arrived at the church, the congregants were already gathering. After quickly surveying the area, he found Emily near the front steps. She was speaking with a young private. The left side of the boy's face had been scarred by shrapnel. He was missing an ear. The wound was enough to make most women of her status shrink back. She, however, was encouraging the man.

"Your Kathleen sounds like a wonderful woman," Evan heard her say. "I would not worry. I am certain she will view those scars as a mark of bravery."

Well done, he thought. *That is exactly what he needs to hear.*

"Thank you, miss," the soldier said. "I appreciate that."

Standing there, Evan realized what a gift she was. Every person Emily Davis came in contact with was blessed in some way.

Including me.

When the soldier tipped his kepi and went into the church, Evan stepped forward.

"Good morning."

Were it not for those broad shoulders and neatly

trimmed side whiskers, Emily would not have recognized him. He looked that different. Where was the scowl? Where were those piercing eyes?

He removed his kepi. The early October sunlight revealed flecks of copper in his nut-brown hair.

"You have returned" was all she could think to say.

"Yes. I thought I would actually step inside the building this time."

Emily blinked. Was that a joke or had he actually spent the previous day in the churchyard? Had he found the congregating mixed company so detestable that he felt he must distance himself from any Confederate sympathizers, lest his loyalty be tainted?

She pushed the thought aside. The smile on his face at present made it difficult to believe such a thing. "Is Dr. Turner with you today?" she asked.

"He did not arrive with me. I am meeting him here."

"Oh."

"Have you seen him?"

The pleasantness of his voice set her heart to fluttering. She tried to ignore it. "I have not, but then I also have just arrived."

The look on his face then grew serious. "I wanted to thank you."

"Thank me?"

"For praying. What you said…'twas true. My pride and my anger were destroying me and bringing grief to everyone around me."

A lump the size of a cobblestone filled her throat. She tried hard to swallow it back. Her heart was pounding.

"But God in His mercy has forgiven me," he said. "And I, by His grace, have forgiven, as well."

She could not believe her ears. Had he really just spoken of forgiveness or had she imagined it?

"Emily!"

Both of them immediately turned in the direction of the voice. Sam and Julia were approaching. Baby Rachael was in her mother's arms.

"You are here!" Emily said, hugging her friend.

"Yes," Julia replied. "Our first outing."

Sam greeted Evan with a handshake. "Dr. Mackay, how good it is to see you again."

"Indeed," Julia said. "We were just speaking of you last evening."

Emily glanced at Evan. He looked like he didn't know how to respond to that. Surely he was wondering in what manner he had been the subject of conversation.

Sam explained, "We are most appreciative for what you have done for our family. We would be pleased to have you join us for supper one evening."

"Supper?" he said, obviously surprised.

"We wish to show our gratitude not only for Rachael's delivery but for your care of my brother, as well," Julia said.

With the mention of Edward, Emily expected his look to darken. It didn't.

"Have you heard from the major?" he asked. "Is he well?"

Is he well?

Emily's jaw dropped, but she closed it before anyone noticed. *It must be true. He has forgiven his enemies.* For a moment she had trouble breathing.

"We have not heard from Edward directly," Sam said. "But we now know that he has arrived safely at Point Lookout."

Evan nodded and then said to Julia, "I pray your brother will recover completely from all of his wounds."

The look in his eyes told Emily his words were genuine. Her emotions further stirred. *Has the Lord answered my prayers?*

"Thank you, Dr. Mackay," Julia said. "Please do come for supper. And, Em, you come, as well."

What? Emily desperately tried to rein in her thoughts, quell her excitement. "Oh...well...I would not wish to intrude."

"Dr. Mackay must have a dining partner," Julia insisted. "And you are the perfect choice."

Perfect choice? When she noticed the agreeable and eager look on *his* face, it took all she had within her to keep her feet on the ground. Was he actually going to accept the invitation? Would this staunch Unionist dine in a Baltimore home? With *her?*

Just then, Emily's mother and father stepped up to join them.

"Well, Doctor," Mr. Davis said, extending his hand, "I noticed you were here yesterday."

"Yes, sir."

"How are things at the hospital?"

Watching, Emily continued to marvel. Evan no longer spoke to her father as though he was a member of the occupying army, reminding a rebel citizen who was in control. He looked at him with the respect a younger man owed an older one.

Her ears were ringing.

"We were just trying to convince the two of them to join us for supper," Sam said.

"Oh?" her mother replied.

Emily gulped. She noted the smile, that interested tone in her voice. The intrigue on her father's face was quite evident, as well. Did they think Evan would make a suitable husband despite the color of his uniform?

No, she wanted to say, for their benefit as well as

her own. *He isn't interested in courtship. He is still in love with Mary.*

Her parents continued to smile. Emily's cheeks burned. All she wanted to do was escape their gaze, flee *his* presence. She couldn't bear the thought of Evan recognizing what was going on. She would be mortified.

Surely it is time for the service to begin. Why don't they ring that bell?

"Well, we will leave you to make your arrangements," her father said. He then looked back at Evan. "When you have finished, Doctor, we would be pleased to have you claim our pew."

No! I shall never be able to concentrate on prayer if he is with us!

Evan nodded. "Thank you, sir."

Her parents stepped away. Emily drew in a quick breath, then vaguely heard Sam say something about next week. Evan mentioned a half day off.

"Then it is settled," Julia said. "Supper, next Friday."

Before Emily knew it, he turned to her. "T'would be my pleasure to escort you," Evan said.

The look on his face made her throat go dry. "Thank you," she somehow managed.

The church bell rang. Sam motioned toward the sanctuary, and he and Julia turned.

"Shall we?" Evan said as he offered his arm.

Thoughts aflutter, Emily slid her gloved hand around his blue wool. She wondered if he could feel her trembling.

Before this morning Evan would not have believed it possible. Yet here he sat in a Baltimore church, a guest of a Southern lawyer and his family. They were to his left. Jacob Turner and Reverend Henry were to his right. He was enjoying himself, and he sang with fervor. Though old and familiar, the hymns seemed so new, so fitting.

How precious did that grace appear, the hour I first believed.

He had to confess, though, that at times his worship was tainted, especially when he noticed certain persons in the congregation. Among the blue was a sprinkling of local businessmen who were well-known gray, yet Evan forced himself to listen carefully to their spoken prayers. The Maryland men did not ask for victory, but for the safety of loved ones, for an end to the bloodshed. With those things, he could agree.

Seated beside him, Emily appeared to be having difficulties of her own. He watched discreetly as she repeatedly knotted, then unknotted her hands. She had never been one to display nervous tendencies before. He wondered if it had to do with him.

He *had* forgiven Andrew's murderers. He *had* forgiven Southerners who had taken lives of Northern men, but in her mind, did his past deeds outweigh his words? He hoped she could see the difference in him, but he supposed that was too much to expect. He had seen the look of surprise on her face when he'd wished Mrs. Ward's brother good health.

Truth be told, he was just as shocked. Where those words had come from he was not certain. He hadn't actually thought to express the sentiment but upon doing so, he'd discovered he did mean each word. He honestly hoped the major would recover from his wounds, that he would be reunited with his family.

Evan had never imagined that family would extend an invitation to dine in their home. He had been so cold

to them. Yet, in spite of his actions, they had modeled
Christian kindness. *Just as she has done repeatedly.*

He eyed her once more. Emily's hands were clasped
tightly on her lap. When they rose to sing the departing hymn, Evan held the songbook for them to share.
She did not lift her voice. He remembered the last time
music had been an issue. His heart sank.

*I blasted her for that rebel battle song. No wonder
she will not sing with me beside her now. No wonder
she trembles so. It is just like that night with the major.
She may wish to show kindness, may wish to look brave,
but inside she is terrified.* He winced at the thought of
causing her to fear. *I must show her that I am not the
man I was before.*

But he did not know how. He didn't have the opportunity to speak with her further, for when the service dismissed, Jacob and Reverend Henry insisted he
meet a Union colonel in attendance. Evan barely had
time to bid the Davis family good afternoon before he
was pulled away.

Emily needed air. While her parents chatted briefly
with several church members, she exited the building.
Julia was outside beneath the maple tree. Apparently
little Rachael had gotten fussy.

"Is she all right?" Emily asked.

Julia bounced her from side to side. "Yes. She just
wished to add a few 'amens' of her own during the service, so I took her out."

Emily watched the baby nibble on her fingers. Most
days she was the spitting image of Julia. Today she
looked like Sam.

"Dr. Mackay seemed most pleasant," Julia said. "Almost a changed man."

"Indeed." Emily could still feel the tingle in her cheeks. The pew had been full. Twice the sleeve of his frock coat had brushed her arm.

"Do you think he might be willing to speak to his commanding officers, to allow you to reclaim your position at the hospital?"

As happy as she was at his presence, Emily knew there was no point wishing for things that could not be. Colonel Cole would never take her back without her agreement to sign a complete oath. "It isn't really up to him."

"Well, I suppose not. I appreciate your willingness to attend supper. I did not think of it when I first asked you, but I imagine it will be difficult to dine with him, given all that has taken place."

It would be, but not in the way Julia thought. "Don't worry about that. I am pleased that I can help."

In truth, the thought of the anticipated evening made Emily practically giddy. *But it will be only as Julia hopes,* she reminded herself. *Gratitude shown to a man for his skills as a physician. I will assist in providing polite, intelligent conversation. He will then return to his work, and I will continue to search for mine.*

Before the ache could fill her heart, she changed the subject. "Did Sally come to the meeting today? I have not seen her."

Julia sighed. "No. Sam and I stopped by her house beforehand, but she said she had a headache."

"Oh. I'm sorry to hear that. I hope she will recover soon."

"So do I, but it isn't the headache that concerns me."

"What do you mean?"

"I worry about her, Em. One day she seems to be doing better—the next she will not leave her house. I know she is still mourning Stephen but… Well, surely you have noticed it."

She had. Since Julia had taken full responsibility for her house following her convalescence, Sally had seemed to retreat to her own. She had come to the sewing circle and had attended church a few times, but that was the extent of her outings. Sally's melancholy seemed worse since Edward's transfer to prison.

"Have you talked to her about it?" Emily asked.

"Yes, or at least I have tried. Beyond speaking of Rachael, she doesn't have much interest in conversation."

"Perhaps we should surround her with company."

"We should indeed, but I fear it will take more than that."

"What do you mean?"

"I hope that Edward is paroled soon." Julia sighed once more. "For her sake and mine."

Evan spent the remainder of the afternoon in Reverend Henry's home. Following a quiet supper with the couple, he and Jacob then returned to the hospital. As the carriage drew closer to Pratt Street, uneasiness filled his chest.

Such begins the real test, he thought. *I do not wish to think and act as I did before, Lord. Please help me.*

"Are you all right, son?" Jacob asked.

Evan drew in a deep breath. Forgiving rebels from the sanctity of a minister's library or within a house of worship was one thing. Actually coming face-to-face with them again, in an arena where he was accustomed to feeling only anger and disdain, was quite another.

"Pray for me, Jacob."

"Already have, my boy. Already have."

The carriage turned. Pratt Street came into view.

Evan jostled atop the bench seat as the wheels wobbled over the uneven stones. The shops were closing for the evening. Businessmen were locking their front doors, returning home. Thoughts of Andrew and his fellow soldiers swirled inside Evan's head.

I have forgiven them, he reminded himself. *I have forgiven them.*

They pulled up to the front entrance of the hospital. Jacob handed the reins to a waiting man, and the two climbed out. Evan straightened his shoulders, forced his feet forward.

Upon entering the building, Jacob slapped him on the back, then headed for his room. Carpetbag still in hand, Evan turned for his ward. Oil lamps cast his long shadow across the buckling floor.

When he opened the door, he glanced about. The beds were full. The odors of blood and ether still prevailed. The smell of rotting fish drifted in from the harbor. The hospital was exactly as he had left it.

But *he* was different.

Evan studied the scarred, pale faces before him. For the first time since his brother's death, he saw not enemies but his fellow countrymen. They were weak and weary and in need of Heaven's grace, just as he was.

His heart squeezed.

God help them, he thought. *May this war come to an end before any more on either side are killed.*

Emily visited Sally's home the following morning. The wreath on the front door had been removed but her friend could at best only greet Emily with a half smile.

"I brought you an apple pie," Emily told her. "Abigail sent it."

"Please thank her for me." Sally set the dish on the

table behind her. She did not invite her into the parlor. Emily could tell this was going to be a short visit.

"Julia told me you were ill yesterday. Are you feeling any better?"

"Somewhat, but I am still very tired."

Emily didn't doubt that. The circles were prominent under her eyes. *Poor thing.*

"Sally," she said gently, "I know it is difficult right now, but is there anything I can do for you?"

Her friend shook her head, her chin quivering slightly.

"Julia and I are concerned about you."

"I know. She was here last night." Sally sniffed. "I know you both mean well. I just...I can't talk about it, Em."

"I understand." Emily hugged her tightly. Sally's black taffeta crinkled to the touch. "I am praying for you...and for Edward."

She stepped back and wiped her eyes. "Pray this war will end soon."

"You have my word."

As she left, Emily did her best to keep faith. The week, however, was long and discouraging. As promised, her father had made several inquiries concerning opportunities for service in nursing and other charitable activities, but his effort was to no avail. The local private hospitals all said they had no need for female nurses at that time. A society that ministered to war widows and orphans stated that due to past problems, they no longer accepted unmarried women as volunteers.

Emily had also applied to the agency that tended to the former slaves in the contraband camps outside Washington. They, too, had turned her down.

I must be patient, she told herself. *I do not believe*

God would give me such a desire for service if He did not intend to use it in some way. He has a purpose. He has a plan.

The last of the Gettysburg wounded had arrived. Evan walked along the dock. Rows and rows of men lay beneath the vast October sky. Their forms were equally emaciated, and one could not distinguish which were blue and which were gray unless they spoke.

By now, the uniforms were all but gone. The wounded were clothed in rags or mismatched donations the Christian Commission had delivered to the battlefield. Those the cannons and mortar shells had claimed had long since passed on. The ones who would succumb to wound fever and infection had already lost their limbs.

The lot before him was filthy, malnourished and suffering from every malady running rampant through the field hospitals. Lice cared not if you were loyal. Dysentery felled the most ardent secessionist. Evan looked on as stewards removed what remained of soiled, infested garments. Nurses boiled items that the men begged to keep.

He moved from pallet to pallet, stethoscope around his neck, sorting out the ones with lung ailments, trying to reassure them.

"Take care. You've made it thus far," he told one particular dark-haired boy.

"Y'all be sending us to prison now?"

The inquiry and accent testified to a home somewhere south of the Potomac. The thought crossed Evan's mind, *How many men in blue have you cut low by your musket?* But when he looked into the boy's eyes, he saw the fear—fear of reprisal, fear of death.

"Right now all you need to concentrate on is regaining your health," Evan told him. "Food will be along directly."

The boy offered a weak smile. "Thank ya, doc. I'm powerful hungry."

At one time Evan would have been tempted to distribute nourishment elsewhere, to stand for the Union by making certain the rebs suffered for their crimes. Now he realized the honor of his country, the testimony of his faith, depended on the attitude he displayed.

These men are in my hands. Will not my example represent my government? Whether this war ends tomorrow or two years from now, reunification will occur. Will the process not be easier, the goal achieved more quickly, if kindness is shown?

Emily had understood that from the beginning. It had taken him this long, but now he did, as well.

The arrival of fresh greens and fruits brightened the eyes of many around him. For the wounded that were too weak for such, Evan ordered beef tea. He hoped they might be able to keep down the broth.

When the last of them had been cleaned and properly fed, Union soldiers who were strong enough for the journey were put aboard steamers for Philadelphia. Very few of the rebel prisoners were well enough for Fort McHenry. Evan conferred with his fellow physicians and the officers in charge.

"We will need to make space for them," he said. "They are too ill to be sent on and the nights are too cold now to leave them outside."

Colonel Cole agreed. He ordered the reorganization of the wards, to place men in the corridors and double up on beds if necessary. Evan suggested those with pneumonia and other respiratory ailments be grouped together in one ward, those with dysentery in another.

"Excellent idea," Jacob said. "The cases will be easier to manage if they are grouped together."

The others, including the colonel, liked the sound of that, as well.

The hospital staff members set about the task. After two days the prisoners had all been accounted for. Evan took charge of the pneumonia ward. Every time he inserted a chest tube, he thought of Emily.

He would never forget the look on her face the night she'd assisted him with the rebel sergeant. She had looked as though she would faint the moment he took up the knife.

But she bore her own discomfort for the sake of aiding another. 'Tis not a finer nurse, a finer woman, to be found.

He looked forward to Friday's supper with immense anticipation.

Chapter Fifteen

Emily paced back and forth across the parlor floor in a gown she hoped was not too ornate or too dowdy. She tried to quell the nervousness she felt about Evan's impending arrival, but her corset was constrictive. Abigail had drawn her laces so tightly that she could barely breathe.

"Stop fidgeting," her mother insisted as she stepped into the room. She then smiled. "You look beautiful, my dear. He will think so, as well."

Although Emily did wish that would be the case, she reminded herself and her mother, "Dr. Mackay isn't looking for a wife."

"And you aren't looking for a husband, I know." She fastened a string of pearls around her daughter's neck. "I am simply pleased you are going on an outing. A pleasant evening of conversation will do you well."

When a strong knock sounded on the front door, Emily nearly jumped out of her skin. Her mother thrust an embroidered handkerchief into her hand. "Here. Take an extra."

"Thank you."

She drew in as deep a breath as her underpinnings

would allow, while her mother offered last-minute advice.

"Keep in mind you aren't going off to the hospital. Remember the social graces."

"Yes, Mother."

Pleased, Mrs. Davis stepped back and, with a nod, encouraged her daughter from the room.

Breathe, Emily reminded herself. *Breathe.*

She could hear his voice coming from her father's library. It held the same timbre, but the tone was far different from that of the hospital. Emily approached the door. Evan was seated in a chair across from her father, his long legs stretched out before him. The moment she crossed the threshold, he stood.

"Miss Davis," he said with a smile. "You look lovely."

Her heart fluttered and Emily wondered just when the change in her had occurred. When had she found that towering, unyielding man in the blue uniform so winsome?

"Thank you, Dr. Mackay."

Between her shoulder blades she felt a gentle nudge. Her mother pushed her forward.

"Dr. Mackay was just telling me that Camp Letterman will be closing soon," her father said.

"Oh?" She looked back at Evan. "Are all of the Gettysburg field hospitals closing?"

"Aye. Soon. The last of our scheduled wounded arrived this week."

It was a comfort to know that the horrific battle was finally drawing to a close. Emily couldn't help but wonder, though, in what condition had the soldiers come to Baltimore?

"Were there many serious cases?"

He shook his head. There was a gentleness to his expression. "Mostly hunger and sanitary ills."

Mrs. Davis politely coughed. Obviously this was not the type of conversation she wanted Emily to be engaging in. Evan must have picked up on it, as well.

"I have something that belongs to you," he said.

He took a step forward. Emily felt the flutter again in her chest as a whiff of something pleasant caught her attention. Soap, and was that shaving balm? From the left pocket of his frock coat he withdrew her volume of Robert Burns.

"I wondered where I had left that," she said.

"You must have dropped it the night you—" He stopped. The smile turned to a more awkward expression.

The night I left the hospital. She took it from him, clasped it close. "Thank you. That was kind of you to return it."

They both stared at each other for a moment as if neither knew what to say next. Her father cleared his throat.

"Well, you don't want to keep Sam and Julia waiting," he said.

"No, sir." Evan replied.

She laid the book on the nearby table and they walked to the front door. Just before she stepped outside, her mother draped a cloak about her shoulders. Emily snuggled it close. The air was fresh but chilly. The evening edition of *The Baltimore Sun* was lying on the doorstep, and twilight bathed her neighborhood in a soft, rosy hue.

"Have a wonderful time," her father called.

I will, she thought. *If only I can remember to breathe.* Up ahead, Joshua grinned at her. He was holding the reins to a horse that looked as though it had marched many miles with the army. The waiting carriage appeared to be at least a decade old, as well.

"I apologize," Evan said, frowning slightly. "This contraption is not of the newest design."

She felt his embarrassment, but the rickety rig didn't bother her in the least. "It will still take us where we wish to go."

The corner of his mouth lifted with just the hint of a smile and he moved to assist her. The moment his hand touched hers, Emily felt a shiver. She let go too quickly and nearly slipped from the step.

"Steady there," he said, catching her squarely by the waist.

"Thank you."

Chagrined, she claimed her seat, smoothing out her hoop and skirts. Evan thanked Joshua for his assistance and climbed in beside her. He clicked his tongue. The wheels began to roll.

The painted sky was darkening and the lamplighter was making his rounds. Emily held her place, straight and quiet as they traveled up the street.

"May I ask you something?" he said.

"Certainly."

"Are you afraid of me?"

She looked at him in disbelief. "Afraid?"

Evan kept his eyes on the way ahead. "That day in the pew, I have never seen you look so fretful."

"What do you mean?"

"You twisted your hands through the entire prayer meeting."

He had noticed that? Her cheeks burned.

He looked over. "You are doing it now."

Emily forced her hands to her sides. It wasn't fear that brought about her fidgetiness. It was sitting so closely beside him. It was the way that kepi sat low upon his forehead, the way the curls at his ears escaped and rolled in rebellion. But what was she going to say? She couldn't tell him any of that.

"You might as well have out with it, lass. I know something troubles you."

The physician was probing. Knowing him as she did, she was certain he would continue until she answered him. Emily swallowed. To be honest, there *was* something that bothered her. She was sure Sally's melancholy played a part, but that day at Stephen's funeral still nagged her. Emily reminded herself that Evan had sought forgiveness for his actions. It mattered not now if he *had* come to supervise their arrest. Still, she couldn't help but wonder.

"There is something. That day in the cemetery, when the soldiers came…"

"Did I send them?"

He glanced at her. She held her breath.

"No," he said. "I did not. I came across the funeral quite by accident. I assure you. Although once there, I did remember you saying who it was for."

Emily exhaled. The carriage continued on. So did he.

"The lieutenant and his men were more than likely just out on patrol. That state flag on the coffin marked you as secessionists."

"And you intervened for Julia's sake…."

"Aye," he said. "And yours."

"Mine?"

"I had watched you among the wounded. You'd spent enough tears on this war already. I did not wish for you to shed more."

Emily was shocked. He had thought that way then? "I'm sorry. I—"

"Don't. Were I in your shoes, I would have asked the same question. Blind allegiance in any human being is a dangerous thing."

"Or army," she conceded. "Lewis Powell taught me that."

He nodded slightly, jaw shifting. "I'd say we have both learned hard lessons from this war." His voice was earnest, and when he looked at her, his eyes were full of sincerity. "Emily, that man in the hospital, the one who cursed your city, mistreated you and the men…he will not return."

She was so drawn to him in that moment that Emily had to resist the urge not to lay her hand upon his arm. "I know."

She said the words with such gentle certainty that his heart swelled beneath his vest. Before his sentiments could show, he focused his attention in front of him.

"Do you ride?" he asked.

"Oh, yes. Well, at least I used to, when I was younger."

"Why did you stop?"

"My mother thought it unladylike."

Curious, he glanced back at her. She smiled slightly.

"You see, my father taught me to ride astride."

Evan grinned. He could just imagine her racing across the fields on some mission of mercy. "'Tis a skill that may still come in handy someday," he said. "With all the pressing matters, I doubt the mission agencies take care to stock ladies' saddles."

She blinked. "How did you know of that?"

"The mission agencies? Your father told me." He paused. "I'm sorry you've not met a more favorable response."

She lowered her chin, but he could still see the disappointment on her face. "I thought of all places I would be welcome in the contraband camps. The former slaves are in such desperate need. I fear my Baltimore address is what caused them to reject me."

He didn't say anything, but he wondered about that, too. Suspicion of Maryland citizens ran rampant throughout the Capitol.

You should have signed the complete oath, he thought. *Then none of this would even be an issue. You could have remained at the hospital. You could have stayed with me.*

"I won't give up hope," she insisted. "I know somewhere there is a place for me."

He wanted her to be happy, but he didn't like the idea of her venturing off beyond the occupied city. The woods and remote roads were full of scalawags, thieves and deserters of *both* armies.

Still, he admired her persistence. "You are a fine nurse, a fine woman. Any relief agency would be privileged to have you."

That lovely smile of hers emerged. "Thank you, Evan. I appreciate you saying such. You don't know what that means to me."

They came to their destination. Mr. Ward was already in the front garden. He greeted them and then assisted Emily from the carriage. Evan's stomach rumbled when they stepped inside the house. Delicious scents drifted about him. He had not had a proper meal since his visit to Reverend Henry's home.

Mrs. Ward welcomed him graciously, then ushered them into the dining room. The table was filled with several vegetables, soup, meat, bread and jam. As Evan helped Emily with her chair he was struck with the thought, *The last time I did such, it was for Mary.*

But when Emily looked up at him and thanked him sweetly, he felt his spirit lift. He took his place across from her. Mr. and Mrs. Ward were seated at opposite ends. Their daughter was in a cradle not far from the table.

Grace was spoken and the dishes were passed. The conversation and the company were pleasant.

"You have outdone yourself, Julia," Emily said. "Everything is so beautiful."

Even as thoughts of Mary drifted in and out of his mind, Evan found himself studying *her.* She smiled considerately as she listened to Mrs. Ward talk of what she and the baby had done that week. She posed thoughtful questions as Mr. Ward spoke of the meeting at the local abolitionist society.

Evan had to admit he was surprised by the Baltimore man's involvement. "Then you openly oppose slavery?"

"Yes, indeed. Julia and I believe that we are created in God's image and, therefore, we should treat others the way God treats us."

"Well said," Evan remarked.

Mrs. Ward spoke. "Samuel recently gave a speech at a city gathering denouncing the continuation of slavery here in Maryland."

"What was the response?" Emily asked.

"He received a standing ovation."

"Is that so?" Evan said.

Mr. Ward grinned at his wife. "Only because I had a very persuasive speechwriter."

"Did you write it?" Emily asked her.

Mrs. Ward blushed, nodded, then smiled at her husband. The love between them was obvious. It reminded Evan of what he had once had.

"They make quite the pair, don't they?" Emily said.

"Indeed." Though by now he hardly knew what he was agreeing to. That quickly he had become distracted. The flickering candlelight painted her curls in an even lovelier shade of gold and her smile was captivating. All he wanted to do was stare. She was indeed a beautiful woman.

"Well," Mrs. Ward then said. "Who is ready for dessert?"

Her husband laughed. "I know I am."

"Shall I help you?" Emily offered.

"No, but it sounds as though Rachael would like to escape from the cradle."

Emily moved to scoop up the whimpering babe. Little legs wiggled beneath a soaked-through gown. "Oh, you poor girl. No wonder you are upset." She looked at Mr. Ward. "I'll see to her."

"Thank you, Em."

He turned to Evan. "Doctor, shall we retire to the parlor?"

Agreeing, he followed him into the next room. A fire was already burning. The home wasn't furnished as lavishly as the Davis house, but it was happy and comfortable nonetheless. It reminded Evan of Pennsylvania.

The men sat down. Mrs. Ward soon returned with a tray of coffee and plates piled high with snow pudding. Her husband eagerly reached for one. Evan did, as well. Snow pudding was one of his favorites, second only to peach pie.

Emily returned with a much more contented Rachael. Claiming a chair across from him, she delicately balanced the baby in one hand and her dessert in the other.

He studied her in the soft parlor light. She seemed perfectly at ease.

When Mrs. Ward took to the piano she played a lively little ditty that made the baby smile. Emily set aside her plate and stood to her feet. Moving in slow, rhythmic motions, she danced with the child. Evan could not tear his eyes away.

The gown she wore was trimmed in ribbons and ruffles, and it accented every curve. The pale hue suited her perfectly. It was not quite blue, not quite gray. She snuggled the babe close, a look of love in her eyes. The pleasure he felt reminded him of an old Scottish prayer, one he had memorized as a child.

As the hand is made for holding and the eye for seeing, Thou hast fashioned me, O Lord, for joy. Share with me the vision to find that joy everywhere....

He was almost persuaded to rise, to take the child and the woman in his arms and waltz them both across the floor.

When she noticed he was staring at her, Emily froze, and nearly begged pardon. The memory of that day among the scrub brushes when he'd spoken of his wife and child sliced her heart. Yet as she looked at him, she realized the expression on his face was not one of grief. It was one of fond memory perhaps, but also something more. On impulse, she moved to the settee.

"Would you like to hold her?" she asked, knowing Julia and Sam would not mind.

He hesitated for the slightest moment, then reached out. Rachael was transferred securely, content in his strong, steady hands.

"Hello, lassie," he said to her. "What a bonny child you are."

Emily was touched, and she thought back to all the moments he had displayed tenderness even when his heart was broken. Now that God was clearly healing those wounds, she wondered just what kind of man Evan Mackay would become. Where would the Lord send him and what purpose through him would He achieve?

Surely it will be a grand one indeed.

Though her desire to make a difference in this war was strong, her zeal for missionary service great, she would gladly lay aside any such plans if it meant being beside *him,* helping him fulfill *his* calling.

Evan could not remember when he had enjoyed himself so much. Love reigned in this home. He could see the evidence of devotion everywhere, from the tintype of the rebel major on the mantel, to the Bible on the table and the abolitionist newspaper beside it. Though he was a stranger, he felt he belonged here. He had laughed. He had bounced the little girl on his knee. He had felt the warmth of Emily's gaze and the pleasure of her company.

When the baby grew tired, Mrs. Ward took her to the nursery. Emily followed. The men finished the last of the coffee and talked of Philadelphia.

"Beautiful city," Mr. Ward said. "I went to school there."

"Really? Where?"

"State Street Teacher's college."

Evan knew the campus well. "I attended the College of Pennsylvania."

"Is that so?" Mr. Ward moved to the rolltop desk in the corner of the room. "I have a Philadelphia paper here. Would you care to read it?"

"I would. Thank you."

"It is a few days old of course, but I have not touched it." He grinned. "In fact, I have yet to even read the news of my own city."

Evan reached for the paper. It was crisp and new. He snapped it open, only to realize his host had given him this evening's Baltimore paper by mistake. The headline leaped out.

Stanton Orders Postponement of Further Exchanges and Paroles.

His breath caught in his throat. He showed the news to Mr. Ward. His eyes widened as he began to read aloud.

"Secretary of war, Edwin M. Stanton, ordered today the postponement of further exchanges of prisoners of war...." He quickly scanned the article. "It doesn't say for how long."

Indefinitely, Evan thought, for he was certain that was what the United States government had in mind. *If the rebs cannot return to the fight, they will run out of men. This will bring the war to a close much sooner.*

A sense of hope filled his chest until he glanced up at the major's likeness. He couldn't help but think of the conditions in which the prisoners would be detained. He also couldn't help but think of the despair that would bring their loved ones.

At that moment the women returned. Their smiles immediately vanished in the somber mood of the room. Both knew something was dreadfully wrong.

"What is it?" Mrs. Ward asked her husband.

He handed the paper back to Evan and went to his wife.

Emily looked to him. "Has there been another battle?"

When Evan showed her the headline, she turned pale.

Mrs. Ward was now in tears. Her husband pulled her close. "Sweetheart, you and I both know the secretary of war does not have final say over Edward's life."

As Evan looked on the scene, he knew not what to feel. Waves of emotion washed over him, satisfaction, sympathy, a feeling of respect for his government for taking measures to finally end the war, yet contempt at the same time for the ruthlessness shown. Never before had his uniform felt as uncomfortable as it did tonight.

"Perhaps we should go," Emily whispered.

"Yes…of course…"

He found her cloak on a peg in the foyer. After returning to the room, he draped it over her shoulders.

"Sam," she whispered, "if there is anything I can do, please do not hesitate to ask…."

Mr. Ward nodded.

Turning, his wife wiped her eyes and apologized. "Thank you both for all you have done."

The *both* surprised Evan, but he nodded in return, then stepped back. Emily accompanied him to the door. The silence between them was thick. He knew he should say something to her, but he didn't know what.

They moved to the front porch. Her face was as pale as the moonlight. The moment he pulled the door behind them, her composure crumbled. Tears flooded her eyes. "Why are they doing this?" she asked.

No matter what he thought of the Union war strategy, his heart broke for her. "It will hasten the end of the fighting" was all he could think to say.

She shook her head. "It will solve nothing. The Confederacy will simply stop the exchange of your soldiers. The prisons on both sides will fill to capacity with sick, starving, desperate men."

He wanted to assure her that all prisoners would be

fed and cared for, but he knew she was right. He had seen the evidence for himself. The army could barely feed and treat the rebels they had now. What would they do with more?

He walked her toward the front gate. He could hear the frustration, the despair in her voice.

"It is all so senseless! So senseless, indeed! They come to us bloody and broken, having fought for a government who promised liberty, yet denies it to so many. And the other side claims they fight for freedom, yet they have not done so here. Joshua and Abigail would still be slaves were it not for my father!"

Though he still believed he was on the *right* side, that in time they *would* bring justice to all, he did not let that confidence cause him to make the same mistake twice. She was clutching his arm with one hand, crying into a handkerchief with the other.

Without hesitation he pulled her close, pressed her head to his chest. Everything in him wanted to comfort her, to take away her pain. "I'm sorry, lass."

"The hatred between both sides will only continue…."

Evan held her tightly, stroked her hair. "That is exactly why you must do as you have always done. Show them differently. Show them that regardless of the color of their uniform, the color of their skin, that life has sacred worth."

"But how?" she cried. "I cannot go to the prison camps. Neither the army nor the commission will allow it."

"I wasn't speaking of the camps. I meant here in Baltimore. Sign the oath. Come back to the hospital." *Come back with me.*

Slowly, she lifted her chin. One of his buttons had

marked her face. The faint impression of *U.S.* stamped her cheek. He smoothed it away with his thumb. Her lips were so close.

"Forgive me," she said, and she stepped back.

Evan couldn't dismiss the disappointment he felt. The mark on her cheek faded but the rest of her face was now as red as that day she'd fallen victim to the sun.

"I shouldn't have gone on so," she said.

Shouldn't have said such things to me, you mean. "You *can* trust me, Emily."

She drew in a ragged breath.

"Evan, I give you my word, I would never provide a Confederate man with a weapon or help him escape, but I will not turn away one who is hungry. I will not report him."

Why must you be so stubborn? he wanted to say. But he realized if he was caught somewhere behind rebel lines, would he not wish for someone like her to take pity on him?

"I understand."

He meant that, but whether she believed him, he couldn't say.

Her chin quivered slightly while she stared up at him. As Evan looked into those wide blue eyes of hers, recognition dawned. He didn't know when exactly it had happened but he knew now that it had.

He had fallen in love.

Chapter Sixteen

Emily lay awake that night for hours, the memory of those moments beneath the lamplight replaying through her mind.

She had not meant to express her frustrations over the war, but Edward's predicament distressed her so. Evan believed the Federal army's decision was a wise strategy, yet he did not condemn her for her thoughts. Instead, he'd taken her in his arms. He'd said he understood.

Never before had she felt so safe, so protected. When he'd wiped away her tears, the feelings were more than she could contain. If she hadn't stepped out of his embrace at that very moment, he would have guessed everything she was thinking.

She could not bear to have him know how she truly felt about him. She had heard his heart pounding beneath his uniform, but she was certain any emotion her presence stirred was one pertaining to Mary.

His behavior afterward only confirmed it. On the carriage ride home, he'd said very little. His forehead had been furrowed, his jaw tight. He had not seemed angry, just troubled. When they'd reached her house, he had escorted her inside, spoken briefly to her parents. They had also seen the newspaper headline. Her father had invited Evan to stay for coffee, but he'd declined.

Evan had turned to her then and politely thanked her for the evening. He'd tipped his kepi and clicked his shoes. Emily had watched him leave, knowing his heart was heavy. But where hers was filled with him and the thoughts of suffering soldiers, his was consumed by the memory of the woman he still loved.

Evan traveled back to the harbor. From the moment he had left Emily in her father's care, he could not get her off his mind. His thoughts were churning. Part of him warned he was simply giving in to loneliness, to a memory, but Evan knew it was far more than that.

He had thought Mary would be the only love of his life but Emily's persistent kindness, her gentleness with just a sprinkling of tenacity, had encouraged him to make peace with his past. Tonight she had given him a glimpse of what the future could be, and he liked what he saw.

Excitement mingled with anxiety. Could he even remember, let alone effectively apply the strategies of courtship? Would she respond positively even if he did?

She said she knew he was not the same man she had worked with at the hospital but he got the impression that was a matter taken more on faith than feeling. Uneasiness still lingered. He knew that because she never held his gaze for very long.

I am determined to change that.

Returning to the hospital he climbed the staircase to his room. There on his cot lay a set of orders. Stunned, he picked them up. In ten days he was to report to the main military hospital in Washington.

Evan sank to the bed and read on. The transfer came with a promotion. His superiors had noted his successes, his techniques. He was receiving recognition for a job well done.

I have been given what I wanted. I am moving on.

Only now he did not wish to go.

A conventional courtship would now be out of the question. Dare he ask permission to correspond with her while in Washington? Would she be willing to wait for his return?

The night was a long one, the following day even longer. Evan found himself praying for guidance, even hoping for a change of orders, yet none came. After his evening rounds, he borrowed a horse and went to see her. He had no idea what he would say, but she had been so upset last night that he wanted to be certain she was all right.

Her father greeted him at the door, then welcomed him in.

"Please excuse me, sir. I realize the hour is late, but I have just finished at the hospital."

"That's quite all right, Doctor. Is something amiss?"

He didn't know where to start. "I...wanted to inquire of Emily. She was rather distressed by the news of the exchanges. I hoped she would be feeling better today."

Mr. Davis nodded. "That is very kind of you. Yes. She is much improved. I'm sorry to say, though, she is not here."

The disappointment Evan felt was unmistakable. He wondered if it showed on his face, for her father then said, "Would you care to join me in the library? Abigail just brought in some coffee."

"Indeed, I would. Thank you."

Upon entering the room Evan's eyes were drawn to

the portrait of Emily hanging prominently above the fireplace. He had noticed it last night. The likeness was astonishing.

Mr. Davis settled into a chair. Evan claimed one opposite him.

"I'm not certain when my daughter will return. You see, she has camped out this evening at Miss Hastings's home."

He searched his memory. "The captain's sister? The lady from the funeral?"

"Yes. It seems the girls have found a way to channel their sorrow into something positive."

Evan blinked. "How so?"

"Emily met with Reverend Henry this morning, inquiring of the Christian Commission's involvement at Point Lookout. As Providence seems to have willed, a delegate has just returned from the camp. They are badly in need of funds and supplies, as they are overwhelmed by the latest influx of prisoners." The man smiled proudly. "Emily immediately took it upon herself to organize a relief effort to facilitate the delegate's quick return."

Evan felt the corners of his own mouth lift with a smile. No doubt she would.

"She and the other young ladies canvassed the neighborhood today seeking donations of winter clothing, foodstuffs and other items."

"Did they meet a good response?"

"Indeed. There is not a family in this neighborhood who doesn't know of some Maryland soldier now held at the Point. The girls instructed everyone to bring their donations to the church on Sunday. The commission man is scheduled to a give a report and all offerings collected that day will benefit the work there."

Evan marveled, "And Emily organized all of this?"

"She did. She and her friends are spending the evening knitting socks, apparently as many as they can turn out before the delegate catches the returning train."

His eyes were once again drawn to the portrait. The woman in the pale pink gown trimmed in lace and pearls could easily spend her time in the leisure of high society. Yet she chose not to do so. She wished to comfort the broken, the destitute, to share Christ's love.

The sudden sound of happy voices turned both men's attention to the door. He and Mr. Davis stood as Emily and the other former nurses stepped into the room. The blush of busy excitement was on her face. Evan thought she had never looked more beautiful.

"You have returned," Mr. Davis said. "I just finished explaining to Dr. Mackay that you were staying on with Sally tonight."

She offered Evan a quick, albeit rather timid, smile, then looked back at her father. "We have run out of yarn. I know Mother has quite the supply in the attic. Do you think she would mind us claiming a few skeins?"

"For this cause? Of course not. Come, ladies," he said to her friends. "Let Emily visit with the doctor for a moment. We'll search for Mrs. Davis."

The group exited the room. As soon as Emily turned her eyes to him, Evan lost the ability to speak. A thousand thoughts marched through his mind. The only one that he could coherently vocalize was, "I came to inquire of your health."

She blinked. "My health?"

"Yes. After last evening, I was concerned for you."

She smiled once more, stepped a little closer. Lilac water drifted about him. "That is kind of you," she said.

He cleared his throat. "Your father told me your news. I must say, it is a wonderful idea."

"Thank you, but I cannot take credit. It was you who encouraged such."

"Me?"

"You suggested that I keep on as before. This was the best way I knew how."

His heart was pounding and he wished more than anything that he had not been given those orders. He may not be able to remain with her, but he wanted to be part of what she was doing. He took out his billfold.

"I am unable to attend tomorrow's service," he said. "But I would like to contribute to your cause."

She looked surprised when he handed her the money.

"'Tis the least I can do after all you have done for me—" He caught himself. "And for the wounded."

The blush on her cheeks darkened, but Evan couldn't tell if she welcomed his compliment or was unsettled by it.

"You are most generous. Perhaps your schedule will allow you to attend our service when the delegate returns to Baltimore. He will give another report then."

"I won't be here."

She blinked.

"You see, I received orders for Washington."

He watched the color drain from her face. "For the main hospital?" she asked.

"Aye."

She tried to smile. There was a tremble to her voice. "No doubt they will fare well from your expertise."

He noticed that she was twisting the wad of greenbacks in her hand. Evan reached forward. The moment he touched her, he saw the expression in her eyes.

That isn't fear.

Emily quickly looked away, as if she had revealed much more than she wished. Evan just stood there, stunned.

Why didn't I recognize it sooner?

Color once more flooded her face but she reclaimed his gaze. "I wish you well in Washington," she whispered . "God keep you, Evan. I shall always be grateful that I met you."

His tongue was thick and heavy. He struggled to find the words. "Emily, I'm sorry...I..."

Immediately, she pulled back. Her father and friends returned. "Please excuse me," she said. Quickly she turned, a blur of silk and lace.

Evan watched her go, wondering how in the world had he, a member of the U.S. Army, captured a Baltimore woman's heart? And what was he going to do about it?

Before her tears could become obvious to everyone, Emily hurried for the solitude of the kitchen. She didn't know what was worse, her broken heart or her shame. He knew. He knew *everything* and he was mortified.

I'm sorry, he had said.

She didn't know what else was coming after that, but she could not bear to hear it. The kitchen door creaked behind her. In stepped Abigail.

"I embarrassed him," Emily blurted out.

Her friend offered her a handkerchief, then her shoulder. "Are you sure 'bout that?"

"Yes. Oh, Abigail! If you had only seen the look on his face!"

"I did see it. Just now, as he left. He looked like a man with a heavy heart."

"I know."

"I'm not sure you do. He don't look like he wants to go to Washington."

She raised her head. "He told you?"

"He tole us all."

The door creaked once more. Trudy, Elizabeth and Sally surrounded her.

"Oh, Em," Elizabeth said. "I'm sorry."

The expression on her face revealed the depth of her understanding.

"You knew?"

Elizabeth smiled gently then, looked at the others. "Of course we did. You light up like a firefly whenever he is around."

Emily sniffed back tears. "That which I shamefully revealed."

"What is so terrible about him knowing?" Trudy asked.

"He doesn't feel the same."

"Don't be so sure 'bout that," Abigail said. "I saw how he looked after you when you left the room."

Inside, Emily felt a spark of hope, but it was quickly doused by the cold water of reality. "He's leaving," she said.

"That may be," Elizabeth countered, "but a lot could happen between now and then."

Evan shut the door behind him and sat down on his cot. He knew what he wanted, was fairly certain now what she wished for, as well. Still amazed, he reviewed his planned course of action.

Officers often took families into the field. She wanted to return to nursing. Within the Capitol district there would be plenty of bureaucrats and high-ranking officers who would have no tolerance for Southern sympathizers, but any suspicion would fall to *him*. As his wife, an oath of loyalty would not be required.

But his impulsive nature had led to a great many heartaches in the past. Was this plan in Emily's best interest? He had no idea how long the war would last, how many postings he would visit along the way. *What will conditions be like? And when it is all over, where will we go?*

Evan had money in the bank, but there was no home to offer her. He raked his fingers through his hair. *What woman in her right mind would enlist for a life such as this? What father would give his permission?*

And, he wondered, *what does the Almighty wish?*

On the desk, beside the tintype of his brother, lay Mary's Bible. He reached for it. Was a comfortable life in the city of her birth what God desired for Emily?

He sighed. If she had come into his life for the sole purpose of drawing him back to his Creator, he would be forever grateful. But he truly hoped she was to be more than that.

Lord, You alone have the answers. Please reveal them to me.

Despite her distracted heart, Emily had to smile. The attendance that Sunday morning was overwhelming. Every pew was filled to capacity. The outpouring of generosity in donations of canned food items and winter clothing alone were simply incredible. Beyond that, several hundred dollars had also been raised.

The contributions were the result of wealthy Baltimore families and Federal soldiers who had attended the prayer meetings or worked at the hospital. Dr. Turner was among them, so was Jeremiah Wainwright. After the service they quickly found Emily and her friends.

"Well done, ladies," Dr. Turner said. "Well done, indeed."

"It is you we should thank," Emily insisted.

The old gentleman smiled and shook his head. "Evan told us what a fine cause this was. It was he who encouraged the attendance."

The emotion she felt at the mention of his name was bittersweet. The thought that the once hard-hearted Federal doctor would encourage his fellow physicians and staff to contribute to a cause that would chiefly benefit *Confederate* prisoners of war was simply amazing.

"When does your commission delegate depart?" Dr. Turner asked.

"Tomorrow morning, the ten o'clock train."

He nodded. "Have you an army to deliver all these supplies to the depot?"

She chuckled. It would take just that. "Yes. The gentlemen of the congregation have all volunteered, and Mr. Griffith and several other delegates are coming, as well."

"After what you have organized, young lady, if that man is smart, he'll make *you* a delegate."

Emily appreciated Dr. Turner's words. Though at one time she would have wished for exactly that, she no longer found such credentials important. She could make a difference right where she was.

The following morning she stood on the platform at Camden Station. The last of the crates were loaded on the southbound train. She had hoped Evan would come, but he had not. Although disappointed, a measure of satisfaction still pulsed through her.

"This will be a great help to Edward," Sally whispered.

"Indeed," Julia said. "I only wish we could have finished more socks."

"We'll send more next time," Emily insisted.

When the crates were secure and all passengers on board, the whistle blew. Reverend Henry uttered the unspoken thoughts of all those looking on.

"Go in peace," he said. "And may God's will be done."

The wheels began to chug. The group watched until the last car disappeared around the bend.

"Well, ladies," Sam said. "I have classes waiting and I suspect all of you would prefer the comfort of a fireside to this cold."

Rachael squealed as if to say she concurred. Laughing, Emily, Julia and Sally could not disagree. Frost clung to the lampposts and the wind was ripping at their cloaks.

Leaving the station, the carriage ride home was just as cold. Sam dropped Emily at her front gate. She longed for a cup of tea and the opportunity to tell her parents about all that had taken place. Emily wondered why they had not come. They had promised to arrive before the train's departure.

She pushed open the door. Her mother met her at once.

"Hurry now!" she said, tugging off Emily's winter cap, then her cloak.

"Whatever is the matter?"

"He's with your father. You don't want to keep him waiting any longer."

There was only one reason a waiting gentleman caller would please her mother so. Emily's heart slammed into her ribs. "Keep *who* waiting?"

Mrs. Davis grinned. "Dr. Mackay!"

Emily gasped. "Truly?"

"Yes, my dear. Oh!" her mother then complained. "Your hands are like ice. For goodness' sake, try to warm them!" She urged her toward the library.

Emily feared that any moment she was going to wake, for this had to be a dream. Sure enough, however, Evan was standing in front of the fireplace, staring at her portrait. The moment he turned around, a smile filled his face. Emily no longer had any doubt.

Breathe! Breathe!

"My dear," she heard her father say. "Dr. Mackay wishes to speak with you."

He then exited the room.

Smile fading, Evan took a step forward. His jaw twitched. This time she recognized the action for what it was.

He is just as nervous as I.

After several seconds of silence, he cleared his throat.

"I have never been very good with words," he said. "I suppose that is why Mary wished me to read poetry."

He visibly cringed. Emily's heart went out to him. Her own anxiety eased somewhat.

"Did you wish for us to recite 'Bruce's March to Bannockburn'? I believe I know most of that."

The corner of his mouth lifted with a smile. He chuckled. "No. Hardly." He moved toward her. Emily's heart fluttered.

"You know I have orders for Washington."

"Yes."

"It won't be an easy place. Conditions will not be comfortable."

"I dare say that isn't the purpose for you being there."

"Aye. I mean, no, 'tis not." He swallowed. "I am to report next week. There…is not much time."

Her heart was now pounding as she waited most eagerly. Evan drew in a quick breath, took her hand and knelt before her. Emily stared at his strong jaw, which at the moment was having such trouble working.

"Emily Davis, I love you. Will you come with me and be my love? Will you marry me?"

The words could not have been delivered more beautifully, but now it was she who was at a loss for them. Tears would have to do.

He squeezed her hand. That smile emerged. "Is that a yes, lass?"

She could not contain her happiness. Throwing her arms around his neck, she cried, "I love you, Evan. Oh, how I love you!"

"And I you, Emily."

Slowly he stood and brushed her cheek with his fingers. Emily felt a shiver as he lifted her chin. Then she lost herself in the strength of his arms and the gentleness of his kisses.

Epilogue

Washington, D.C.
March 4, 1865

Evan steered his wife and infant son around a large puddle, inching as close as they could to the East Portico. Weeks of rainy weather had left the Capitol grounds wet and muddy, yet thousands still had gathered.

"Can you see him?" he asked.

"I can now."

A hush fell over the crowd as President Lincoln began to speak.

"Fellow countrymen, at this second appearing to take the oath of the presidential office there is less occasion for an extended address then there was at the first...."

The late winter wind ruffled cloaks and tugged at the hats of those around them. Evan drew Emily a little closer. She looked up at him and smiled. One glance from those wide blue eyes still tied his tongue.

She had left the luxury of Baltimore for the dark, near-destitute conditions of the military hospitals. Never once had she complained. Side by side they had worked, he mending wounds and she the broken hearts of count-less men in blue and gray.

"Let us judge not, that we be not judged. The prayers of both could not be answered. That of neither has been answered fully. The Almighty has His own purposes..."

Aye, Evan couldn't help but think as Lincoln con-tinued. *And God's greatest purpose is to draw all men unto Him. May we now seek His guidance, chart a new course for this nation.*

The wind gusted again and little Andrew twisted his face in protest. Emily snuggled him close. Four years ago, if someone had told Evan that he would fall for a Southern woman, that he would make peace with the rebels, he wouldn't have believed it possible. But she had taught him the healing power of forgiveness and the strength to be found in grace.

Emily had managed to soften the hardest of hearts, even here in Washington. She had collected numerous funds and items for the Christian Commission, sup-plies that would be distributed to wounded soldiers and prisoners of war.

Evan did not know when the battles would cease, but he knew eventually they would. The process of healing had already begun.

"With malice toward none, with charity for all, with firmness in the right as God gives us to see the right, let us strive on to finish the work we are in, to bind up the nation's wounds...."

Emily looked up at him and smiled. Evan knew that together, they would seek to do just that.

* * * * *

Dear Reader,

Thank you for choosing, *An Unlikely Union,* the second book in my civil war series. Although spared the destruction other Southern cities faced, Baltimore still witnessed the high cost of battle. Throughout the war it served as a distribution point for thousands of wounded soldiers and Confederate prisoners. Despite Federal occupation, Southern sympathy remained strong, particularly among the upper class. Supplies and information secretly flowed even as the U.S. Army tried desperately to maintain control. Martial law was instituted. Searches, seizures and arrests (often of innocent civilians) were common. Sadly, slavery remained legal throughout Maryland until a new state constitution took effect in 1864.

Yet amid the abuse and desire for retribution on both sides, there were those committed to charity and reconciliation. The U.S. Christian Commission was one such example. Born out of the YMCA's commitment to mentoring America's young and the noontide prayer meetings of the late 1850s, the Commission provided relief for soldiers, sailors and prisoners of war by attending to both physical and spiritual needs. Hundreds of delegates sacrificed their own finances, health and, in some cases, their very lives to share God's message of love and forgiveness on the battlefields, in the hospitals and camps. The volunteers treated their fellow countrymen with dignity and respect, regardless of which uniform they wore. Little by little, hearts were softened and the war-torn nation inched its way toward healing.

The work however, is not yet complete. May we continue what they started.

Let your light shine,
Shannon Farrington

Questions for Discussion

1. How does Evan's prejudice toward the people of Baltimore affect the way he treats Emily? How do her preconceived notions concerning "Yankees" influence her opinion of him? Have you ever made assumptions about people who were different than you?

2. Why does Evan become so angry when Emily plays the role of the dying sergeant's wife? Should she have done so? Why or why not?

3. Although Emily respects many of the Federal physicians in the hospital, she perceives Evan as an enemy. How does her realization of such change her attitude toward him? What influence do you think Abigail may have had?

4. Why does Evan recommend Emily for the position of night nurse?

5. Why is Evan so secretive about his past? How does this affect his relationships with his fellow physicians in the hospital?

6. Emily slowly realizes she is attracted to Evan. In what ways is he the man she dreams of marrying? In what ways is he different?

7. Evan is hesitant to pray, because he fears God's rejection. Have you ever felt this way? What did you do about it?

8. When Emily learns her interaction with Ben Reed provides an opportunity for another prisoner's escape, she regrets her involvement. Have you ever regretted an act of compassion? If so, what lesson did you learn?

9. How does Evan's attitude toward Confederate prisoners change once he realizes God has forgiven him for his past mistakes?

10. When Emily learns that prisoner exchanges have stopped she is devastated. How does she cope with this reality?

11. Which character can you identify with most in this story? Which scene is your favorite?

12. Can forgiveness bring about healing? Is love truly more powerful than hate?

REQUEST YOUR FREE BOOKS!

2 FREE INSPIRATIONAL NOVELS
PLUS 2
FREE
MYSTERY GIFTS

Love Inspired.
HISTORICAL
INSPIRATIONAL HISTORICAL ROMANCE

YES! Please send me 2 FREE Love Inspired® Historical novels and my 2 FREE mystery gifts (gifts are worth about $10). After receiving them, if I don't wish to receive any more books, I can return the shipping statement marked "cancel." If I don't cancel, I will receive 4 brand-new novels every month and be billed just $4.74 per book in the U.S. or $5.24 per book in Canada. That's a saving of at least 21% off the cover price. It's quite a bargain! Shipping and handling is just 50¢ per book in the U.S. and 75¢ per book in Canada.* I understand that accepting the 2 free books and gifts places me under no obligation to buy anything. I can always return a shipment and cancel at any time. Even if I never buy another book, the two free books and gifts are mine to keep forever.

102/302 IDN F5CN

Name	(PLEASE PRINT)	
Address		Apt. #
City	State/Prov.	Zip/Postal Code

Signature (if under 18, a parent or guardian must sign)

Mail to the **Harlequin® Reader Service:**
IN U.S.A.: P.O. Box 1867, Buffalo, NY 14240-1867
IN CANADA: P.O. Box 609, Fort Erie, Ontario L2A 5X3

Want to try two free books from another series?
Call 1-800-873-8635 or visit www.ReaderService.com.

* Terms and prices subject to change without notice. Prices do not include applicable taxes. Sales tax applicable in N.Y. Canadian residents will be charged applicable taxes. Offer not valid in Quebec. This offer is limited to one order per household. Not valid for current subscribers to Love Inspired Historical books. All orders subject to credit approval. Credit or debit balances in a customer's account(s) may be offset by any other outstanding balance owed by or to the customer. Please allow 4 to 6 weeks for delivery. Offer available while quantities last.

Your Privacy—The Harlequin® Reader Service is committed to protecting your privacy. Our Privacy Policy is available online at www.ReaderService.com or upon request from the Harlequin Reader Service.

We make a portion of our mailing list available to reputable third parties that offer products we believe may interest you. If you prefer that we not exchange your name with third parties, or if you wish to clarify or modify your communication preferences, please visit us at www.ReaderService.com/consumerschoice or write to us at Harlequin Reader Service Preference Service, P.O. Box 9062, Buffalo, NY 14269. Include your complete name and address.

LIH13R

Reclaiming the Runaway Bride

Seven years and two broken engagements haven't erased
Garrett Mitchell from Molly Scott's mind. Her employer insists
Molly and Garrett belong together. To appease the well-meaning
matchmaker, the pair agrees to a pretend courtship. But too late,
Molly finds herself falling for a man who might never trust her.

Garrett is a prominent Denver attorney now, not the naive
seventeen-year-old who always felt second-best. Surely the string of
suitors Molly's left behind only proves her fickleness. Does Garrett
dare believe that she has only ever been waiting for him? The third
engagement could be the charm, for his first—and only—love.

Charity HOUSE

Finally a Bride

by

RENEE RYAN

*Available November 2013 wherever
Love Inspired Historical books are sold.*